Shattered Hopes

DAYA DE SILVA

PRESTIGE

PRESTIGE BOOKS
3/28, East Patel Nagar
New Delhi 110 008

ISBN: 81-7551-104-4

Printed at Chaman Offset Press, New Delhi 110 002

For

CR

with deep appreciation and affection

and

Vassy and Ruwan

Wherever you are and wherever I am

I'll be cheering for you, always

This is a work of fiction. Most fiction is based on real life experiences. However, any semblance to any person or any incident mentioned in this work, is purely coincidental.

Acknowledgments

There are almost a million South Asians living in the United States today, many of us are first or second generation immigrants. We are an influential group especially within the academic and scientific community. Like any other immigrant community, we are lost in nostalgia, often idealizing our homeland. Some of us feel exiled, some feel displaced, some of us have assimilated, some are tough, some feel cheated and the stronger of us have somehow survived. *Shattered Hopes* arose out of those experiences we shared in our adopted country—our pleasures and pains, joys and sorrows.

One of the greatest gifts that life has blessed me with are my friends—some of whom read through the early drafts of the manuscript and gave me invaluable comments and much needed encouragement. Carolyn Rhodes, lover of literature and former Professor of English at Old Dominion University, Norfolk, Virginia, guided me from the very beginning and taught me the art of fiction writing. Her tremendous patience in going through the first draft of this story in its very rudimentary form and returning every page of it with blue pencil marks and helpful comments, gave me much courage to carry on. Tessa Bartholomeusz, Professor of Religion at Florida State University, encouraged me, saying that this was a good story. Susilie Wilson, former librarian of the University of New

Brunswick at Fredericton, read through the whole manuscript and gave me comments which helped me to polish up rough edges. Professor William Whitehurst and Janie, very kindly read through the whole manuscript and shared with me their thoughts. I owe a word of gratitude to Anita Fellman, Sujatha Moorthi and Louisa Carinho Igloria, all professors at Old Dominion University, for their comments. Professor Antoinette Burton of the University of Illinois, as always, was very supportive. The beautiful cover is the creation of Paul Arroyo of the University of Illinois Press.

Our son Ruwan, during his short break in between business school final examinations and his first step into the world of business, read the whole manuscript with the keen eye of a detective and pointed out inconsistencies and factual errors in the story. CR encouraged me from the very beginning and lifted me out of despair on numerous occasions when I was on the verge of giving up. He showed me that we could do mostly anything if we set our hearts to it.

I am grateful to Rohit Dhawan of Prestige Books for his advice and assistance in the production of this volume.

Daya De Silva

PROLOGUE

That sound—almost like a cat's scratch—on my door that morning in mid-December was faint, but yet, it still echoes in my ears as loud as a drum beat. Little did I realize at the time that the knock was going to transform the course of my life forever. It was two weeks before Christmas. I had just returned from a research trip to the Folger Shakespeare Library in Washington D.C. and I was seated by my study window trying to write a paper I was scheduled to present at the Shakespeare Conference in April. The north wind across Lake Michigan brought drifting snow flakes towards the city. Distracted, I watched the flakes as they hit the windowpanes, melted into icy water and dripped down the glass panes. The heavy snow blurred my vision of Lake Shore Drive. The snow-capped roof-tops of the high-rise buildings were faintly visible making the surroundings a lonesome but peaceful spectacle. The last time I had experienced a snowstorm of this magnitude was in Maine almost eighteen years ago.

I had loved the Maine winters, almost like the Arctic. The immaculately white landscape was so breathtakingly beautiful that I did not mind the cold. I remembered one day in April in my second year in high school, we were working on some Math problems. It was around eleven in the morning. I was looking out of the window when I saw snow flakes beginning to form with the drizzle. I was thrilled and surprised—snow in late April? I forgot I was in class and shouted that it was snowing. Of course, no one believed me. Lindy, who was sitting next to me, without even looking up from her book, said Nelu is such a romantic. Snow in Spring! But soon everybody saw it—it was snowing hard.

A few days before on Easter Sunday, it had been so warm we walked outside in our T shirts. The winter had been cold but there was little snow. That very morning as I walked out of the door on my way to school I remember telling my mother, "It's not fair. We don't get to see the snow but we have to walk in the cold."

That April day, sensing that a big storm was approaching, the principal closed the school at noon and we were asked to get ready to be sent home in the school bus.

"Will there be school tomorrow?" someone wanted to know.

"If the snow does not stop by four in the morning, the plows will have no time to clear the roads which means we cannot re-open school. Anyway, listen to the radio," Miss Bartlett, our social science teacher said. While we waited for the school bus, we watched the snow piling up on the sidewalks and draping the trees. The snow plows were already rolling and the school telephone kept ringing—parents calling about their children's walk back home.

When I came home, mother was sad. "It's spring, and it's supposed to be warm." She was worried about her tulips which were in full bloom. Officially, it was Spring but two and a half feet of snow blanketed Brunswick that afternoon. Father and my brother Roshan came home early and together we celebrated the arrival of snow—the first real snowstorm that we witnessed in America.

"It's an opportunity to revel—a genuine New England blizzard," I remember my father saying as he enjoyed the storm. We heard over the radio that airports in Portland and Boston were closed. Falling trees cut the power lines and knocked out electricity in schools, offices and homes. Thousands of people in the north had to do without electricity. Roads were also closed and a state of emergency was declared in Maine. Across Brunswick, winds gusted to nearly fifty mph in the evening. It was beautiful to see the snow constantly coming down in the light of the street lamp in front of our house. We saw the wind blowing the snow in different directions through the lights in the nearby college quadrangle. The trees in our backyard were swinging with the wind—first the big branches started to swirl and then the little branches followed suit. It was fun to see what was happening outside as long as you had a warm place to stay. That was Maine weather.

Chicago, where we lived next, was not much different. But Chicago was not as beautiful as Brunswick during a snowstorm. And it is windy here too—this is the Windy City.

Our family moved to Chicago during the years of Mayor Richard Daley. Mayor Richard Daley Welcomes You to Chicago, was the first billboard that caught our eyes as we left O Hare Airport in a taxi to go to the house assigned to my father by the Newberry library. Chicago as told to us, is the city of fresh air from Lake Michigan, the city of the Magnificent Mile, of quiet ethnic suburbs where the gardens were laid out in immaculate order. I had been told to expect many school trips to the world-renowned Museum of Science and Industry and the Museum of Natural History. I had been waiting to see the great lions that guarded the Art Institute of Chicago, to visit the planetarium and the aquarium where the big whale jumps out of the water to welcome the visitors. We drove past the luxury high-rise buildings off Lake Shore Drive. They loomed above the traffic, offering their occupants magnificent views of Lake Michigan. It seemed to me not a lake, but a part of the ocean dropped in the middle of this enormous landmass. Just as we reached the northern end of Michigan Avenue, the taxi turned to East Bellevue—one of the finest residential areas in the city. The driver stopped at a three-story stately-looking house.

"Here we are," he said as he got out of the taxi to help father to take our bags out. I looked around me and was overwhelmed by the beautiful condominium complex in front of our house. It dwarfed our house by its gigantic size and its magnificent appearance. I could see hundreds of candle-like lights of the gold chandeliers burning inside and the doormen in their brass-buttoned coats and black sailor caps opening doors for ladies who had just arrived at the porch. "Oh! what fun to live here," I remember shouting with glee at the time.

When we were preparing to leave for Chicago, father's friends had advised him against living on the south side of the city.

"There is a huge unemployed black community there. The city itself is designed to keep the blacks and whites separate, so if you live in the Oak Beach area you are safe. But just a couple of blocks to the west of Newberry there are slums," one friend had warned father.

"The violence gives these unemployed youths a sense of power, a sense of control. They have a minimal education and therefore no hope to get a job—nothing to look forward to. So they turn to crime. It's very important where you live in Chicago. As you know, crime free areas are the most expensive," another had said.

We were fortunate to get a place to live in the most exclusive residential area in the city. Our apartment was on the second floor of the building. It was a beautifully furnished apartment, with wall-to-wall carpeting and new furniture. The kitchen was spacious and clean and the two bedrooms had large, comfortable beds in them. The first morning when I got up and looked out of my bedroom window, I thought my eyes were playing tricks on me. Fur-clad ladies, the kind I had only read about or seen in movies, stepped out of chauffeur-driven limousines and walked into the building in front of our house. What a delight! I had not seen anything like this during the last two years in Brunswick, but now I felt like a poor relation living among rich folks here. This is real America!

As we settled down to live in our new house we felt that the evenings, as in Brunswick, seemed long and dragging. For some reason unknown to us, mother couldn't bear the twilight. Back in Brunswick I remember we took some time to get used to the evenings in America. The winter darkness came so fast, so suddenly. Mother dreaded the evenings. She would call us together and we gathered by the fireplace in the cosy sitting room in our Brunswick house, and talked about the evenings in Sri Lanka, until the night arrived. Evenings arrived slowly in Sri Lanka where we'd all assemble at dusk to watch the sunsets, while Mary, our cook, prepared our evening meal. We'd talk about the birds flying to their nests as darkness enveloped the world around them, the bats coming out of their hiding places and our neighbors coming home to rest after long hours of work in their offices. We'd talk of the farmers, weary and hungry after a hard day's work in the paddy fields, coming home to eat and sleep. In Chicago as in Brunswick, our evenings were different. The year arrives differently. Many days in Brunswick we felt a longing for those evenings in our hometown in Sri Lanka, and the same feeling was coming back to us in Chicago.

Nevertheless, we spent some of our happiest times in America in that apartment. Father enjoyed going to the Newberry Library and doing research there. In fact he said that year was one of the most productive for his academic writing. Back at St. Peter's College in Brunswick where he had been a Visiting Professor for two years he had not received a full professor's salary. We were far from being comfortably off, but mother managed the household expenses with utmost care and father worked hard volunteering for extra courses, toiling over students' recommendations for days. When at the end of the two-year period, he had to leave, there was a Resident Fellowship waiting for him at the Newberry Library which had an excellent collection of literature on Shakespeare—father's speciality. He envisaged that, with hard work and a little bit of luck, with his writings and publications, during the year at his disposal, he would be able to land a lucrative position at the end of his Fellowship. Hopes were high when we came to Chicago. We all assumed he could move on and up, as he always had, to Princeton, Yale or to one of the other Ivy League universities on the East Coast. After all, father's Ph.D. from Cambridge

University was a prized possession that only a minuscule fraction of those in the academy could boast of.

Now I live by myself in one of the finest condominium complexes on Lake Shore Drive, built on the world's most expensive real estate. My father, if he were alive, would be so proud to see me as an academic. It's been eight years since he passed away. A year after he died, I entered the Graduate Program in English Literature at the University of Chicago. He never got to read my Ph.D. thesis or to know that it was commended by my examiners as an exemplary study on Shakespearean drama.

On my way back from the airport last evening I drove down Michigan Avenue after the snowstorm hit Chicago. The Golden Mile, as Michigan Avenue is so appropriately named, was illuminated with millions of tiny light bulbs and the place looked heavenly to me. Hundreds of shoppers were walking hurriedly from shop to shop looking for gifts. I never realized how lonely and miserable it could be until the Christmas holidays arrived. From the time I moved out of my mother's apartment, except for a period of three years when I spent Christmas holidays with Sanjeev—my former boyfriend—I had been alone in my apartment on Christmas day. I had my job and did things I most liked to do but the holiday season brought wistful memories and made me go to far away places, to scenes filled with scents and sounds and warmth and happiness I shared with my parents and my brother Roshan. Though we were not Christians, this was the time that evoked strong images of family togetherness for me. More than anything else the holidays made me envy what my friends enjoyed and I had lost. A time of year that once was so joyous, which we all had looked forward to, had become unbearable to me. Thanksgiving, Christmas and New Year's eve became days to suffer rather than to enjoy. I felt a special pain when I thought of my father who had made Christmas so special to me by lighting up both inside and outside of me. The passing away of my father altered my life, and our family togetherness was lost forever. I have parties to attend and gifts to buy. To get into the holiday spirit, I even decorate my apartment—yet in my heart there's emptiness and such deep sorrow that I find it even difficult to pretend.

I miss my father, especially now—now that I have achieved something that he could not achieve for himself in America. Some of the recent immigrants here, like our family, were pushed out, literally, from their country by economic hard times, political and ethnic strife. We Sri Lankans, like many from other places, were pulled to America by its democracy and freedom, economic opportunity and boundless optimism. My parents struggled to make it in America, working, saving and investing in their children, their futures. We, their children, in our turn inched our way up the social and economic ladder as we adapted and assimilated; eventually some of us achieved a measure of success and prosperity—the American dream.

Being a university professor had always been my dream. This was my life's ambition that I achieved through hard work and determination. I remember standing in the middle of the bedroom and staring at the real first pay check, bigger than I had ever imagined. A three thousand dollar pay check appeared like a million to me that afternoon and how I wished that my father and mother were there to enjoy the look of it. To feel it and know that it was real. I felt guilty at the time, because I felt that my mother deserved to share that moment with me—she had worked hard all her life to make things better for us, for me and my brother. Now it looks as if I was the only one who benefitted from my parents' efforts. My parents worked hard and I have learned from their experience that hard work only was no guarantee of success. Success is only a dream—that never came my father's way. Now I know that success comes to those who are lucky enough to be in the right place at the right time and be able to reach out your arm and grab it when it passes your way.

Now I am mature enough to look back and see my early life more clearly. I am full of gratitude for the world that made me. Adaptation to the American way of life was not easy. Though we were young when we arrived in the country, we had already become used to a set of behavioral patterns that we found difficult to cast aside. I also now realize, even after living in America for almost twenty years, I will remain a person-in-between, an outsider looking in. However much Coca Cola I sip, however deep red I paint my lips and how well-pressed my Calvin Klein suits appear, I will never be All-American. There were times when I wished my eyes were blue and my hair was blond. It once offended me very much when people asked me where I came from. I couldn't understand why they asked me that question. After all, all Americans, except the American Indians, came here from somewhere outside the shores. I knew what they wanted to know—my country of origin—but then why do they want to know? But those days are gone now. I feel, it's here I belong.

My father's sound advice on life comes to mind often these days, though his face remains a distant memory. I sometimes think of the long discussions I enjoyed with father on democracy, about affirmative action, and the Elgin Marbles. We argued till late into the night. My arguments were noisy and sometimes foolish—and I knew they were. Some days father would talk about his experiences in the classroom. One such day talking about the bad behavior of university undergraduates, father said that in America there exists an exaggerated desire for democracy where no one is ever anyone else's superior for any reason or under any circumstances. This feeling, he said, made it difficult to enforce discipline among students in class and even among one's own children. "Think of those children who sue their parents because they had been told to behave in a manner that the parents thought was the best. Children's rights are being impinged upon; constitutional rights are being violated—these make headlines in the newspapers. Civil behavior is transformed from one generation to the next through parent-child and teacher-student relationships. If as in present day American society, parents and teachers cannot take responsibility of being culturally and intellectually superior, who is going to teach those of the next generation civility towards each other? Wouldn't that mean the decline of American civilization?" He would throw the question at me and I listened, open-mouthed, completely lost in his ideas.

How I wish he was around now! Sometimes, I still think, I see him around crowds—I see his crown of black hair around the bald top of his head—just a few heads away from me, just a little too far away to reach. Very often I ran to catch up with him, only to see a stranger looking down at me and giving me a confused smile.

I face difficult situations in my day-to-day teaching career. I would have received plenty of sound advice from my father but in his absence, I have to rely on books. I do talk to senior professors and I do read about survival in academe. My father would laugh at me if he were to see the books on academic life in the form of survival guides on my book-shelf. I have a book on my table written especially for women academics who are motivated by the feminist desire to change the world of academics for women. These books have attracted much attention both among young men and women in today's job market and their ideas reflect conventional wisdom on many campuses. I read about the women in academe, including essays such as the effects of hairstyle, clothes one wears, one's weight and disability, on job prospects and promotions. There are books that say to have any hope for a happy life as an academic, you must work on what you love, on what gives you intellectual pleasure. At the same time there are books that advise junior faculty to keep quiet until they get tenure. Only with tenure secured should they push for change if they want any change. One's preferences and concerns should be restrained for the sake of fitting in. The message is, "only those who somehow get tenure can ever change the situation." In fact, some books advise to give high grades even for weaker students, and be sure of "good teaching evaluations from students." These days, I read anything I can get hold of about special problems faced by academics.

Though it's been a long time since I left Sri Lanka, I still think back of the life we left behind. We lived together as an extended family—my father, his brother and his family and their parents. We were used to having people around all the time. The cold Chicago climate and the formality of Western culture inhibit casual visits and closeness. This in turn promotes a sense of loneliness and isolation which further contributes to depression and to making back at home seem glorious. Some summer evenings coming home after a long session of reading in the library, I sit outside on the balcony and indulge in a glass of wine. When I am on my second glass of Chardonnay, I dream a little bit about my family. I think of hot days in Kandy, my hometown back in Sri Lanka, with scorpions and centipedes under the doormats. Mother, frisky after a day's work, tucking her legs up underneath her, waiting in the evening heat for the servant to bring her a drink. Not a single day passes without my thinking of my parents and brother, especially at dinner-time, for it was then that we got together and exchanged our day's experiences. I make something to eat and sit down at the kitchen table, and the memories keep coming back. As I lift the fork to my mouth, I can feel my family around me, as they always had been. I know just which way to turn my head to look up and see mother trying to get more food on to father's or Roshan's plate. I know just what father would have been doing, reading the *New York Times* while pretending to be part of the dinner conversation. Then I feel it is a mistake to think of them. I feel a sob rise in my throat and I swallow it down; I cannot see my plate. My eyes would remain dry, I cannot cry.

I saw my father in a dream on the night I was the awarded the Ph.D. I had been writing a critical review of a Macbeth play produced in a London theatre and had stepped out of my study to take a break. My father was there in the corridor. I noted my dream in my diary the next morning. He was wearing his blue jacket with brass buttons, I wrote. He smelled of Old Spice aftershave and I felt his arms around me when I hugged him. I said, I love you, something which I had found difficult to say when he was alive, for fear that he would laugh at me for being so American. He didn't say anything, he only looked at me—his eyes glowing with the kindness that only my father could give, I wrote. It felt completely real, with all the details of his presence—smell, feeling, look, silence—very clear. I woke up sobbing. I added in my diary, When will we meet again? I saw him again in a dream last night—this was after a period of long silence—almost three years. Sometimes I feel that there lurk in me some remnants of the beliefs of my ancestors; believing in dream-lore. Whenever I dream of my father I feel that something significant would happen in my life. What would it be this time? Would it be the arrival of a Prince Charming to erase the curse of solitude that had taken hold of me? I wish my father were with me now. I've felt incredible loneliness since I dreamed of my father last night. What's the point of a great job or a great day or something spectacular happening if you don't have your family around you to share it with? When I look back on my childhood my mind focuses first on the bad times I had with my mother and the day I left her to begin my own life. I am a person for whom time doesn't soften rough edges so easily. I sometimes wish my past were different so that my future would not be difficult for me to face.

My thoughts had been drifting towards my past for almost an hour. I had just woken up from my reverie and turned back to my desk and started working on my paper when I heard that sound on the door again. I wanted to spend more time at my writing. I wanted to fill each day with work and fun, in balance. I stopped my day-dreaming and read what I had written earlier—it felt good to finish work before getting ready for Christmas. I had already re-read an essay by D.H. Lawrence on, Why the novel matters, and one by Conrad that compares writing a novel to an act of creation. Reading literature, sitting by my study window and appreciating the beauty of the falling snow and the dim light of the winter noon—these are the things I mostly treasure in life now.

I was distracted by the knocking.

I

A faint knocking sound came from my front door, like someone's scratching. Who would be visiting me in this weather anyway? Did I hear it again? This time there was a more persistent knock. I set aside my book and with the pen still in my hand, I walked to the door and opened it. There in front of me stood two policemen in their full snow gear.

"Are you Professor Fernandez? Ma'am?"

"Yes," I replied, bewildered at seeing them. They took a while to respond to my inquiring look. The stockily built one opened his mouth and stammered, "There has been an accident, Ma'am."

I knew that nobody in my family, except for Uncle Henry, my mother's brother, was aware of my address—so it must be one of my friends. My eyes were intensely glued to the policeman's lips and my ears were eagerly waiting to hear what he had to say.

"Mrs. Fernandez has been in a car accident," he mumbled.

"Who? What did you say?" Loud words, in an angry and shocking tone came out of my mouth.

"Your mother, Ma'am. She is at the Methodist Hospital."

For a moment I thought I was dreaming, but then I heard the policeman's voice again bringing me back to reality. "Her condition is said to be critical. She is in the Intensive Care Unit of the Methodist Hospital. From the Accident Ward she has been transferred to the Intensive Care Unit. We've come to take you there."

"Oh God! My mother! What's happened?" It's strange—I've been thinking of my family this last hour. Maybe my father saw what happened to my mother and appeared in my dream last night to convey the news to me; and here the policemen were his messengers. A million thoughts flashed across my mind as I slipped on my boots and grabbed the heavy winter coat off the hook and followed the policemen to the car.

The falling snow had covered the roads and the snow plows had not started to clean up some parts of the city yet. Driving was treacherous. While traveling in the police car, I wondered why my mother had been on the road at a time like this. Hoping to find out what exactly had happened, I prodded, "Do you know what happened? How did my mother get involved in an accident?"

"We don't know yet, Ma'am. The police are working on it."

"What time did this happen?"

"It happened yesterday afternoon just before the snowstorm hit the city. I am sorry it took all this time for us to reach you. We found Dr. Henry Pereira's address. His card was in your mother's wallet. He tried to reach you last evening—your phone rang, he said, but nobody answered. We came here looking for you—I think around ten in the night—but you were not in. Dr Pereira is at the hospital right now."

"Who else is there?" I was thinking of my brother and the question just slipped out.

"There were two ladies and your uncle by your mother's side when we left," one of them responded.

"Two ladies?" They seemed to ignore me. Perhaps Uncle Henry's wife, Aunt Viva, and their daughter Maya were there. But then where was my brother Roshan? If only I knew how to reach him now.

I had been driven to this same hospital in an ambulance some ten years ago when my father suffered his first heart attack. Now seated in the police car and looking at the falling snow, every little detail of that incident that led to his heart attack kept coming back to my mind. It occurred one afternoon while he was working in the garden after mother said she wanted to send pictures of our house back home to Sri Lanka. She wanted to show her mother and father's mother that we were doing well in the United States. She wanted flowers in the front garden and a picture-perfect house with newly painted front door and windows. My father was in no mood for beautiful photographs that afternoon.

"Why won't you take pictures of our neighbor's beautiful house instead? Your mother will be really happy?" I remember father shouting and realized that I had never heard my father shouting at my mother like that before. That afternoon he must have been very angry.

"You want to do as the Joneses do—act like rich people?" father went on. Our neighbors could hear them but father didn't seem to care. I listened from the kitchen—first mother cried out, then father ranted and then both shouted at one another. Then, I heard the front door bang and then there was dead silence everywhere. Father went to their bedroom. Mother followed him slowly and closed the door. I heard the creaking of the door. She turned on the radio, maybe to try to bring down the unpleasant noise of their argument that she expected.

"So you want me to work? You think you own me because you work? All I do is spend your money? I live on you—a parasite!" Father went on shouting.

"You are a failure! You know what you are? You are a loser." As I heard my mother's angry voice, I heard a sudden terrific crash—my father had fallen on their bedroom floor. I ran in there to see mother bending over father who was lying on the floor beside the bed.

"Quick, Nelu call 911," shouted mother. It was that evening that father had his first heart attack. He didn't die. He lay unconscious on the floor. The paramedics arrived within fifteen minutes and strapped him to the stretcher. The ambulance parked just in front of our house seemed to spin with its red lights blinking all the time.

"Oh no! Please don't die!" mother shouted with fear. Three of us, mother, my brother and I were pushed into the ambulance and I felt the ambulance screeching headlong forever to the hospital. I remember looking at my father's face, his eyes closed, cheeks drained of blood. Any other time and day he would have been bringing back color to my drained face—pale with fright. Mother bent over him. Then suddenly we were there at the hospital entrance; the same hospital that I was being driven to in the police car today. Hospital workers carried my father into the emergency room. We followed them there only to rush out when the doctors rushed in. We waited outside.

It was a miracle—I did not know that my mother prayed or that she knew how to pray—but she threw her hands heavenwards and asked a deity—a deity who they say comes to the help of the helpless—to help father to live. Not knowing what else to do, I imitated my mother and pleaded to the same deity I had just begun to have faith in—a deity I never believed existed. When I was in despair, when my parents had those loud, heated arguments over flimsy things I had asked this very same deity to make my parents happy. I wanted a miracle—a real miracle. Not only for my father to simply survive but for things like this never to happen again. I prayed for my parents to live like before they came to this country—a peaceful, happy life. So many things I wanted—I did not know how to pray—to ask God to help me to get them, not for me, but for my parents to get their life back.

Two weeks later, my father came home. I had not cried at all during my father's stay in hospital. I had forgotten how to cry, I only prayed. I had never been so scared in my life. Now that he was at home, he did not need my prayers any more. I wanted to cry—cry for what had happened to our happy family since our arrival in Chicago. I cried all afternoon coming back from school one day and then after dinner too, crying past the point when I did not know what I was crying for. I fell asleep on the couch in the sitting room and when I woke up in the middle of the night—a pillow had appeared under my head.

While seated with my gloved-hands on my lap in the back seat of the police car, I wondered why I couldn't cry now—not a tear appeared in my eyes! I just couldn't understand why mother's pain did not hurt me. Why couldn't mother keep out of trouble anyway? Why is it that when mother is in danger I keep thinking of her clumsy ways of driving? In Brunswick she was reluctant to drive, because she said that in America everybody drives so fast that she was afraid to sit at the wheel. But after much persuasion from father and because of sheer necessity as there was no public transport there, she took the old Ford Escort out. I remember it was exciting to watch mother getting ready to drive the car. Once she sat at the driver's seat, she would take about five minutes to settle down—look in the rearview mirror, try the gears, pull the handbrake down and pull it up again, look behind and front of her and behind again. Not satisfied she would adjust the side mirror again. Even if she was the last person to have taken the car the evening before, she would go through the ritual once again.

The police car passed slowly through the snow covered street. The sky over Chicago looked gray and the bumper-to-bumper cars coming into the city along Lake Shore Drive had their headlights on. It was around ten in the morning and the temperature at the time would have been below twenty degrees. The pedestrians on the sidewalks walked quickly ignoring each other's presence. We had been traveling for almost forty-five minutes and it seemed like an eternity to me. Finally, the police car jolted and stopped at the entrance to the hospital. Following the two policemen, I walked along corridors that seemed endless until they guided me into a large room filled with medical equipment. Beyond that large room was the Intensive Care Unit. One of the policemen opened the door for me. I entered the room with so much fright that my knees began to wobble.

There at the end of a long row of beds, I saw her. Neither her bandaged head nor her leg hanging from a hook attached to the ceiling obstructed the beautifully shaped nose that was visible on her face. Yet, I would not have recognised her if Uncle Henry and my two aunts, my mother's two sisters who lived in Indianapolis, were not standing by her bed. I could not believe that this bandaged body on the bed was my mother. My eyes were filled with tears and I could hardly see her. My heart filled with grief, a grief so great that words flowed out of my mouth and I shouted, "What have they done to you, Mom?"

Hearing my voice, I imagined I stirred my mother to open her eyes slightly, and she looked up at me. I did not expect this. Mother's eyes were half closed but I could see the redness in them. Tears oozed out of her eyes and flowed down her cheeks. On each arm, IVs pushed drugs and fluids into her body. A tube running through her nose and into her stomach, hooked up to a machine on the floor, drained out her stomach. Her face looked blank as if she didn't mind at all the coils of plastic tube that had invaded her body. There was a tube down her throat, a ventilator, Uncle Henry said, because she couldn't breathe by herself. More tubes looped down from the bottles and bags that hung from above the bed and they met at her neck. The valve was masked by light brown tape, as were the electrodes on her temples and chest.

I held her right hand, bandaged from wrist to shoulder. I sobbed, because holding her hand was something I had not done for years now. Fate had brought us together here, in this hospital. I sobbed louder because my mother who was so beautiful and at times vain, who had used her beauty to get most things in her life, was now lying in this hospital bed with her mouth gone crooked and her cheek bones broken. Those full, sensual, red lips were dry and cracked.

Suddenly there was a flurry of beeps from the machine. In an instant doctors and nurses crowded around my mother's bed. The sound increased. I feared that something terrible was happening. I stepped back from the bed to let the nurses and the doctors surround the bed and stood beside Uncle Henry dumb and helpless. He squeezed my sweaty hand.

"Why don't I go ahead and attend to this patient, and you do the next one?" I heard the older of the doctors say. The young doctor in the green coat nodded in agreement as they approached my mother's bed. They could not see my mother at first because of other hospital staff standing in their way. There were two nurses on the left, two doctors in green coats at the foot of the bed and a tall black doctor in a long white coat on the right. As the older doctor approached mother's bed, I observed the tall black doctor adjusting the pressure setting on the respirator. The doctors in green coats were obviously concerned. Their eyes showed their worry. I saw the shaking hands of one of the nurses.

"There's got to be some sort of explanation," said the senior doctor, taking hold of his face mask that was hanging on the back of his neck. The beeps from the machines stopped suddenly. "Is she all right?" I heard the young doctor's voice cracking with emotion.

"Everything seems to be normal," said the senior doctor. "Blood pressure, pulse, temperature all perfectly normal. However, her pupils are dilated and they do not react to light," he said as he pointed a penlight into my mother's eye and held it open.

"This is not a good sign. It probably means there is brain damage to a limited extent." The doctors spoke in whispers. I experienced a sickening feeling rising up within me. I felt helpless and desperate and held on to my uncle's hand.

"Oh! Uncle Henry. Why should this happen to Mom?" I questioned, my voice quivering. The commotion was over in five minutes but it gave us the worst scare in our lives. The senior doctor came to where Uncle Henry and I were standing. He held my hand.

"You are her daughter?" The doctor looked into my face. I instantly noticed his kind eyes. I knew he would do whatever was possible to get my mother out of danger.

"They've taken a CAT scan and we are waiting for the radiologist's report," he said looking at Uncle Henry. Just then the radiologist walked in with the negatives in his hand.

"Here are the pictures," he said while handing over the negatives to the senior doctor. The doctor turned away from us and examined the pictures. "Her brain is swollen slightly. That explains it," he said to the young doctor.

"What's the verdict?"

"Touch and go."

"Touch and go? What does that mean?" Uncle Henry jumped in.

"Serious cases like your sister's can recover only to die tomorrow," answered the doctor.

"If she does make it, would she be all right?"

"I cannot be certain at this stage. She could be blind; she could be paralyzed. I understand your worry. We'll do whatever there is to be done to make her survive." Then he looked at me and said in a very kind voice, "Let's pray. You have to have faith. She will recover. Once your mother's condition stabilizes, she'll have to go through a series of operations to set her broken bones. We need you to sign some papers. Please step into the office before you leave," and he was gone. It was so kind of him to try to console me. His words comforted me a little but I could hardly see my mother now—my eyes were a pool of tears.

I was dumb with grief and misery. When the doctor told us that mother had to go through surgery, I recalled the only other time I had seen mother after surgery. That was the day she went to the plastic surgeon to get a face-lift. What had happened to that beauty who got an eye job done when father was around? Every little detail of the scenario of the day that mother announced she was going to get plastic surgery flashed across my mind. Father was very angry that day, while mother kept her cool. For father, anyone undergoing plastic surgery for sake of beauty was a sign of mental imbalance. He said so, and added that he could not believe that mother had reached that stage in her life so soon.

"Go on and get the eye job," father told her sarcastically. "It's unnatural, it's violence against women to allow themselves to be sliced up and mutilated. Whom do you want to please?" True, mother was approaching middle-age, but she had not lost an iota of her good looks. Did she know that the plastic surgeon would slice open the top of each of her eye lids, peel the skin back, and trim the fat underneath with a scalpel or a laser? Mother could suffer blindness but she thought that was most unlikely. She counted on looking prettier than ever. I remember mother laughing at father that day. She said that cosmetic surgery was an art and that there was nothing wrong with it. She reminded father that we all go jogging, or do body building or do aerobics, or wear fashionable clothes. All these activities manipulate our bodies to make us look more beautiful. But surgery after an accident is different; it repairs the damage done. Of course she could not know at that time—almost eight years ago—that she would be going through surgery to look ordinary and healthy. I just could not believe that my mother's beautiful face could turn into this thing that was now a mask of white bandages.

Uncle Henry leaned forward and gently pressed down a piece of tape that had come off from one of the catheters in mother's arm. He looked up at the battery of machines each of whose purposes Uncle Henry had insisted on having the hospital staff explain. Now, he systematically checked them, scanned each screen, valve and fluid level in the bottles to make sure everything was as perfect as it should be. While doing this Uncle Henry explained to me that all this was computerized and that alarms would sound at the central monitoring desk in the doctors' office, if anything were to go wrong, but it was best to see for himself. Satisfied, and still holding my mother's hand, he announced he had to go. Maybe it was my guilty conscience that kept me saying to myself that if I had been with my mother this accident would not have happened. I found it difficult to leave mother's bedside and it was almost mid-night. My aunts said they would stay with mother and wanted me to go with Uncle

Henry. Since there was nothing I could do by staying, I decided to go and return early the next day morning.

As he drove me back to my apartment, I told Uncle Henry that it was difficult for me to understand how my mother could have met with an accident so serious as to come just a breath away from death. I told him that mother was so careful and it was father who made mistakes when driving.

"However careful you are, you cannot avoid accidents. You know you have no control over other people's actions," said Uncle Henry. I told him how sometimes my brother and I thought father made mistakes consciously to see mother get agitated. In the first few weeks after our arrival in the United States, every time mother saw traffic lights turn red, she would caution father, "Careful Nalin, red lights!" Father acted as if he was color-blind. "They are green, aren't they?" he would ask pretending to be very serious, and if there was no other vehicle in sight, he would just drive through and my mother would land her left fist hard on father's shoulder. I told Uncle Henry about the first time when we went to see Niagara Falls; father drove in the opposite direction on a one-way street (this time it was a genuine mistake) and five other vehicles followed our car! The on-coming traffic, confused to see all these vehicles intruding on their right of way, perhaps thinking a motorcade was bringing a local celebrity to some function, let the vehicles pass through. Father calmly turned at the very next intersection and stopped mother from getting a heart attack! There were numerous occasions when he lost his way; instead of getting out of the next available exit, father would take a U-turn on the highway when there were no vehicles around, and drive on as if he had done nothing illegal.

Uncle Henry listened in silence to my stories and walked with me to my apartment. I wanted to tell him then what had been bothering me since I heard of mother's accident—maybe the idea had crossed his mind too. Considering mother's frustrations in life, could she have caused the accident to put an end to her life? But I dared not present my outrageous opinion to

Uncle Henry. He would not like it. My mother was not only his sister but his favorite sister as well. Observing my silence, he told me to try to get some sleep as there were lots of things to attend to tomorrow.

Once he left, I felt a kind of loneliness I had never felt before—a loneliness that I had not experienced even on the day that I left my mother, just a few weeks after my father passed away. It happened quickly, even before she could get back to her normal life pattern. I could not live with her anymore. I was so angry that when I left her, I planned never to see her again. I blamed her and held her responsible for what happened to my father's grief-stricken life and for the disappearance of my brother.

Where was Roshan? I had to find him somehow. He needed to know that mother was in danger. I sat on the sofa in my sitting room for a long time, thinking about how to find my brother, when my eyes caught a photograph amidst my books on the shelf. In it my mother is in a dress and she is smiling at me—that sweet, captivating smile of hers—her lips brighter than the red rose that appears next to her ear. Roshan took this photograph on one of his visits home during college vacations.

"I want to take a picture of you, Dad," I remember Roshan following father to the garden, getting his camera ready.

"Not now. Go and take your mother's, I am busy now," father refused.

"It will only take a minute. Please Dad," Roshan pleaded.

"All right." Father waved his hand above his head and grinned. Roshan looked through the camera viewfinder. I could almost see the heavy gold ring father wore on his left hand middle finger shining in the afternoon sunlight. That ring was a gift from my mother's mother, given to father when my father married my mother. His hair, streaked with grey was thinning above the forehead. His face looked a little tired. Roshan snapped the camera shutter.

"Now, go and take one of your mother." Father sent Roshan away. Those were the good days that I will never see again.

"Mom! Can I take a picture of you now?" Unlike my father, my mother liked to pose for photographs. Mother didn't take long—she came out dressed in a long, red dress—she knew she looked radiant in red. She applied lipstick, darkened her eyebrows and gently sent a brush through her dark black hair. She walked out into the garden and touched a red rose.

"Why won't you stand at the front door so that I can take the house as well in the background?" Roshan asked, looking through the viewfinder.

"No. I want my picture taken with the red rose," she said firmly.

"Take the picture now."

Her radiant smile lit up her face. I noticed the pair of earrings she had put on especially for the photograph. She has wrinkles under her eyes but she hardly shows her age. She looks as if she has been forty-six for the last ten years or so.

My mother believed she was beautiful. After Roshan snapped the shutter she plucked the rose and wore it behind her ear. I remember, after the photograph was taken, Roshan and mother ate ice cream in the kitchen. I was with them listening to their conversation. A cool wind blew through the kitchen curtain. After eating, mother walked out through the kitchen door to the backyard and sat on a folding chair beckoning Roshan to sit on the other. Roshan followed her. They were the best of friends.

I have to find him somehow.

On my bookshelf, there is a photograph of me, also taken by Roshan that same day. I am sitting on a wicker chair, hunched forward, staring at the ground, hands tightly clasped on my lap. I remember Roshan's camera aimed at me and I can now almost hear his voice saying, "Say Cheese, Nelu!" I was imitating my American friends then in dress, in smile and in walk and was appreciative of my mother's comments on how American I had become.

I have another photograph of my mother, on the shelf near the television. I feel her compassionate eyes looking at me. She is wearing my favorite of all her sarees—a deep purple one that rippled with light when she moved. My mother's hair, its blue-black hue, shone in the light like a wreath of dark feathers. I remember her dressing for that photograph. She was seated on the black stool in front of the dressing table mirror in their bedroom back in Kandy. The dressing table top was crowded with fragrant jars and beautiful bottles. My mother told me that those bottles held the secrets of her beauty. Much of what I knew about mother's vanity I learned in front of that mirror.

Looking at my mother's photograph, I thought over and over again of something I had suspected all the time when I was growing up; that my mother was a flirt—she flirted with the mirrors and cameras and then with the admiring glances of father's friends. I remember her telling me one day, getting ready to go to the doctor two years after our arrival in Chicago, "It gives you a top of the world feeling to look sexy. It is wonderful!"

It had been a long, difficult day. The photographs brought back some memories of my life with my parents and Roshan. Instead of cheering me up those memories tormented me and I was haunted by thoughts of Roshan. I wanted to talk to someone. I believe it is easier to bear any pain of mind if you can share it with those closer to you. It was too late in the night to call my best friend Lindy or any of my other friends at the university. I must contact them tomorrow. Not having engaged in any religious event for some fifteen years or so following high school, I found it impossible to seek solace in religion. Whom could I ask for help if I didn't believe in the existence of any superior being who, they say, comes to the help of the helpless?

II

The moaning of the wind woke me up in the morning. Beyond the panes of my bedroom windows, I saw patches of blue sky. For two days in a row Chicagoans had lived with this snowstorm and now it seemed as if the snow had brought me loneliness and I faced the day with a confused state of mind.

I wished for my brother Roshan to be there with me. If only he knew what mother was going through, he would be the first to be at her bedside. He would be there holding her hand and wishing that his mere touch would transfer some of his life energy to her body and bring her back to consciousness.

In the depth of my heart I had a faint feeling that I would see Roshan yesterday in the hospital. In fact, when I heard of mother's accident, one of the things that first crossed my mind was the opportunity to see my brother again.

I hadn't seen him for eight years now. Would I be able to recognize him? He might have grown a beard; his hair must have grown longer, perhaps to his shoulders; would he be displaying a little pony tail? Without mother to feed him, he must have lost weight. When I went to the hospital yesterday I planned to ask mother whether she had heard from Roshan—but then I never imagined that mother's condition would be so critical.

About a week or so after Roshan broke away from mother and me, I remember mother telling me that she was so grief-stricken, she covered herself from head to foot with her quilt and closed her eyes, and vowed never to get up from her bed. Then she had a vision of Roshan through the bedroom window, walking towards the house, laughing and waving at her. It was then that mother had jumped out of her bed and phoned the local paper and placed an advertisement, phoned the local missing persons office and every evening walked from night club to night club on Rush Street hoping to see Roshan. After work, before coming home, she walked the crowded streets of Chicago, something that she detested. On weekends she sat on the grounds for hours at classical music concerts in Grant Park. She had looked into almost all the young faces coming out of the subway stations hoping to see Roshan. I joined mother in these very same things for a while but gave up. My efforts were useless. But my mother never gave up—maybe she now knows where Roshan is.

One day, before I left her and that was almost six years ago, when I had gathered enough courage to ask her if she had heard from Roshan, she didn't say anything—instead her eyes swelled with tears and she turned her head away from me. That day I decided never to bring up the subject again.

Before leaving for the hospital that morning, I thought I would talk to Lindy, my best friend from Brunswick school days. She now teaches piano at the Catholic school in downtown Chicago. I respected her and I could find some consolation in her kind and friendly words. But, I couldn't reach her; she had her answering machine on. I left a message asking her to come to my apartment in the evening.

Feeling hopeless, I decided to drive to the hospital. As I inserted the key in the ignition, I imagined I faintly saw Roshan's face in the rear view mirror of my car—the picture of him driving away on the highway—just like the very last time I saw him. I was shocked and confused and yearned to talk to someone. I sat in my car for a while before taking a short walk down Michigan Avenue. I thought that the beautiful place that I had taken refuge in so many times when I was in despair would help me to get over my confused state of mind. I was confused because I was upset with myself over my guilt—my guilt of running away from my mother after father passed away and after Roshan left us. I felt terrible leaving her on her own when she needed me around so badly, that I now thought of excuses for my selfish actions. If only I had stayed with her this accident would not have happened—but then at that time I blamed mother for all the misfortunes that fell on our family.

I pushed my way through the lingering crowds down Oak Street, out into the drizzling December day. Once outside and without any particular destination in mind, I just walked, aimlessly, lost in my own thoughts. I turned on Cedar Street and then walked on to Michigan Avenue. The snow collected on the sidewalks made it difficult to walk but yet Michigan Avenue was crowded with holiday shoppers. I felt the light rain fluttering on my hair and against my forehead. Small droplets gathered and dripped from the tip of my nose. Despite the doctor's consoling words last evening, I could not remember ever feeling so helpless and isolated. I felt totally alone. Sudden fears of being an orphan invaded my brain. I thought of the worst; my mother dying in hospital before coming out of her coma—before I could ask her for forgiveness for leaving her and neglecting her all these years—before I could hold her hand and tell her that I love her very much. In the middle of my tormented musings, I felt my right foot slide as I put my weight on it. I steadied myself with my hand on the nearby lamp post and looked down to see that I was walking on a thin sheet of ice. The drizzle that had developed into a light rain was gradually ceasing. Icy cold water dripped down my face, and I wiped it with the sleeve of my coat.

I had just walked past Nikeland that morning and recalled my visits there with mother. There was a period in her life when she was crazy over American tennis stars and she wanted to play the game like them. She would then go and buy the most expensive tennis shorts and shoes from Nikeland.

"You should have the expensive, classy stuff. If not these folks won't take you seriously. You have to get yourself noticed," she told me when I asked her why she was spending so much money on sports wear.

"When you are a foreigner and especially when you have come from the Third World, you have to show good, expensive taste. It's very important."

"Everyone here is a foreigner, Mom. They all came here from somewhere else, didn't they?"

"Now you are talking like your father. Face reality, Nelu," mother retorted and refused to talk anymore. Here was an instance when mother showed me that silence was power. When she got angry she did not talk. I remember how this behavior of hers infuriated my father. In the midst of a heated argument she would shut her mouth, letting father talk and receive no response.

By accompanying mother on her shopping expeditions sometimes I learned a little patience. Very often she took me to Marshall Fields on Michigan Avenue. She was pleased at the way women-clerks used to compliment me on my ability to get interested in shopping for my mother's clothes. She would make me sit inside those elegant dressing rooms and watch her try on clothes—one outfit after another. She never got tired. She put one on, stood in front of the long mirror, took a 180 degree turn, then gently touching her hips with both her hands and turning her head slightly would ask my opinion. I was just thirteen years old—she wanted my opinion! I would sit there like a dummy. Words would not come out of my mouth, inhibited by all that grandeur around me.

"I like it—you look beautiful in it," over and over I said. Every single garment that she tried seemed perfect for her. If she was not in the hospital now, my mother would have been on Michigan Avenue joining hundreds of holiday shoppers, jostling, weaving in and out of stores, carrying packages and colliding with other shoppers. Though it was a hassle, I wanted mother to take me on these trips. Even though the prices at stores like Nieman Marcus and Saks were too high for her wallet, mother never missed rushing into them. As we passed the jewelry store,

I wondered who would have the money and who would be so dumb as to purchase a $ 400 ashtray? Where you buy things was absolutely critical for my mother. To carry a Saks shopper's bag was a status symbol for her.

Walking past F.A.O. Schwarz, the toy store, I was reminded of my mother's childish behavior. But there were times when I really admired the child in her. One Saturday morning we were walking past the toy shop when we noticed a crowd gathered in front. Mother held my hand and pushed her way through the awestruck children and their parents. We heard a robotic voice on the elevator announcing, "I am Go-2-Floor-2! I am happy that your journey has brought you to the galaxy of toys!" Hearing the announcement, I looked at my mother's face. Her face was gleaming with joy; she was a child that moment. I was happy, too, just to see the wonder around me!

I can almost hear my mother's voice on a shopping spree in New York. That particular day, she took me to Tiffany's where the average American's salary was petty cash to regular customers. To get into the shop we stood outside the store's iron grilled door looking serious. A doorman admitted us to an anteroom where a showcase of some of their lower priced items, say $8,000, were on display.

"What are we doing here, Mom?" I whispered, clinging on to her arm.

"We must see these things. We are in America," she hushed me up.

Mother used to buy all of father's clothes but after coming to Chicago where she began to earn more than father, she took control of family finances and her life style changed. Then she stopped buying for father. Yet she walked into Bijan, a men's exclusive boutique. A brass plate near the door announced, "by appointment only." A white-gloved doorman stood blocking the entrance.

"This is the land of $2,500 cashmere sweaters and $350 ties," mother whispered in my ear as we stood at the doorway.

"You can go in," the doorman said with a smile to my mother who showed her beautiful white teeth and smiled back in appreciation. Perfumes for men started at $350, a salesman in double-breasted pinstripes said, but the cheapest piece of apparel was a $75 silk pocket handkerchief bearing the shop's logo. From there we walked to designer Geoffrey Beene's tiny Art Deco boutique. I was terrified when mother showed interest in a $90 pair of Beene's wool gloves trimmed with fur.

"You are not going to buy that?" I asked in horror.

"No. I'll go for this instead," she said, handing the salesman a set of four linen mats and napkins, in white with contrasting hemstitches, priced at $85. Now she could impress her friends at dinner parties at home, but would her friends even notice?

How my mother's shopping style has changed. My thoughts went back to the leaner days at Brunswick when mother would break off and steal a thumb-size piece of ginger from the supermarket. Seeing my wide-open eyes, she would say, "It's not worth weighing—it's too small," and would place it in her pants' pocket. I knew to keep the secret from father—for if I did not, I would not be accompanying mother on her small shopping trips in Brunswick again. I thought of those Saturdays in Brunswick when I followed mother in her shopping sprees. She did not have much money to spend then but we certainly had great fun—she and I. We used to buy one ice cream cone and sit on the steps leading to the summer house in the town square and take turns licking the ice cream while we talked and laughed. We used to walk down Maine Street; window shopping. There was one particular store that I liked—mother knew I liked it so she took me there whenever we walked to town. I couldn't take my eyes off the exquisite costume jewelry there. I remember mother one day grabbed a pair of ear rings which I was admiring and threw it into her handbag and walked out of the store! She handed the earrings to me the next day as if she had done nothing wrong. How could I be so ungrateful to let myself forget what little things mother did for her only daughter?

When I got tired of walking, I sat on the steps at the entrance to Marshall Field on Michigan Avenue and watched the crowd walking in and out of the store. The beautiful young women carrying bags of shopping brought back images of mother. My mother was so beautiful to me, it was as if someone had made her up out of a desire to create beauty in the world. Mother told me that she and her sister did not have much money to spend on clothes when they were young. Both her parents were teachers. They believed their mother when she told them that because of their beauty, both of them would marry rich men.

Many a time mother's advice to me was, "Always look as if you are having a wonderful time." To my mother, virtue consisted above all in keeping up appearances. "Nothing is more important than how you look and how you dress," she told me over and over again. "Use your looks. Show off what you have," she advised me. Those days back at home with her own mother, she said, she made her own dresses. She would lay the fabric on the floor, cut it out, and with her mother's old Singer sewing machine, make beautiful dresses for her and her sister Edith. When she and Edith went out, people stared at them because of their beauty—and they had lots of fun enjoying their "admiring stares." My mother had a charming figure and she carried whatever dress or saree she put on exquisitely. Style means a lot to women. Many women spend a lifetime without any, or trying to figure out what theirs is. My mother seemed instinctively to know. She was smart enough to know and courageous enough to try what style worked for her—what was best for her and her physique. She had cultivated a great deal of social poise and in the library where she worked she said she found it difficult to make friends among women because some of them were envious of her beauty.

"When you get older and lose your beauty and your figure people treat you as a normal person. Women make friends with you but men don't treat you like a special person," she told me.

"A man proposed to me on the elevator today," I remember mother shouting triumphantly, stepping into the apartment one evening, coming home after a day's work in the library. She was radiant as always. I cannot remember her face showing fatigue ever. Given the choice of attending a boring dinner party or reading a good book seated by the fire on a wintry evening, my mother would choose the dinner party. She was so upbeat that she would have kept the others at the party in high spirits. She loved to show-off and be around and be seen. Although I didn't really understand why, I had the suspicion that all men were secretly and madly in love with my mother. She was the most beautiful and charming of all women. How else could I explain my father's blind devotion to her?

The smell of perfume emanating from the cosmetics department through the revolving door, as it opened every time a customer walked in and out, reminded me of mother's favorite perfume, *Blue Grass*. She loved it and kept it in *eau de toilette* and in perfume. During the first few years of our stay in America and when we did not have much money to spend on perfumes, she was very careful with her bottle of *Blue Grass*. Her fragrance was mild and sweet. The perfume seeped from a thin wad of tissue hidden on the left shoulder underneath her blouse. She wiped the mouth of the *Blue Grass* bottle with a piece of tissue, folded it into a small square and tucked it in there. I would have thrown the tissue into the waste paper basket.

III

I had been walking for almost an hour, thinking so much of my mother's shopping habits that I did not feel the time pass. It was late and I couldn't postpone going to the hospital any longer. The freezing cold and walking on the snow-covered sidewalks were not pleasant but they made my guilty feelings fade a little. I dreaded to think what my mother must be going through now. Maybe she had regained conciousness. Maybe she was out of danger now. Why was I so scared? Come on, Nelu, look at the brighter side of life! I cheered myself as I walked back to the car.

It was raining when I finally made it to the hospital in the afternoon. The freezing rain-drops that poured on the hoods of cars made puddles on the hospital parking lot. I wondered if the weather would delay Uncle Henry's arrival at the hospital. As I stepped out of the car, the freezing rain-drops hitting my shoulders, I looked across the lot for the familiar Volvo. Yes, to my great relief, Uncle Henry was already there.

I went into the hospital through the main entrance. The inevitable crowds were occupying every seat on the corridors. There were people of all ages, waiting, forever waiting. These were not people seeking attention in either the clinic or the emergency room. They were people waiting for a relative or a friend to be admitted or discharged or perhaps they were patients who had been treated and were now waiting to be picked up and taken home. There was no conversation and no smiles. The dense crowd stood in my way to the elevator as well. I forced my way through the crowd and to my horror found myself standing in front of a man (or was it a woman?) whose eyes were surrounded by dark patches of blood. The person's nose was swollen and distorted. Two wires came from the nostrils and they were taped to either cheek. It was like seeing something out of a horror movie. I tried to keep my eyes on the elevator numbers to avoid the frightful sight. When the landing light lit eight, my mother's floor, I jumped out of the elevator and ran towards her room.

Ignorant of all the snow and rain outside, mother lay still in the privacy of her coma. Her battered cells were silently coming back to life but there was no change in her outward appearance. For three days she had been unconscious. The doctors had removed the air tube down her throat and had inserted one instead through a little hole cut neatly on the left side of her neck. They fed her plastic bags of brown liquid through the tube that went up her nose and down into her stomach. Three times a day the physiotherapist came and worked on her limbs to stop her muscles and joints from wasting away.

While Aunt Edith stayed at mother's bedside that afternoon, Uncle Henry and I walked out to the adjoining waiting room. We talked for a while and stretched ourselves on the couch for a minute. Maybe we dozed off. I felt the presence of the young good looking doctor who gave injections to mother the previous evening, standing near the couch. He touched Uncle Henry's arm. In the dim light I noticed the doctor was wearing a green coat and his face appeared sad and worried. I heard him tell Uncle Henry that my mother, even if she regained consciousness he doubted whether she would be able to walk ever again. Feeling exhausted and helpless, I walked up to the coffee machine in the corridor outside the intensive care unit and watched the rain gusting in great swathes across the parking lot. An old man was wrestling with the wind to keep his umbrella over his head and two nuns in their black robes were being swept like penguins toward their car. The clouds looked low and mean enough to bump their wimpled heads. The coffee machine gave a last gurgle and I extracted a cup and took a sip. It tasted revolting, but at least it was hot and it was some liquid. I walked slowly back into the unit and met one of the younger nurses coming off the shift.

"She's improving," the nurse said as we passed.

"You think so?" I asked looking at her. Surely the nurses knew well enough not to say such things without thinking hard.

"Yes, of course," she paused for a second at the door and it seemed she wanted to say something more. But she thought better of it and pushed the door open. "Just keep massaging her muscles," she said and disappeared into the darkness outside.

Improving? What did she mean improving; I wondered as I walked back to mother's bed. As I approached her bed, I noticed another nurse changing the dressing on mother's arm. Aunt Edith was watching her. I went and stood by my aunt. The nurse looked up and smiled and went on with her job. It was the only job I couldn't bring myself to do—changing dressings and massaging. The hospital staff encouraged relatives to get involved in the treatment. Aunt Edith had become quite expert at the physical therapy and most of the other things that had to be done, like cleaning mother's mouth and eyes and changing the urine bag that hung beside the bed. I could barely look at my mother's body lying lifeless on the bed, let alone massage it. Her limbs felt like dead fish to my touch. During this time in hospital, I learned that there are really two kinds of people in the world—people who became hard and efficient in times of terrible trouble, and those like me, who scream, shriek, go limp, sink to the floor, become worse than patients themselves.

"It's healing nicely," the nurse said. My aunt nodded and I forced myself to keep watching. The stitches on her left arm made long curved scars and were a vivid purple. The nurse saw the terrified look in my eyes.

"I think her tape's run out," she said pointing towards the Walkman on the pillow beside mother's head. The nurse gave me an escape from the scar and I gratefully took it. I ejected the spent tape, which contained the *mahapirith*—soothing sounds of the *sangha* chanting Buddha's teachings—soothing sounds for mother to hear and come back to life to the blessings of *sangha*. This had been my aunt's idea—what lengths we go to when we are in despair! Who knew whether mother could hear the chanting and what it could do to a brain so bruised?

Aunt Edith wiped a trickle of saliva from the corner of mother's mouth and put back a strand of hair from her forehead. She let her hand rest on mother's forehead and kept looking down at her face. After a while Aunt Edith became aware that the nurse had finished dressing the arm and was watching her. They smiled at each other. But there was a trace of something close to pity in the nurse's eyes and my aunt looked at me and quickly broke the silence.

"Workout time!" my aunt said and pushed up her sleeve and pulled a chair closer to the bed. The nurse gathered up her things and left us leaving Aunt Edith and me at mother's bedside. Aunt Edith, as instructed by the physiotherapist, started with mother's left hand. She held it in both her hands and began working the fingers one by one, then all of them together. Backward, and forward, opening and closing each joint, feeling the knuckles crack as she squeezed them. Now the thumb, revolving it, massaging and kneading it with her fingers. I could hear Aunt Edith's whispers, humming the *pirith* following the sound emanating from the tape. When my aunt turned my mother's arm over, I observed mother's pale skin and her lifeless wrist with the veins, blue in color, flowing from the wrist joint. Aunt Edith moved on to mother's elbow, opening and closing the joint, twenty times, counting each time as she did so, then massaging the muscles. It was hard work for Aunt Edith and she said sometimes her hands and arms ached at the end of every session; but she never complained.

I wished I could help her but could never muster enough courage to do so. Soon it was time to move around to the other side of mother's bed. Aunt Edith laid mother's arm gently down on the bed and was about to get up from where she was seated, when I noticed something. It was so minute and so quick that I thought for a moment I must have imagined it. But no—it really happened again and I saw it. I saw one of mother's fingers in her left hand quiver. That was the hand that Aunt Edith had been working on all this time. In my excitement, I almost shouted to Aunt Edith and both of us waited to see it happen again. It didn't. Aunt Edith picked mother's hand again and squeezed it.

"Leila," she said quietly.

"Leila, it's me. Your sister Edith. Can you hear me? Please squeeze my hand. Give me a smile." Nothing happened. My mother's face remained blank. The only movement was the top of her chest which rose and fell in time with the respirator. Maybe what I thought I saw was only the hand falling over from its own weight. My eyes shifted from my mother's face to the stack of machines attached to her body that monitored her functions. I didn't know how to read what went on, on the screens. Only Uncle Henry learned it all. But I didn't want to miss a second of what I thought would happen, so I didn't run to Uncle Henry who was still in the adjoining room. The heartbeat screen had a little electronic orange heart on it and it had been moving at a rate of a constant seventy for the last two days and now I noticed it was moving faster—at eighty-five, eighty-six. I looked at Aunt Edith. She looked around. There wasn't a nurse to be seen. I was as usual in a panic, but not Aunt Edith. She held mother's hand again.

"Leila?" she squeezed her hand—the monitor had reached hundred.

"Nelu, go bring Henry," my aunt instructed me. I wasn't going to budge from mother's bedside. But as I looked up there were two nurses and the young doctor—the one who talked to us just a little while ago. The change in heartbeat had been picked up on the central screens.

"I saw her finger move," I said panting with excitement.

"Keep on squeezing her hand," the doctor instructed Aunt Edith. He opened one of mother's eyes and looked into it with the help of the penlight he took out from his coat pocket. The nurses were observing the reaction on monitors. The heartbeat had reached a steady hundred and ten.

"Talk to your sister," the doctor asked Aunt Edith. For a moment Aunt Edith was lost for words.

"Talk to her!" he repeated. "Say anything that comes to your head," he said in earnest.

"Leila, it's me—your sister, Edith. Can you hear me? Time to wake up. Look at me. Your girl, Nelu, is here."

"Keep on talking. It doesn't matter what you say. Don't stop."

"Blood pressure is one fifty," said the nurse.

"What does that mean?" I couldn't keep my mouth shut.

"It means your mother is responding," I heard the doctor's voice. He took my mother's hand from Aunt Edith, still holding the eye open with the other hand.

"Leila, I am squeezing your hand now. I want you to squeeze back—you can do it, I know you can—Try hard." The doctor squeezed my mother's hand, looking into mother's eyes all the time. "Good girl. Now do it for your sister," he said and gave the hand to Aunt Edith. My aunt took a deep breath and squeezed my mother's hand gently.

"Squeeze it, so that she will feel it," said the doctor.

"Leila, we love you. Here's Nelu. Show us that you are with us." It took just a few seconds for my mother to open her eyes. She heard our voices. We felt that she was regaining consciousness. She was coming back to life. I felt Uncle Henry's presence by my side. His eyes were filled with tears of joy. He bent down and kissed my mother's forehead leaving a tear there.

"Soon," the doctor said softly, "she should be able to breathe on her own without the help of the respirator. We all have jumped the highest hurdle. Still, the road ahead is cluttered with numerous obstacles. We have a long way to go." He looked at us with a triumphant smile and walked away from mother's bed.

We stood there for a long time, all four of us, around mother's bed, talking with excitement and relief, that we didn't feel the time pass. It was already late in the evening. Though I found it difficult to drag myself away from mother's bedside, I had to leave as I had asked Lindy to come to see me. My aunts seemed like angels to me, who had appeared from heaven not only to save my mother's life but to save mine too. Without them I could not have managed the situation. They assured me that they would stay on as long as mother's condition remained critical and I was free to do whatever I had to. After hugging them with deep gratitude, I walked with Uncle Henry to the parking lot.

On the way he told me he had been to the police station but had not found out anything new. The officer-in-charge of the case had informed him that the heavy snowfall just after the accident had made things difficult for the police investigators. Added to that there were yet no witnesses to the accident. " I am planning to go to the police station in the morning, I told him.

"Good," he said. "The police will speed up with the inquiry if we show our concern."

Uncle Henry waited by my car until I got in and started the engine. Then he walked away looking for his car which was parked nearer the hospital entrance. I watched him as he disappeared beyond the dim light of the street lamp. At the time I realized how fortunate I was to have a pillar of strength in Uncle Henry. I needed to lean on him in my despair.

IV

Lindy did not turn up at six o'clock that evening. Maybe she did not get my message; maybe she was not in town. As it was still early, I decided to wait for her. I made a mug of coffee and made myself comfortable in the sofa, thinking how comforting it would have been if Roshan were around. I had hoped to see him at mother's bedside but no one spoke about him—not even Uncle Henry. Roshan had drifted away from my life, further and further, carrying with him a part of me into oblivion. Did the disappointments mother had experienced with my brother's disappearance lead to the accident? The thought crossed my mind several times that evening.

Every family has its troubles—scratch the surface of any family and you will find an ugly source of pain and disappointment—the father can't get a job that satisfies him, the son has thrown away the opportunity for a good education and has gone astray. There were many times when I tried to explain to mother that there is a difference between circumstance and choice. Roshan and I grew up under the same circumstances; in fact he was given more opportunities than I—but we made a million different choices on the way. Circumstances we could not control, but the choices were ours to make. There were times when I asked myself the question, How can a brother be so different from the sister?

But now I realize why, because my mother explained to me that one asks the question only until one has children. Is the mother's body only a sort of nourishing pipeline creating a variety of humans, each one conceived different, as a whole different individual? My mother did not listen to me—she did not take me seriously. Even when I was in college, mother treated me as her little girl and little girls are not smart. Little girls are not expected to think ahead, to think maturely.

I hated it when she ignored me. But the truth is, the same advice I gave mother during the days when Roshan made a mess of his life, I find hard to follow now. This pattern of realizing principles that I could not act on made mother and me so much alike. Sometimes when I think of what happened to my family, I find it difficult to enjoy the stable and comfortable life I earned with so much hard work and determination.

The bonds between parents and children have always been tight in our families—too tight, I now realize. Our parents believe that the harder they cling, the more they can protect us. If only that were true. Our parents had protected us so much and so well that we have never known risk; never been in danger. I remember back at home in Sri Lanka, when Roshan wanted to join his friends to go swimming in the pool at Suisse Hotel in Kandy, mother stopped him.

"Too many accidents happen these days in pools," she said. Mother was afraid of the darkness then, so she wouldn't go out alone in the night. She said there were ghosts and spirits who came out when darkness took over the world waiting to pounce on living creatures. She forbade us from taking showers after dinner for fear that food would not be digested and we might throw up on the bathroom floor.

"Don't walk back home alone from school," she advised me. "Wait for Roshan and please, Nelu, don't hang around with fast ones." On days when Roshan stayed late, she told me to join some girls to walk back home from school. If something happened on the way one of them could always run for help. I found it difficult to tell her that I preferred to walk back from school alone, that it gave me time to think of what happened in school that day.

Sipping my coffee, I thought of the days when our parents talked to us about American schools, American school children and teachers even before we arrived in the United States. They made it clear to us that we were here in the United States because they wanted to give us the best in life and that, to them, was an American education. After our arrival in Brunswick and for days before that first Fall semester, their advice to us became a regular thing at dinner table. For mother, doing the right thing had great importance. Approaching new situations with great caution meant less risk of mistakes and more opportunities for making the right impressions and getting ahead of others. I thought she recognized this more than father because she herself was planning to go back to school. She planned to go back to Library School to become a professional.

"When dealing with Americans one must be assertive," mother told Roshan many times. At home, we were taught to shut up and listen but out in society we should be able to get up, make a speech, sing or do anything which we would be called upon to do. We had to force ourselves to assume an assertive style that was not familiar to us. Roshan and I knew that we would find this very tough to handle.

"With the Americans you have to speak up, loud and clear, or you'll never be heard," said mother. Back in Sri Lanka, as children, we were taught by example the importance of silence, even punished for being too loud and talkative. The old adage, empty vessels make the most sound, had been repeated to me many times. American children are encouraged to speak up, quite a contrast to the Sri Lankan don't talk back.

"Being a foreign student," father said, "you have to get one step beyond everybody else. You do this by judging them by their motives. Don't ever just accept a person by what he is saying. Because they would say one thing to your face to please you and behind your backs they will say something else." Mother fully agreed with father's analysis. She always showed a suspicion of the outside world. We thought that mother knew it all because she had experience working in England back in the days when father was studying for his doctorate in Cambridge.

Mother was very much aware of social status. She observed American behavior and was sensitive to criticism. So she wanted us to adopt the manners of upper-class American friends, their social graces. It was important to mother that my brother and I enter the American society as well-mannered persons. She reminded us of this many times, especially at the dinner table.

Observing Roshan lifting the bowl to pour the remaining soup into his mouth one evening, mother demonstrated how to dip the soup spoon and how to lift the bowl gently with your left hand thumb and forefinger to scoop out the last remaining soup in the dish.

"I have shown you the difference between the fish knife and a butter knife, but you, Roshan, keep buttering the bread with the fish knife. If you don't learn things at home, you will disgrace me when you go out for a meal with our friends." Roshan nudged me in the ribs and father winked at me and smiled. Mother ignored their reactions and went on to tell us that when you sit at table, there is an exactly right time to put the napkin on your lap.

"Since we came here we have not had many opportunities to attend social gatherings except at college where gatherings seemed pretty informal to me," mother said. "But back at home we attended many dinner parties and cocktail parties where we had to observe strict etiquette. I remember reading books on observing etiquette before attending dinner parties held at ambassadors' residences. I even subscribe to *Good HouseKeeping* magazine to learn how to behave in the presence of others. Observing strict etiquette shows one's upper class breeding."

She went on to explain to us that here in America very often both parents hold full-time jobs and what is called the great socializing vehicle, the family meal, has disappeared. "That's true," my brother sometimes added. "The other evening when I dropped in at Bryan's to discuss our debate topic, he was having his evening meal all by himself. His parents were at work. He was eating Chinese food straight out of cardboard cartons. I actually couldn't help laughing when I noticed the way he was attacking the food with the fork!"

"Most parents in America are so busy that they depend on schools to teach their children basic manners. I think if you have to learn social manners in school it's an embarrassment for the family for that shows that you come from a not well-bred background," said mother. "So you must learn your manners at home and I am responsible to teach you your social manners. Roshan, it's important you go first and hold the door for your sister to walk out the door," mother told Roshan many times. But when it came to rushing out of the door in the mornings to go to school Roshan forgot what mother said the evening before and just rushed out.

"Little things matter most, you know," my mother would insist.

Every weekday after school, father helped us with our school work. Roshan and I brought our school satchels to the dining room. Mother very often worked until late in the library. Whenever she was around she kept insisting, "I always came first in class; besides I had a good memory. You both are just like me—you should have no difficulty in doing your school work. It's much easier here." Mother's so frequent, "you are just like me," made my brother furious. We sat around the dining room—the three of us. I scrunched over my books, my elbows resting on the table while father would look at Roshan's books. His work was attended to first, my work came second. In our family, as in all Sri Lankan families, boys' education was more important than girls'. After we finished our school work, Roshan would talk to father for hours. I wondered why he needed all this time to get father's help to do his school work. Roshan, unlike me, was considered smart and he worked hard too.

Sometimes Roshan told father things that troubled him at school. I confess that I found out by eavesdropping.

"Most of the time I don't understand what the boys talk about, so, I feel left out," Roshan told father.

"Is it their way of speaking that you cannot follow or is it the contents of their conversation. What do they say?" father inquired.

"Well . . ." Roshan was hesitant.

"Go on, son. You can tell me," encouraged father. Roshan was feeling embarrassed. I could see it in his face.

"Roger, the boy who is in my Math group said that his girl friend's sister, who is still in High School, got pregnant and had to leave school."

"Hmm," father only made a sound.

"Those boys read the *Playboy Magazine*. Do you know what it is Daddy? It has pictures of nude women." I have seen father reading the *English Language Review* and burying his head over the *New York Times*. What does my father know about the *Playboy Magazine*? I know more about the magazine than both of them!

Roshan continued. "Cindy wears falsies, one of the boys told me. Cindy is the girl in my French Class. I work with her during recess. He also said that girls in the French Class are real shits. I listened to them and I don't quite understand, don't quite believe them either. They screw their girlfriends, they say, and they dress up in their sisters' underwear! I feel embarrassed most of the time when they tell me these things because I don't follow them. They hoot and lift their hands and touch each other's palms and call it high-five. What's high-five Daddy?"

"It's a very American thing—high-five." Father stood up, and not knowing how exactly to advise Roshan, just uttered, "In time you'll grow up, Roshan," and walked out.

Mother did not have time to help us in our school work but whenever we had something to show off, like grades for an assignment or the end of semester class report, both Roshan and I ran to mother first. I remember on many occasions when I got straight As and told my mother, she was indifferent. But she never failed to shower praise on Roshan's academic achievements. If the son in the family excelled in academic matters, the whole family took credit for it. At times like that I could not hide my frustration. With my fists clenched and my body stiff, I would begin to perspire.

When my brother was still in high school, mother had decided that he was going to study to be a doctor. She had high ambitions for Roshan. I couldn't say whether father had a say in the decision. I remembered mother talking to Roshan for hours, almost everyday, trying to persuade him to be a doctor.

"You will bring honor to the family. Your sister can marry a doctor. Think about it." Roshan was deaf to mother's pleadings at first. He had by then been brainwashed into American attitudes. "Do your own thing. Do what's best for yourself." But Roshan went along with mother's decision. It was much later that I realized, that like most Sri Lankan mothers, my mother also considered her son the measuring stick by which she would be judged as a mother. If he studied hard and became a doctor, mother would be the model Sri Lankan mother. If somehow Roshan could not become a doctor, mother was a failure.

A vivid picture of the day that Roshan left for college flashed across my mind. Mother cried that day. To keep his emotions down, Roshan laughed and made fun of mother's red nose.

"Mom's nose is getting red," he said.

Mother and I helped him to pack his clothes. I ironed his shirts while mother neatly folded them. Roshan had a case full of science fiction books that he had already read, but he wanted to take them with him. Father held Roshan close to him for a long time.

"Going to college means you are leaving home. It's like holding on to the tail of a tiger. You can't let it go—it will jump on you. You are in a slow fight for the rest of your life and you will notice that the lightness of youth will leave you. You will not have the time to think about your surroundings. My blessings go with you, son. Make the best of it," father advised him again. I kissed him on both cheeks. When the time came for him to leave, "Good Bye," Roshan said to me. I looked up at his face and saw that his eyes were red. He reached out to mother and held her hand and walked out of the door with her. "I love you, Roshan," mother said. I remember how Roshan got into the car and waited silently for father to start the engine.

"Going to college does not mean he is leaving the family," mother consoled herself. She couldn't hold her tears anymore.

Once he got into college Roshan showed signs of a brilliant academic career. When he came home from college for short breaks, he shared with us a little of his college life. The life he described seemed to me a lonely one. It sounded as if he was becoming a recluse. There were names of friends he mentioned, but none seemed close. There were girls he said he was friendly with, but none he was serious about. By his own account, most of the time, he spent reading and studying for the courses he had signed up for. Mother remarked that Roshan had grown quieter and that he spoke only when he had something important to say or only when spoken to. Father said, "He is taking his college studies seriously. Isn't that good?" and he found nothing unusual about Roshan's quietness, surely it meant he focused attention on his studies.

But at the end of his sophomore year, Roshan suddenly decided to take a year off from college. It was then that my mother received the first severe blow in her life. Her life long ambition of seeing her son as a doctor seemed terribly threatened. For days she wouldn't even talk to father. She wanted father to force Roshan to change his mind. I remember father talking to Roshan a few times but Roshan stuck by his decision. Needing someone to put the blame on, mother said he was not convincing enough and wouldn't talk to father for days. Living at home became very unpleasant. We didn't talk to each other. I hid in my room for fear that mother would jump on me. My mother became a different person overnight. When I look back now I realize that Roshan's decisions affected the relationship between my father and mother.

Then a week or so later, Roshan announced that he had rejoined the Prudential Insurance Company in downtown Chicago where he had worked during his summer vacation the year before. He started going to work every morning dressed in shirt and tie and sometimes wearing a jacket, and my mother gradually began to respect Roshan's wishes. We all knew that she loved to have Roshan at home, but it was more important to her that he should finish his education and become a doctor.

V

I had been thinking of my brother and his relationship with my parents for a few hours; it was time to sleep. Obviously Lindy was not coming after all. I lay awake that night reliving the events of my life, going over and over certain scenes, wondering whether I could have done anything to change my brother's life. Lying in my bed in the still darkness around me, I let myself mull over the mystery of how my brother became gay. Memories of my brother's life began to unfold in precise detail, vivid and clear.

Now I know that Roshan's tendency towards a gay life started way back in Kandy. Though it never occurred to me then, now when I think back of those days in Kandy, there was a priest whom my brother was attached to. The priest, who was from Belgium, came to Sri Lanka for missionary work and, after a few years, decided to make Sri Lanka his home. I remember him as a handsome man of around forty-five or so. He lived in the seminary about three miles from our house. Father met him through one of his university friends when father was looking for a teacher to coach Roshan Latin and French. Roshan went to the seminary every weekend and some days he spent the whole day there. The day we left Kandy the priest came to see us off. He hugged Roshan and asked him to think of him whenever Roshan needed help. I remember Roshan walking with the priest to the gate, holding the priest's hand all the way.

During the senior year of his high school days in Brunswick, Roshan began to be a recluse. I remember he played every possible trick to avoid playing games with other boys. He started growing his hair until it reached almost down to his shoulders. Yet both mother and father did not ask him to cut it. I thought it was funny that he should grow his hair that long. I began to notice on some evenings he powdered his face and started acting like a girl. He even wore uni-sex clothing. Mother said at the time, "That's in vogue now. It's nice to see him enjoying his youth."

In retrospect, I don't know what to think of my parents' reactions to Roshan's behavior—whether they were naive or whether these were their denial devices.

When he came home after the second semester in college, Roshan appeared to be a different person. We could hardly recognize him. He wore an earring in his right ear and tied his hair in a neat pony tail. He wore a gold necklace and a wrist band on his right wrist. He began to look and act more and more like a girl. I remember mother noticing Roshan's silky eyebrows and telling me that my brother was growing up to be a beautiful young man.

I remember while having our evening meal one day father laughingly questioned, "Who is the girl in the family, or do we have two girls? I find it difficult to pick out the girl. You both look the same to me now." Mother laughed at this and I looked at Roshan inquiringly. Roshan walked out of the dining room. That was the last time we sat together for a meal. He refused to have any meals with us after that. He became completely anti-social and wanted to spend his time alone. I was very hurt and angry with my brother at this time because I waited for the holidays for him to come home and spend time with me, but he hardly ever spoke to me. He was my only brother. He took his plate and walked into his room and ate by himself. Sometimes mother served his meals and took the food to his room. At that time my parents said Roshan was going through adolescence, and we all had to be considerate for it was a very difficult period in his life. He was nineteen years old at that time.

During the summer vacation after his freshman year at college, Roshan worked for Prudential Insurance Company as a clerk. There he made friends with a tall and lithe Italian-American guy named Angelo. He brought Angelo home many times. Angelo had come to Chicago from Evansville, Indiana, to become an artist, and ended up being a dancer in a gay night club in downtown Chicago. He told me that as a young artist he settled down into the routine that so many artists of the day had experienced: the cheap apartment by the University of Chicago, the burdensome but necessary night job, endless cups of coffee at a cheap Polish coffee shop and the nights at the Gay Night Club. Angelo was friendly and I enjoyed talking to him. I actually liked him. I liked his good manners and found him funny and warm-hearted. On a few occasions, I had heard him addressing my brother as "cutie," and sometimes as "my girl." He took my brother out in the evenings.

I think my parents suspected what was happening to Roshan and they were trying their best to believe that whatever was happening would go away. They just wanted to believe that gay people are children of other parents. One episode that should have alerted them happened when Roshan started going for dancing lessons. A brother of a friend of my mother had seen Roshan dancing in a night club in downtown Chicago, a gay night club. He had been slow dancing with a man, with his eyes closed and his head on the man's shoulder. I listened to this conversation taking place in mother's bedroom between my mother and her friend.

That same day in the evening when Roshan came home my mother took him to her bedroom and talked to Roshan for a long time—all in whispers. I could not hear a word. That night after dinner, I came upon my parents engaged in intense conversation. My father was obviously agitated. He paced back and forth, biting his lips as he usually did when he was angry. Their conversation continued in whispers for a long time, way into the night. A few words from here and there that came my way made me understand that the topic of conversation was my brother's sexual orientation.

"Roshan's behavior is weird. Laura said they call him 'queer' in the streets." Mother's broken voice came through soft sobs. I heard her crying for a long time that night. Father's voice was softer. Mother began to weep.

"I am dying inside. There were times when I questioned his strange behavior but never suspected this," she said. She grabbed a tissue from the kleenex box on the bedside table and blew her nose loudly.

Then came the day that Roshan spoke openly to mother. It must have been about six weeks after Roshan started work. One evening both of us were seated in the comfortable sofa in the family room and Roshan read aloud a quotation from a book he said he picked up from the local bookstore. "On a cold evening a fire is such a comforting element, yet, normally it's so destructive. It's the opposite of love. Love is such a positive force in one's life yet at times it's nothing but negative." Roshan then moved over to the fireplace and bending deeply, stirred the logs with the fire stick. Just then mother walked in; she had heard what Roshan read out to me.

"What's up? You are getting all philosophical, Roshan. Are you two keeping a secret from me?" inquired mother, laughing and making herself comfortable next to me on the sofa. She wanted to join us in our secret conversation. There was silence in the room for a minute or two.

"I have fallen in love, Mom," Roshan said, facing mother.

"Oh! I am so happy." She jumped from the sofa and hugged Roshan. "I've been waiting to hear this from you for sometime now. She must be very pretty! Tell me about the lucky girl," mother's face brightened up with happiness.

"You will not approve of it, Mom. I've fallen in love with a man." Sure, at first, mother did not want to believe what Roshan was talking about. I was puzzled at first when I had eavesdropped on Roshan and Angelo. Later, I suspected this was coming because Roshan talked to me many times about his special relationship with Angelo—the guy he met in Chicago during his summer vacation the year before. I was horrified at the time. Indeed, now I understand that my brother had no option in his yearnings. Choice, if any, was between repression and honesty. I treasured the close brother-sister relationship I had established with my brother and didn't want to ruin it by letting my parents know about his strange friendship with Angelo. To Roshan there seemed nothing strange or unlikely in the love that he felt for Angelo. It seemed an inevitable thing for him, as much a part of himself as his breathing. I remember the evening when the door to Roshan's room was left ajar slightly; as I walked past his room I overheard my brother and Angelo talk in low voices.

"Would you put some lipstick on? You look so passionate sweetie," that was Angelo s baritone voice.

"I have to live here with my Mom for a little while longer. I am not ready for it yet. You understand, don't you?"

"Of course." What was I hearing?

With the corner of my eye, I saw the two of them standing by the window. They were looking at each other and were drawing close together. "Angelo, be careful, for God's sake—the door is open—my Mom," I heard my brother's voice. Angelo's hands dropped from my brother's shoulders and I saw his lips touch my brother's. I couldn't believe what I witnessed then. Roshan was in love with Angelo! I could see, that his eyes, as they say, were drawn to the stars and never gravitated towards the earth.

My brother had changed. He had become polite, cool, appeared to listen but took no notice. Where was my brother? This young man standing in front of mother was not he. After a minute, which seemed like an eternity to me, mother stared at him, suddenly turned pale with shock.

"You are mad," she mumbled slowly, "you're raving mad." She banged the door behind her and walked out of the room.

"Mother makes me suffer because she knows I love her the way I do," Roshan said to himself. He sat on the edge of the sofa and with his hands holding his drooping head began to sob. I noticed his eyes filling with tears which I knew was caused by the pain he had just caused mother and his longing for Angelo.

There followed a long, almost breathless silence, while Roshan sobbed with his head buried in his hands. If a leaf had dropped, its minute, soft falling could have been thunder at the time. I could have heard the creak of the branch that had let its leaf fall on the ground.

What I see, looking back, was a lonely boy wanting to have a best friend to confide in, to ask for advice when there was confusion around him. Then the silence was broken by the front door being opened and my father's footsteps approaching heavily.

"Roshan, you are not going to tell father. Please, you are not going to let all hell loose around us. I understand your plight but please save us from this," I pleaded with Roshan.

"I won't have you interfering in my life," he said and brushed me off. I could still see the amazement on my mother's face when Roshan gave her the news. I think the revelation of Roshan's sexuality not only affected the relationship between my father and mother, it also devastated their lives. I think it hit my father deeply; he never recovered from the blow. I try to put that evening behind me but it keeps coming back, torturing me.

I cannot bear to let my memory linger on what happened that very next day. We, mother, father and I were having breakfast when Roshan walked out of his room and announced he was going for a jog down Lake Shore Drive.

"Have a waffle with some honey—there's Sue-Bee. It's good for your body, son," mother said, beckoning Roshan to sit with us and enjoy breakfast. He took offence at that and quite unexpectedly, flared out at mother and father.

"In your own way you always decide what's best for me, mother. To you I am still your naive, little boy who always needed your hand to hold. I never had any say in my own life. Your leading hand has put me in chains now."

My parents stared at each other with a shared sense of surprise and disbelief. I immediately recognized Roshan's speech; this was a pent up declaration that he said he wanted to tell my parents for some months. But I had no clue that it would come so soon. I wanted to say something, something to make Roshan go easy on my parents. I wanted my voice to sound strong and assertive to drown Roshan's harsh words, instead it sounded hollow and dull. I began to speak but my voice came out in an embarrassing squeak. Swallowing the last drop of saliva left in my throat, I started again, "Whatever Mom and Daddy have done for us is for our own good . . ." but Roshan shouted me down.

"Did you ever stop to think that maybe I should have had some say in what I wanted to do with my life? Both of you decided what college would be the right one for me to attend and I should go in for medicine. The college, of course, had to be a prestigious one and I have to be a doctor so that you could brag to your friends about me. You never thought that maybe I wanted something more than school and books, but that was never important to you. You only wanted me to be academically successful so that your Sri Lankan friends would be impressed. That's why you wanted me to be a doctor. I was never consulted. You never realized that I wanted a life. To make real friends for once in my life. There was nothing in my life that you let me have any control over. When I finally met someone who meant something to me, you couldn't handle that. Please don't force me to break the only real relationship that I have ever built up for myself. To you I am disgracing the family . . . what will everyone say? That's what's bothering you!" Then with a sense of relief, Roshan shut the door behind him. I heard the sound of his footsteps vanishing down the corridor. My father and mother just listened and didn't utter a word in response. They looked at each other and pretended nothing had happened.

"I've never felt quite at home, at home, because of my sexuality," Roshan told me later.

He returned after an hour or so with Angelo who had his right arm around Roshan's waist. I remember the horrible scene with every detail. No other episode in my life has left with me with such a powerful impression. I now shiver when I think of the intense atmosphere in the room at the time. Roshan went to the rocking chair where father was seated, reading the *Sunday Tribune*.

"I am moving out with Angelo," he said. He spoke only to father, not even looking at my mother and me. We were seated on the couch opposite. Father looked up from the paper. Roshan hesitated. I noticed Angelo nudging his elbow into my brother's ribs.

"As I discussed with you earlier, I am taking a year off college. I want to find myself first. I am moving in with Angelo," Roshan's voice was full of emotion, hardly audible, yet firm. "Finding out one's own self" is a very American thing. I thought my father would explode. On a few occasions when he had his differences with mother, he responded with fury. But now he was so overwhelmed with what he just heard, he didn't even try to say anything.

Mother tried to say something but her sobs drowned her words. She fell silent, fearing to lose her son. Roshan did not move. Perhaps he sensed that his whole life depended on his behavior at that moment. He stood there for a few seconds without letting anything shake his determination. Then he walked to his room. Angelo followed. Soon the two of them carried the bags—already packed—and went to our front door. Roshan turned and looked at mother, his eyes now filled with tears, and walked out.

I kept staring at the floor. The floor around me became an ocean and two little dirty specks on the floor transformed themselves into two boats. It was a quiet sea, a still sea. I looked for Roshan's boat docked beside mine on the floor, but could not see. Roshan had sailed away leaving me there. I closed my eyes.

Memories of those days in Kandy, when my brother and I were the greatest of friends, rushed back to my mind. We remained friends until one of his school friends appeared. They came during week-ends to spend the day with him and no sooner had they arrived, he would ignore me and join them in harassing me if I was around. His best friend in school was a Dutch boy named Hans, whose father was an economist advising the government of Sri Lanka at the time. The two of them gave me a hard time, sneering at girls in general and pretending to throw stones or throwing stones which were aimed to miss me by an inch. They ran off up the hill behind Grand Ma's house to lose me. They helped me to climb the guava tree in Grand Ma's backyard, which I could not climb by myself, then ran off, to enjoy watching me trying to climb down.

When I asked Roshan one day after he befriended Angelo, if he remembered what a difficult time he and Hans gave me, he was surprised. He had no recollection of treating me unkindly. As long as there was no boy around he was sweet and kind to me. It is odd I think now—holding in your memory where someone else is so alive and that someone else doesn't remember a thing. When I opened my eyes, I noticed it had begun to rain. The sound of rain drops poured into the silence that had engulfed the room. Finally, father sighed in despair.

"What have I done to deserve this? Roshan is punishing me. I failed to be a strong father figure. All hopes I built on him are shattered now." I heard father's broken voice. Mother was crying; her eyes were red and her face was swollen. I watched the two of them. My parents were in denial. They thought that things like this could happen to somebody else's son but not to their own flesh and blood. My parents refused to stop pretending to see something that was not there in Roshan, most of the time fooling nobody but themselves.

Thinking back to what happened then, now I believe that my parents held back as long as they could. They didn't talk to Roshan in case they might chase him away. The strange thing was that I had not a single tear, not one flicker of feeling for my parents. Can one do anything for oneself without hurting anyone else in the meantime?

Months after my brother left us, I remember an evening when my father, watching the next door neighbor's two little children playing with their dog, said to me, "Yes, that's what you were like too. Such lovely little things you were, and look what your brother turned into. It's not worth it!"

"Oh! Come on," said my mother, even though she surely must have agreed with him, "You are exaggerating!"

"Oh, no, I am not," said father. "What's exaggerated about it? I bet if you ask most people about it, they'd say, it wasn't worth it; raising children, all the hard work and worrying about them and then they blame us. They turn into third raters and leave us."

My father fell silent. The look in his eyes told me all I didn't want to know. My father was a moral traditionalist who had faith in his religion, country and family. He often talked of the days when he was young, when morality was absolute and virtue was held in highest regard. My mother, in contrast, was modern in her outlook. American society had changed her views of life. She was willing to accept change and welcomed the fact that families were no longer patriarchal in America. She thought that American society was somewhat better than Sri Lankan because one group could no longer impose its ideas of what's good and bad on another. In some ways, my mother wanted to be both traditional and modern at the same time. She honored religion and family and also wanted to accommodate herself into the realities of modern American society. My mother once told me that she only believed in doing what is right and avoiding what is wrong.

"Out there, there are lots of people, Nelu. You can't please everybody. So do what you have to do to please yourself."

At the same time she was not what one would call a moral traditionalist. I think she has changed her thinking because of her son—to accommodate her son she would do whatever it takes. She perhaps did not believe that she had the right to tell her grown-up son the right way to behave. She did that when we were young, when we were being introduced into American society.

"I don't want to meddle with his life. Roshan is grown-up enough to judge for himself and choose what sort of life he wanted," she told father a few months after Roshan left. These words, coming from my mother, made me wonder how far she would go not to lose her son. Afraid of chasing Roshan out of her life, mother adjusted her attitudes.

"I don't like homosexuality. But gay people deserve respect because all people deserve respect," she said.

My father used words like abnormal, immoral, sinful, unacceptable, sick, unhealthy, wrong, perverted—whenever the subject of homosexuality was raised. He could never understand how some Americans, in this puritanical society, had accepted homosexuality as an alternative life style that is the moral equal of any other. My father said that homosexuals believe that sexual identity is a big part of what defines a person. He knew that his strong condemnation of homosexuality created an atmosphere of hatred between him and his son as well as bitterness between him and mother. He did not blame this odd behavior of some individuals on biology or genetics, for then he himself would have become a part of it. He said that it was socially constructed, dependent on the company one keeps.

"They are different because they want to be different. I just don't believe that people are born that way, so I wouldn't want a child of mine to adopt that life style." He was firm in his beliefs. After some time father just refused to discuss the subject, as if the mere mention of the word would pollute his morality.

Mother consoled herself by saying, "I think it's something we have to accept because it's part of their nature." Observing how understanding mother was, I recalled a day in Brunswick when, for the first time, I heard of homosexuals and asked mother about their life. I told mother about some "queer girls" that my friend Rose's mother had met at work. "Be careful what you tell your mother," Rose warned me when I told her that I was going to ask my mother if she had met any "queer girls and lesbians." "Lesbians—who are they, Mom?" I asked her after coming from school. My mother's eyes widened and her mouth opened in shock at my question.

"Where did you hear about such people? There is nothing worse on the face of this planet than a stinking, disgusting lesbian." At the time she just dismissed my question without even trying to explain what the word meant.

Did she change her views for her son's sake, or has she really become tolerant?

VI

Roshan did not leave us altogether. He came home occasionally and talked to mother and father. Mother talked to him but father did his best to avoid meeting Roshan face to face. In response to my mother's questions, he usually hesitated for a while before giving mother an answer. I felt at that moment he tried to decide which would be better for mother; the truth or a lie. I could sense—and I am pretty sure mother did too—he went for the lie. Don't we all?

I talked to him; on some occasions he gave me one word answers in response to my inquiries about his day to day life. On other days he would talk to me for hours. One evening, after I had been prodding him on as to what he was doing at work, he came out with the story of what Angelo was doing which opened for me a new side of Chicago. It was Chicago's night life. In the evenings, Angelo worked at Billy's Topless, down Rush Street.

"The name should explain to you the activities that take place inside," Roshan said with a timid smile. He said that Angelo was in charge of recruiting dancing girls and scheduling their appearances in the half a dozen Topless Bars that Tony Salvio owned in downtown Chicago. While listening to Roshan, something that happened to me during my graduate days on my first visit to the Newbery Library by myself one evening, came to my mind. I told Roshan that several blocks from the library on Rush Street a large sedan slowed and pulled to the curb next to me.

"The window came down and a middle-aged man in a dark suit leaned across the front seat; I thought he wanted directions." Roshan laughed when I told him that the man inquired, "How much?"

"The man smiled pleasantly and said, 'Get in and we'll negotiate. I've got fifty bucks!' It took a while for me to realise what he was after. I backed away from the car and only then did I notice the video stores with their pink neon lights and the Peep Show signs displayed across the front windows."

Whenever I walked with my friends past this bar, they talked with a giggle and referred to it as a forbidden place for us. Billy's Topless on Rush Street had been in operation for more than a decade in the two-storey building. The ground floor served as a gay meeting place while the upper floor was reserved for topless dancers.

When Roshan visited Angelo in his workplace for the first time, Roshan had been surprised to find the doorbell to Angelo's cramped office buzzing, pulling Angelo away from talking to Roshan. He told me that a delivery boy arrived first, bringing a pizza which Angelo wanted to share with Roshan. Then, the girls had walked in—Eva, Joanna, then Annette—all wanting to know where they would be on display in the next week!

"Am I going to Pussycat on Friday night?" Eva had wanted to know. "Eva, sweetheart, we are in the midst of something important. Can you come a little bit later?" Angelo had requested. "But then you asked me to come between five and seven in the evening," Eva had said. Angelo had then looked around for the wall clock which had been hanging on the wall cluttered with framed photographs of Billy's Topless clients. The time was six in the evening. "Come back in an hour." Angelo had sent the girls away and sat with Roshan to enjoy the pizza.

Roshan told me how on the dance floor beneath billows of blue smoke, three topless women moved to the tempo of a Fleetwood Mac song. "The chairs around the small stage where the girls danced were all empty. It was still early in the evening. A dozen or so customers sat at the bar, some sipping drinks, some watching the dancing, others watching a basketball game on television. There was a Bulls' photograph on the wall. Occasionally a customer stood up, walked over and handed a dancer a dollar bill. All of a sudden we heard a jeer from the small crowd and what I thought to be an obscene remark. To my amazement one of the dancers, named Tanya stepped down from the stage and wrapped a towel around her body. Then she walked towards the entrance to the room where Angelo and I were standing. We began talking. Tanya told me that she had been educated in a convent. Seeing the shocked look on my face, Tanya asked me, "You know why I work here?" Before I could say anything she went on to say, "I am a single mother and have two kids. I have no skills to sell. There's no touching, no hustling here. If I cover my breasts these guys won't be here. They'll say they can see the same thing on the Oak beach." I sensed the bitterness in her voice. "I've never seen anything like that in my life before, but now I am used to it—I am there every evening. Sometimes I help Angelo in his work. Don't tell mother though," Roshan requested.

About six months after Roshan's decision to leave us, he came to see mother one evening, agitated and depressed. He talked to mother in soft whispers and kept his head down looking at the tip of his shoes while talking. As he talked I noticed tears flowing down his cheeks. Mother was worried and kept asking him questions. That evening Roshan left before father came home. "Angelo is dying of AIDS," mother told father. She knew father had no sympathy for Angelo and was furious with Roshan. "Roshan wants me to meet Angelo's mother and persuade her to see Angelo before he dies," mother informed father.

"Why does he want to see his mother now? They remember their parents only when they fall into trouble. Otherwise they don't even know that their parents exist in this world. Can she perform miracles? Where is she anyway?" There was nothing but anger in my father's tone.

"Roshan is begging me to. Angelo's mother has said she never wanted to see him again. Now he wants to give her a chance to say good bye." Father showed his indifference to the request. The next morning I heard mother talking to Angelo's mother over the telephone before going to see her at the cafe where she was working as a waitress. It didn't take much time for my mother to become friends with Angelo's mother, Elma, who belonged to a completely different social class from ours. She had raised her son by herself when Angelo's father had abandoned her when she told him that she was carrying his baby. Angelo's father had never set eyes on him. Working as a waitress in a coffee house in the outskirts of Chicago, Elma had saved enough money to send Angelo to school hoping like any other mother, to make her son somebody useful to society and also hoping that one day Elma could lead a life free of financial worries. But it was not to be. During his first year in high school a teacher had told Elma that Angelo showed signs of being depressed and even suicidal. Noticing Angelo's apathy about girls, Elma had decided to ask one day after school, "Do you like guys?" while holding his hand. "Yeah," Angelo had replied in a hushed voice. It had been a painful revelation to Angelo's mother, who had said those days she was so innocent of the world around her, that she couldn't even say the word 'gay'. His troubles at school had started in the first semester of his second year with a few pushes in the hallway. Tables would empty when he sat in the cafetaria. He had regularly found the word 'fag' scrawled across his locker. By the end of the semester the harassment had escalated to threats of death and other violence.

"You know what we do to queers?" one boy had asked Angelo who had put his head down on his desk and pretended to sleep. "We cut them open, dig out their insides and burn them. . . ." "I didn't want to hear anymore," Elma had told mother. "I don't cry over much but I cried when my son said, I hate myself because God made me a freak. I will tell you as a mother my heart broke because I knew how hard his life was going to be." Elma had cried while relating the painful story. Angelo had finished his senior year in work-study program at another high school.

"If it was happening to my son, it's happening to other kids," Elma had consoled herself. As mother told me about Angelo, it came to my mind that Roshan was quieter, preferring to play the piano during school lunch breaks rather than spend time with his friends. Roshan started to withdraw in his late teenage years.

When Angelo went to Chicago his life style had changed completely. "I don't care what people think," Angelo had told his mother. He became cocky and spoke openly about his sexuality which Elma couldn't face. "There was no way I could help him. Some people now brand the gays as a special group trying to paint themselves as victims." Elma had poured out her sorrowful tale to mother. "Every group in America is trying to do that right now," my mother had said then.

Angelo had fallen into "bad company" after his high school days and had moved into Chicago where his circle of friends was all gay. He had moved out of his mother's house at the time when he was "coming out" so to speak—after telling his mother that his sexuality was different from others around him. When Angelo left her, Elma had been devastated and she had told my mother that she could never forgive her son for leaving her. "He is queer, Leila. You don't understand the shame I've been through because of him. But that's the way he was born." Elma had cried out loud when mother told her about Roshan. "Those who live in the cities don't care—but those who live around here can't even tolerate it let alone try to understand it. If someone chose to be gay, it's their choice—so unchoose it or perish."

"Doesn't genetics play a strong role in everyone's sexuality? We did not choose our sexuality but we believe that gay people chose theirs. Is that fair?" Mother had tried to explain to Elma. But she had refused to see her son saying her son was "queer."

"Stop calling him names. Show him a mother's compassion before he leaves this world. Give him some strength to die." Mother, at first, had been angry at Elma's intolerance. Then she had calmed herself and had hugged Elma and coaxed her into changing her mind.

"Come, Elma. I will drive you to the hospital. I will be with you when you are at Angelo's bedside. Let him see his mother before he leaves this world," my mother had said. My mother's gentle persistence had made Elma change her mind. The mother and son had not seen each other for almost six years—he was twenty-four now. Thanks to my mother's persuasive powers, Angelo had died after making peace with his mother and Roshan had been at his bedside holding his hand when he passed away.

"Has your son got himself tested for HIV?" Elma had asked mother.

"I didn't ask. To tell you the truth, I am frightened to ask," mother had responded.

"Tell him to do it for whatever it's worth," Elma had said showing concern in her voice.

The day Angelo died my brother came home, he kept walking behind mother following her every footstep with his head bent down. I heard mother asking Roshan if he had got tested for HIV. He said it was of no importance now as his life was empty without Angelo.

"Angelo helped to raise my life to an exhilarating height. I think myself the luckiest of men to have shared his warmth. He made me laugh until I cried. No one else could do that. I will miss him forever," Roshan told mother before he left that evening. He left before nightfall and did not come back to see us for some time. His visits became less frequent and whenever he came he talked to mother and avoided father's attention. But he came to see mother—the love between mother and Roshan was too great for him to stay away completely.

Since I have not seen my brother for almost eight years now, I cannot help but wonder whether he got himself tested and whether he met the same fate as his friend Angelo. There are certain situations in life that are so dramatic, so filled with sorrow, so much a matter of life and death, that they seem to bring almost the end of life itself. Some are beyond our comprehension, some we make for ourselves. The former, some of us attribute to an unseen super being or to *karma* because we cannot explain them. Some seem to come in unimaginable ways, just like the revelation of my brother's sexual preference. And now with the spread of AIDS virus and the links established between homosexuality and the AIDS virus, my brother's life had gone down in flames. I almost feel the anger, betrayal, despair and the hopelessness that my father must have gone through because of his son.

For eight years and more my mother must have waited for her telephone to ring or someone to bring the news that Roshan was still around. The first few months after Roshan left us, my phone used to ring at least twice a day and no one answered when I picked up the receiver. That happens to everyone, I told myself then. To everyone.

As I weep for Roshan I feel wrenched backward into events and circumstances that seems so long years ago. Though half a decade apart, we were both raised in Kandy and then in Brunswick with the tender love of caring parents. He fled from us to go on with his chosen life style. That morning when he came to mother with the news that Angelo was dying of AIDS, standing in our living room in the Hyde Park apartment, I told him I feared for his life. He cried as I took his hand. I was educated enough to understand that my mother wanted to believe that her son's sexual orientation should not make her son a pariah in society.

"All my life I'd tried to make him happy. To keep him safe we brought him here to America, and now here in America I watch him destroy his life," mother said with tear-filled eyes.

After my brother's disappearance, I felt as though a part of me had been cut away. I questioned my parents' actions then and still do. Did I not reach out soon or earnestly enough for him? I feel guilty. For weeks after he left, I woke up in the middle of the night, crying after a dream in which I sat next to him in the park, holding hands trying to convince him to see things from my parents' point of view. How I wish we were younger, still playing in Grand Ma's backyard in Kandy, with no cares in the world to engulf us. Those carefree days are only a memory now.

In the darkness of my room I lay awake breathing in and out slowly to calm myself. I didn't have much sleep these last three nights, I had nightmares. The moment my eyes closed, my brother Roshan appeared in front of me and I would wake in a cold sweat. Big and small episodes from my childhood and early adolescence follow me so closely with my present life that I find no escape from my past. We all have them don't we? Mortifying moments that put us on the very edge of the cliff. Ones that keep hopping in our dreams all too often, haunting us. I think about what my brother must be doing at this very moment while I am reliving the life I had with him. I have to find a way somehow to shut him from my mind and think of how to deal with the situation I am faced with now—but I can't. Memories keep rushing back.

VII

Though I had not had a wink of sleep, I got out of bed early in the morning, made a cup of coffee and sat by the kitchen window. It was still snowing lightly; I watched the tiny flakes as they drifted aimlessly with the wind. The remains of the huge snowstorm of the last four days still fringed the Lake Shore Drive. Ice on the road made the vehicles move slowly. Watching ice form on the lake I felt a loneliness more intense than any I could remember since my childhood days in school in Brunswick. The early morning was incredibly still. After two mornings in solitude and three nights of silently dwelling in my past, I felt as if I were poised at the edge of eternity.

A thin silver lining though appeared amidst dark clouds last evening—my mother showed some signs of life. I was so eager to see my mother, that instead of going to the police station as planned, I decided to go to the hospital. It was very early, yet there was no lack of visitors there. I joined the crowd and walked up the steps and entered the foyer. There I blew my fingers while walking in place to encourage the circulation of blood in my feet. I always had cold feet and hands from November to March. I blew and stamped and waited for a moment looking around to see any friendly faces. Seeing none, I rushed down the hospital corridors crowded with breakfast carts. As I passed the people waiting along the corridors I got agitated and started to run thinking that something awful had happened to my mother. The arrival of breakfast carts added to the appearance of utter chaos at the entrance to the elevator. Every time I went to the elevator, there was confusion and delay there. A man repeatedly pushed the "up" button as if manhandling the button would bring the elevator more quickly. The floor indicator above each elevator suggested that the elevator was taking its own cool time, slowly moving up or down from floor to floor; obviously dropping and picking up passengers in its usual slow motion. "Damn the elevator! Where are the stairs?" I heard somebody muttering impatiently and running down the corridor. Several followed the impatient man. I thought of following him but decided against it and pushed my way into the elevator. It seemed a wonder to me that the right patient, received the right drug, therapy or meal in this chaos. I pressed the eighth floor button and allowed myself to be pushed to the rear of the elevator. Once the doors closed, the smell inside was overwhelming and there was a *potpourri* of human beings there with every possible ailment. The air inside was heavy and hot and there was one passenger smoking despite the No Smoking sign. The people inside didn't look at each other, they stared blankly at the light progressing from number to number, as I, wishing the door would open and close more quickly. When the elevator reached the seventh floor I pushed my way to the front and got out at the next floor. The atmosphere changed immediately but the smells—of medicine—remained the same.

Once outside, I almost ran to my mother's ward and saw my aunts there standing by mother's bedside—such faithful souls. What are siblings for, if they are not around at times like these? My aunts, with the boring slog of physical therapy, hour upon hour of it, until their limbs ached like mother's, have brought back some life into her muscles.

"They are doing a fine job," the nurse who was overseeing the patients in the ward said to me referring to the dedicated work of mother's two sisters.

"Not much progress in her condition—but she's doing fine. It's only a matter of time now. We would eventually have to seek the help of a good physiotherapist. She is on the way to recovery," the nurse reassured us.

My aunts told me that nothing had changed since last evening. When they talked to my mother and held her hand, they felt it tighten inside theirs. My mother though conscious still found it difficult to open her eyes. I found it odd to hold her hand and talk to her—I had not done that for six years now. Yet when I did talk, I did see her slightly open her eyes as if she recognized my voice. Just like what my aunts had experienced, I felt her hand tighten inside mine.

My mother was in the best care possible—my aunts were looking after her. I could go in and out of the hospital with the knowledge that there was somebody by my mother's bedside all the time. I was grateful to my aunts. I stayed on in the hospital until noon and left for the police station to find out more about the accident.

VIII

A difficult task loomed ahead of me now. I was afraid of what I might learn from the police regarding the accident. I was well aware of what my mother went through since our arrival in America. The dreams that she had built around her family had been shattered and she was living a lonely life. I questioned whether she drove recklessly to cause the accident to put an end to her sufferings. I kept thinking—what if the police report confirms my suspicions—I would be partly responsible for mother's situation, because I left my mother at a time when she needed me most. I left her just a couple of months after father passed away—guilt entrapped me so severely that I felt my eyes go blind and almost lost control of my car. "Let me not think of the past now," I said and pulled myself together.

By the time I reached the police station, the light snowfall had given way to rain. It was just a drizzle now and the sunlight behind the clouds gave the sky a pearly glow. Rain drops gathered on the leaves of the New Zealand pine under which I parked my car, fell heavily into puddles with a faint smacking sound. I parked my car and walked carefully on the icy parking lot to the building across the narrow lane and entered the building. I was so exhausted by the flood of memories of the last few years that flashed across my mind that I sat on the bench in front of the reception desk and waited for a while. I found it difficult to explain even to myself why I was behaving so weakly—a woman who had to struggle hard to carve a place in this world as a university professor now sitting and waiting, afraid to hear what the police officer had to say. I consoled myself thinking that these things happen to the strongest of individuals when they are caught in a shroud of guilt. I might have been there for longer than I should, because the officer at the desk, getting no inquiry from me asked, “Ma’am, can I help you?” It took me sometime to ask because I somehow was afraid to hear the answer.

I introduced myself to the officer and told him of my mother’s accident. “Have you found out how the accident occurred?” I asked without a pause.

“Of course. Give me a minute,” he said and punched on the keyboard of his computer and asked for the name of the person involved in the accident.

“Leila Fernandes,” an almost inaudible mumble came out of my lips. The officer punched a few more keys and led me to a room at the far end of the hallway. He knocked on the door and opened it just a little to put his head through and said something to the person inside and showed me in. There was a police officer seated at the desk. He looked up at me, placed his hands on the papers that he was working on and beckoned me to sit and inquired the purpose of my visit. I repeated what I had said to the officer at the reception desk. Then he wanted to know my relationship to the accident victim.

“I am sorry Ma’am. It was a very nasty accident. How is your Mom?” I felt his expression of sympathy to be sincere. “We have not been able to make much progress in the last four days. As you know the weather has been a factor that hampered our investigation. The snowstorm that hit the city took place almost around that time and it erased evidence that might have been useful for us. The snow made it extremely difficult to trace even the tracks of the vehicle. In fact your mother’s vehicle is still in the police premises,” he said.

My mother was in a coma. There were no eyewitness accounts yet, the sergeant told me. People do not want to get involved; they are busy with their own lives; they prefer not to get involved and waste their time making visits to the police station to help solve mysteries.

"We received a couple of anonymous telephone calls regarding the incident. One of them said she observed a hit-and-run vehicle. A yellow cab, she said, but the thick fog over the city that evening had made it impossible to read the registration number of the vehicle. We have to collect more information to arrive at a definite conclusion as to how the accident took place. But from what little information we have got so far, this does not look like any other accident. It might have been a case of reckless driving. When the police went there, there was no other vehicle involved in the accident at the site. But because the anonymous caller said there was a hit-and-run-car, we kept track of vehicles that were involved in accidents during the last few days but found none that would reasonably fit the description of the vehicle we are looking for. But my investigators have managed to trace faint tire tracks on the road that indicate another vehicle, which seems to have been traveling at around sixty miles an hour, and that was probably the vehicle that hit your mother's car. My guess is that, that vehicle might have slid sideways at the exit to Washington Street and crashed into your mother's car. And as it collided with your mother's car, it turned your mother's car upside down making it stand on its roof. The vehicle probably drove away without stopping. We also have to consider whether a mechnical failure in your mother's car was responsible for the crash. The company that manufactured the vehicle your mother drove recalled some models recently because of potential problems with the steering mechanism. We still have to do a thorough examination of your mother's car to make sure there were no mechanical problems. We have to do more work on this case to prepare the report, it could take up to three weeks."

Continuing the work he had done with the investigation, the police officer informed me that investigators had not determined how fast my mother had been driving before she was hit and lost control of her car, but was quick to point out that the speed limit was fifty miles. My mother's Toyota Camry, heavily damaged, remained in the police station.

The police officer continued to talk to me about the information his investigators had gathered. I saw his lips move and I heard his baritone voice, but after a while his words faded from my ears. I felt a cold shiver running down my spine. The picture of my mother's bloodstained body being pulled out of her Toyota appeared in front of my eyes. I saw the paramedics bringing a stretcher from the ambulance and lifting my mother's lifeless body on to it. The ambulance with its numerous red lights flashing, its siren deafening the ears of those around, sped away towards the hospital. For a moment I was lost in my thoughts and kept staring out of the window, forgetting that I was still in the police officer's room.

"Miss Fernandez, are you all right?" I heard his voice, but did not pay heed. He got up from his chair and perhaps seeing the helpless look on my face, touched my shoulder gently and said, "I know it is difficult to hear what your Mom went through. We'll do our best to find the culprit. Give us a little time." Then, he shook my hand and walked with me to the steps leading down to the parking lot. As I thanked him and descended the steps, I heard him say, "Be careful out there. Walking on ice is dangerous."

IX

I came home in the evening from the police station in a confused state of mind. Though I learned little new from the police officer, that little information helped to increase the suspicions I held regarding mother's role in the accident. If only there was an eyewitness to the accident these doubts I held would be cleared. Uncle Henry and I were waiting for somebody to come forward in response to the appeal we published in the local newspaper asking anybody who had witnessed the accident to contact us. For two days we waited for a phone message but it hadn't arrived yet. Maybe somebody would turn up. We kept hoping.

I heard rumblings in my stomach and realized that I had not eaten anything since dinner last night. I made myself an omelette and a mug of coffee and sat at the kitchen table. The steam rose slowly from the coffee and blended into the cool evening air above my head. My thoughts were restless. I stared through the rising steam thinking of the work I had to do. Through the kitchen door I could see my books on the study table, untouched and undisturbed since that knock on my front door five afternoons ago. I was in no mood to start work on that conference paper. Instead, memories of my father getting ready to present his papers at the Annual Meetings of the Modern Language Association came to my mind. When we lived in Brunswick, he had attended two MLA meetings, once in Washington and once in Los Angeles. He read a vast amount of literature and took quite some time to write his papers. The papers were highly advanced and full of academic jargon which, at the time, puzzled me. I did not understand what he was trying to convey. While preparing the paper, he told mother that, publication was the only way to sell one's self to prospective recruiters. There were hundreds of job seekers at these meetings, all looking for an opening leading to a tenure track job. It was always a nerve-racking experience for him, especially as mother objected to father spending money and time on attending conferences. She called his efforts futile exercises.

"Instead of writing an article and looking out for an opportunity to further himself, he just goes to socialize with friends," mother sometimes complained. Father's friends said that his work was 'brilliant'. But although several universities expressed interest in his work in the first year when he was at St. Peter's College, he did not have any job interviews.

I can't remember him without a book in his hands. He read whatever books on English literature he could lay his hands on. He would fish out his reading glasses from a leather pouch rigged to his belt, make himself comfortable in the sitting room couch—the study room chair was not cosy enough for him—and begin to read. If I happened to sit with him in the same room doing my school work, he would glance up at me. His black-rimmed glasses placed on the bridge of his nose, he would read aloud what he thought might interest me. He would overpower me with his enthusiasm. That enthusiasm made me a student of literature as well. "Treasures of an earlier generation," he would say. "Think how literature is taught now. Today, we are not supposed to look at context but simply analyse the text and draw multiple meanings, some of which the author never dreamed of. Shakespeare might as well have lived in the nineteenth century." There were times when father got himself lost in his favorite subject, Shakespearean drama. I loved to listen to him then.

"They say they are impressed with my work but the trend now is feminist theory and poststructural stuff, of which I know very little," father told mother. She walked past us, attending to housework. Mother didn't understand him or didn't seem to care.

While in Chicago father had attended the Annual Conference of the Shakespeare Association of America which was normally held in Washington. It was for this year's meeting of the same organization that I was preparing a paper now. The year he went it was attended by over six hundred Shakespeareans from eighteen countries. Though the belief among the academics was that Shakespearean studies were waning in popularity, father said that he learned at the meeting that more and more college students were taking up Shakespearean studies. He said that the Association had announced that Shakespeare was the most frequently studied author of all. "When politicians and journalists are at a loss to describe the awful and the important, they often look to Shakespeare for a metaphor. Margaret Thatcher is Lady Macbeth and Jackie Kennedy is Desdemona," father said laughing. "'some are born great, some achieve greatness, some have greatness thrust upon them,' that's Malvolio in *Twelfth Night*, Nelu," father said, looking at me. He was in one of his lighter moods. I admired my father especially when he quoted from English literature to get out of bad situations with mother.

"Where do you fall into in this, Nalin?" mother wanted to know. Father didn't have to think long—out came his response, "The second, of course."

"Where is this greatness that you have achieved? Why am I oblivious to this greatness?"

"I have you! I achieved my greatness when I married you!" Father lifted mother in his arms.

"Please Nalin, put me down," mother struggled to put her feet on the ground.

It was my father's enthusiasm for Shakespearean literature that made me gravitate towards his subject. In his day-to-day speech he used Shakespearean language. Not until my high school days did I realize the extent to which my father was quoting or paraphrasing Shakespeare. When mother brought him his morning tea, he would say, "My kingdom for a cup of tea, My kingdom for a kiss," and kiss mother on her lips. "To thine own self be true," was a common expression he often used and it all sounded quaint to me then.

"If it weren't for Shakespeare and the Bible, the English language would have been a provincial tongue. When Shakespeare was writing his dramas, the English language was still being created—that explains why his language is so different from what we use today. But Shakespeare's true genius lies in his incredible ability to understand human nature—what he said then, most of it, applies to our daily lives now," father explained to me, sensing my interest. He convinced me that Shakespeare has relevance to everyday life.

Those were the days when father could joke about his job situation—days when he was confident that he would be invited to fill in a prestigious professorship in a university on the East Coast. That was mother's dream and he very much wanted to make that dream come true. Father had married a woman who had set her eyes on higher things. Mother would not be satisfied if my father taught at any American university—it had to be an elite institution on the East Coast, because, for my mother, that was where the sophisticated and the cultivated live.

"I don't see any reason why I shouldn't get a job teaching Shakespeare," father said quite confidently when in Brunswick. Little did he know at the time that those wishful thinking days were numbered. After four years and mailing over ninety applications he ended up without a single interview. He told me later, that he could never find the right time, nor the right place in the house, to tell mother that he had received yet another letter bringing the news of rejection. There was mother, always with her lovely smile and her eternal faith in father—the man she had grown to love over the years, the man she believed at the time would one day fulfill her wishes by becoming a respected academic in America—just the way he was back in Sri Lanka.

During the time when I was moving out of mother's apartment, I came across a case with my father's belongings—in it was a bundle of letters. I couldn't resist the temptation of opening the bundle and looking into my father's private life. I thought they were from some old flame of his, back from his university days—but no, they were rejection letters, all from universities. They were arranged in chronological order of the days the letters received—a time span of almost seven years. At first, the Ivy league universities from the East Coast, Yale, Harvard where he was once a Research Fellow at the Humanities School, Swarthmore College and the most recent came from two-year Community Colleges in the Mid-West. There was a letter from a two-year college saying my father was over-qualified for the position they advertised, advising my father to try a research-oriented big university. The reject letters began, . . . Thank you for your interest. . . . You are undoubtedly a strong candidate, but we had a very strong applicant pool. . . . My poor father! Now I can understand his plight. He bore the pain of rejection by himself, packed those letters neatly in a case and kept the bad news all to himself. At first, I remember he shared the news with us, but as the number of rejections increased, he must have just stored them, some, without even opening the envelope. He knew, by then, that a thin letter without a telephone call meant a rejection.

It took him many years to realize that securing a full-time academic position in the United States was an impossible task for him. Hiring was directed towards new and younger Ph.D.s at the assistant professor or lecturer level so that universities with leaner budgets could save money while getting good, though somewhat inexperienced instructors. It was this very strategy that, later on, opened doors for me in academia.

One day after receiving yet another letter of rejection, father sat on his bed holding his head between his hands and the letter slipped through his fingers. After four years of denial and distress, he reluctantly embraced the kind of teaching that he thought was not his.

"I am destined to be an adjunct professor and I have to settle for that for the rest of my life," he said one evening, coming home after teaching in one of the three different two-year colleges he was teaching in the Chicago area. He taught some

English literature but these students were not interested in English literature except to obtain credits to complete general education requirements for their diploma. Father, who had been a full-time professor for two and a half decades, now became a part-timer. I now understand the pain of mind he would have experienced at the time. What he taught at the two-year colleges were not the advanced courses he taught on Shakespeare back in Sri Lanka and at St. Peter's College, but freshman composition. He was elated when a dean of one of the colleges had asked him if he would like to teach a course on English literature in the British Commonwealth, but the enrollments were not encouraging and the class was canceled. He must have been deeply disappointed, for once the class did not make it, he avoided all reference to it thereafter.

What father regretted most was losing touch with his field. He was used to teaching the same course, year in and year out, reading new books on the subject to refresh the course which at the same time helped him in his writing. As an adjunct he did not get to teach any courses on Shakespeare—where his expertise and love of the subject lay—those were reserved for tenured, senior faculty. He taught four courses per semester as an adjunct—they were standard composition courses which needed little preparation. So he prepared lectures whenever he found the time, in between travel from one college to the other. Not having a permanent job even in a small college, must have been humiliating. His first job in Sri Lanka was tailor-made for him and he just walked into it after completing his Ph.D. at Cambridge. That was back in the sixties.

Father considered himself too conservative and too old to learn computer skills. He did not want to be a university administrator—anyway as he told me later, he did not possess any experience in the administrative field. Back home in Sri Lanka, father had reveled in the perks and privileges of being a university professor. During the first two years at St. Peter's College, mother was so enraptured by the comforts and the status of academia that she did not encourage father to try something else. Father said, many times, that he had underestimated the pressure on faculty here in the American universities—the absolute need to publish in order to get ahead, and the desperate competition among thousands of Ph.D. holders to get even the most thankless of university posts.

I remember one afternoon, when father opened his mail and found yet another rejection letter, mother made a suggestion.

"You don't have to tell me what you just found out. Nalin, I have been thinking of this for sometime now. I would very much like you to be a professor and do what you like doing best. But let's face reality. Both of us make just enough money to meet our day to day expenses. We are not young and how long do you think we can work like this? We don't have any savings. We know now that it's not possible for you to get a position in any university here. So don't you think it's time you change your subject field? Read for a law degree or enter a Business School and get a professional qualification? This will help you to join with Henry in his business. Just think of the money you can make! Don't forget we have two children whom we have to help through college!"

"Please don't even think of me working with your brother. He is your brother, I know, but I can't stand the man's arrogance; the way he puts on airs just because he had made it good here in this country!" Father dismissed her idea. It was originally Uncle Henry's idea that mother gradually put forward now. Sensing father's refusal to join him in his business ventures, Uncle Henry also showed his contempt for academics. "Who needs the intelligentsia? Wouldn't the world be better off without those sniping, backbiting intellectuals? Just because they read a few books—and they have the time for it—unlike others like us who have to work to make a living, they think they are smarter than everyone else. And if they disappeared with their snooty literature and know-it-all attitudes, would anyone really miss them?" Uncle Henry had convinced my mother that if father were to work with him, my parents would never have any financial worries. I had heard him telling my mother, that if father worked with him, he could give mother a mansion with half a dozen maids waiting on her all hours, two chauffeured limousines, a sailboat and trips to Paris every summer! Uncle Henry was not joking. He had made money through business and thought that for the effort they put in, university professors did not earn enough money to provide a comfortable life for their families. Perhaps Uncle Henry judged all university professors by my father's situation.

"Me? A businessman? Are you serious?" Father's voice sounded angry. Before an eruption from mother, he walked out of the room. In the back of his mind, father was thinking of going back to Sri Lanka where his Cambridge Ph.D. was still valued immensely. After seven years of writing up applications, revising resumes and all that money spent on telephone calls to his friends asking them to write recommendations on his behalf, father was still nowhere near a permanent job. Not even a year's full-time position. He talked about the incredible amount of work that went into the futile exercise and how much debt he had fallen into.

"I don't think I'll get an academic job as we had planned. I wake up each morning dreading that there will be another rejection letter in the mail," father told mother one day. "I am too set in my old ways to change careers." He wanted to go back but then he would have to invent a story why he came back to Sri Lanka. He looked a defeated, insecure soul. If he went back home to Sri Lanka he would have to live with the stigma of failure in the land of opportunity. "There isn't anyone out there who hasn't had a setback in life. Is there? That's life!" I heard him say to himself one day, trying to console himself. Father became depressed in mind and spirit.

Though I could spend days reading without talking to a soul, father's reclusiveness bothered me. I insisted that he go out and meet his old friends at the Newberry library. On several occasions, I had observed my father sitting by the living room window and staring across the road with a pensive look on his face. I wanted to walk up to him and talk to him—hug him and talk to him—as I did many years ago—I was his little girl then. I was not that little girl anymore. Well, yes—I will remain father's little girl forever, but I was a grown woman. I was twenty years old. I felt odd to touch him the way I did when I was little. I do remember the times I had sat on his lap and pulled the numerous black hairs that appeared on his chest. I used to call him the big chimpanzee because of his hairy body.

One morning when mother had gone to work, I walked into the kitchen and found my father drinking coffee. He liked instant coffee. He didn't care for *express, cafe latte* or *capuccino*. Just *Taster's Choice* was good enough for him. As I entered the kitchen, he looked up at me, his mug held between his palms; he nodded. A slight lift of his head and nod was enough for me to gather enough courage to inquire from him what was bothering him so much that he had almost become a recluse in his own house. His face was unshaven. He looked at me with tear-filled eyes and gave me a slight smile.

"Tell me, Daddy, did mother shout at you again? Why are you sad?" I asked him.

"It's my *karma*, Nelu. Nothing else, nobody's fault, it's all my *karma*. I am paying for something bad that I may have done to somebody in my previous births. How else could you explain what has happened to our family? You remember how happy we were back home in Kandy, Nelu? What did we lack? We had everything—we belonged to the elite there, didn't we? Your mother was happy—well, that's what I thought—but she wanted more. I had the best job in the world and I had friends. I often think of the great times we had then. Of course, you and Roshan could not have gotten a good education there. For that I am grateful. But then, when I think of what happened to Roshan, I blame myself for coming here." He believed in *karma* and said that sins of parents descended on their children. He looked at my brother with a sense of failure on his part. Many days he regretted coming to America. "I should have been firm with your mother. I gave in to most of what she wanted because I loved her very much. I still do." As father opened himself to me, his hands shook like the dry leaves in the wind. He paused, overcome by a rush of memories. His voice choked, his eyes blinked and tears welled in his eyes. He started to cry and the words ceased to come out of his lips.

Mother was cruel at times. I realized later that she ill-treated father not merely because father couldn't get a position in a high-powered university as she had wished, but also because she thought that father was stubborn. "When you found that you couldn't get a position in a university you should have prepared yourself for some other position without lamenting over something that you cannot get," I heard mother shouting at father a few times. I was used to a mother who was kind and generous—generous to all of us with her time and words and deeds. None of those things existed in her any more. She had become hard as steel. Instead of kind words, sarcasm dropped out of her lips.

"I have to work, earn money, buy the groceries, cook and feed you and clean up after that. I am not going to do these things any longer. I am not a slave." Mother shouted one evening and stopped cooking for us. We were used to waiting for her to come back from work and cook us all something to eat. What she cooked tasted so delicious then. We—father, Roshan and I—sat on the front door step and craned our necks to get the first glance at mother appearing round the corner. Those were the days in Brunswick and those days had gone for ever from our lives.

Father longed to go back home to Sri Lanka, 'the paradise on earth,' as he called it. He stayed on to keep the family together and he knew that his wishes—of either getting a university position or going back to Sri Lanka—would never be answered. Some evenings, I used to sit with my father and listened to him go back to fifty-six years of memories, the images of loss—great and small. Sometimes the memories would expand to a point that he found almost unbearable to relate. A university career that stretched back twenty-six years had faded into uselessness and so had the vision of Sri Lanka and its peace and stability. As I listened to him I felt his quiet, bottomless sadness and bewildered rage.

There was a long streak of sadness that ran through my father's family. His father was a lawyer and lawyers make money by inventing lies and putting the opposing party in trouble. There was a belief in Sri Lanka among our friends that a lawyer's children would suffer for the sins of their parents. How else could you explain that my father's elder brother who also had a Ph.D. from Cambridge University in England couldn't get a suitable position and is teaching high school children there? His eldest sister, married to a Tamil doctor had to emigrate to Australia because of racial tensions in the country and was without a steady job. His younger sister married and divorced soon after, was known to have 'lost her grip' on things. And now my father. . . .

It was during these times on a dull Fall day, my father, then aged fifty six years, went to teach in one of the two-year colleges, just as he had done every other day for the last seven years. He came home in the afternoon looking tired and distressed. When I told him that he looked exhausted after a long day's teaching, he just smiled from the corner of his mouth and walked into his room. Even he didn't know what was happening to him that afternoon. When I took a cup of tea for him later, I noticed that he experienced a little trouble in speaking, but that didn't seem to bother him much. The next morning, getting ready to go to work I heard his faint voice calling me. Mother had already left for the library. "Nelu," my father mumbled. "I am having trouble getting words out of my mouth." I quickly made my father lie on his bed. "I am numb from the waist down," he said as he dragged himself to the bed. He could hardly walk. I sat with him holding his hand for a while, and called the ambulance. Then I phoned my brother Roshan. When my brother arrived he found father lying on his bed,—father couldn't get up; his speech was slurred and soft. By the time the ambulance arrived father couldn't speak at all. My father, as we would come to understand in the next few hours, had had a stroke.

As soon as he was taken to the emergency room, he was given a blood thinner. "These are only effective if administered shortly after symptoms start," the doctor told us later. My father also had a cerebral angio-gram taken.

"This provides a map of the blood vessels that supply blood to the brain," the doctor explained. One of two carotid arteries which carry the blood to the brain, was fully blocked, the other, ninety percent. The only option was surgery to open the flow of blood through the one artery that still was allowing some blood to pass through. The blocked artery couldn't be reopened. Father lay on a stretcher, and my mother, who had just arrived in the hospital, with Roshan and I, each held his hand for a moment and kissed him. His speech was so slurred we could barely make out his word.

"You don't need to worry, I'll be all right," I thought he said, in the way he had always given us comfort and reassurance. As he was wheeled to the operating room, he raised his right arm and waved, a kind of good-bye in mid-air. In an instant, the double doors of the operating room flapped open and closed behind him.

But I cannot tell how long we waited that morning for word of my father's surgery. I can only think about how much fear and grief filled that room. Even now, when I think of that day I feel a sharp object pressing against my chest, an object that wouldn't let me breathe. My brother sat with his head in his hands much of the time while my mother paced up and down the waiting room, her lips moving constantly. Finally, after what seemed like forever, we saw the doctors solemnly walking out of the operating room dressed in their green coats and caps, removing their blood stained gloves as they disappeared down the corridor. The very next day after surgery we were allowed into see him. He couldn't speak—where there were slurred words before, now there were no words at all. His mouth and tongue had lost their function. But he could raise his arms and legs off the bed. While we were at his bedside, the nurses lifted him out of bed, guided him to a chair and strapped him in. The nurse fed him as she would feed an eight-month-old baby. The beginnings and endings of life—how remarkably alike they look, I thought at the time, but to totally different effect. By mid-morning, father's situation had taken a turn for the worse. He could not move his right arm or leg. He was immediately taken for a scan of another sort. We waited again. The scan had shown a pool of blood between the skull and the brain. He had to go through another operation, the doctor informed mother. I was standing by my mother then.

"Oh! God," mother sighed in despair. In the night the doctors operated on father for the second time in thirty six hours. But our prayers were not answered—father did not recover. What pained us most was, things happened so quickly that neither of us could do anything to help father, even at least to console ourselves.

A few days after father passed away, Roshan came to see mother. He talked to mother and me for a short time and sat on the sofa in the sitting room silently—the whole afternoon deep in thought. When the evening came, he walked into mother's room and said he was leaving. I walked with him to his old Toyota and waited until he got into his car. He climbed in and shut the door gently and closed his eyes for a few seconds. He looked at me with his tear filled eyes; a look that remains in me and causes me so much pain everyday. He reversed the car, shifted the gears into first, and headed for the highway. I saw him looking at me, or was he checking through the rear view mirror, for it is important to be cautious when you enter the highway.

That was the last time I saw my brother—he left me never to return. Why did Roshan desert mother and me in our grief? This is a question for which I cannot find an answer. A question that had come up in my mind many times. Perhaps he did not want to burden my mother with added grief—has he been tested positive for HIV? His physical appearance made me think of the worst. He was half his size, with just enough flesh to keep his bones and skin together. His eyes, I noticed were red and almost popping out of their sockets. His cheek bones stood out on his once good-looking boyish face. He has aged beyond his years. Even his voice had lost its enthusiasm for living. The possibility that he had been infected with the AIDS virus had gone through my mind a million times—a possibility that I dread and refuse to believe. Every time I think of the loss of my father and the disappearance of my brother, the images of my father raising his hand to wave good-bye as he was wheeled into the operating room and my brother's tear-filled eyes as he looked at me while starting the engine of his old car, become clearer and clearer. Those images do not seem to fade with time. I had told this story to my Uncle Henry many, many times. I have been lost in my thoughts so intensely that I did not realize that it was almost midnight. I should try to get some sleep and be fit to face another day—who knows what unexpected things would happen in these uncertain times?

X

I heard the telephone ring twice on the other end before it was picked up. "The Life Insurance Company, can I help you?" I immediately recognized the friendly voice of Veronica Shields, mother's agent. She handled our parents' insurance policies—auto, health, house and life. Since my parents entrusted her with all four policies, they earned discounts on them and had bought an umbrella liability policy. At the beginning they paid something like one hundred and fifty dollars a year for a coverage of one million dollars. Since insurance premiums increase with age and physical condition, as the years passed, my parents paid over eight hundred dollars a year on insurance alone.

"The main thing is to keep your policy limits up-to-date," I remember Veronica advising my father those days. "You don't want any unpleasant surprises."

"Morning, Veronica. This is Nelu Fernandez. I spoke to you yesterday afternoon regarding my mother's—Leila Fernandez's—accident." This was a call I had to make and I made it with much reluctance.

"Oh! Yes. How are you Nelu?" Before I could answer she said, "How is your mother? She's getting better?"

"Well, since she showed signs of regaining her consciousness, the doctors think she's out of danger for the time being."

"I am happy to hear that. It's a big relief. Well, let me see." There was a pause and I heard the sound of shuffling papers.

"No eyewitness, yet?" she wanted to know. "No," I said rather annoyed, for if there was, she would have been informed by now.

"Have you thought of getting a note published in the *Chicago Tribune* and the local paper asking for anybody who had witnessed the accident to come forward? Sometimes that helps—it urges people to talk who otherwise are reluctant to get involved," she suggested.

"We've done that. It's five days since the accident. Police are still working on it."

"Nelu, it will take a few more days for me to get the papers ready. We haven't seen the final police report yet. Last time I spoke to the officer-in-charge of the case, he informed me that they still cannot rule it as a hit-and-run accident. Since Leila can't remember anything of the incident and considering all the difficulties she had to go through recently, he said that distraction when driving that evening might have led to negligence. Our inspector visited the scene of the accident—his report says that the weather conditions were so severe at the time that there was ice on the road surface which explains why the car didn't leave any track marks—no skid marks. He had gone to the police station and had seen the car. It's a wreck. He assesses the market value of the Toyota Camry around four thousand dollars. Your auto insurance has a comprehensive policy going up to a hundred thousand. I will get the claim papers ready as soon as I get all the necessary information. In the meantime, will you call me as soon as you get any additional information that you think I should be aware of?" Veronica's voice showed concern. "One more thing, Nelu. Can I see your mother one of these days? I'd like to say Hi to her."

"Sure you can. She'll like that, but don't get disappointed if she cannot recognize you. Anyway give me a call when you are free, I'll take you," I assured her. We said good bye and hung up.

After talking to Veronica I wanted to get dressed, for Uncle Henry had said he was coming with me to talk to mother's Insurance Agent. But I had so little sleep these last few nights that I had fallen asleep on the couch. It was only when I heard a pounding on my door that I opened my eyes and remembered that Uncle Henry must be at the front door. When I opened the door for him he looked bewildered.

"What's up? Were you in the bathroom or something?" he inquired.

"No. Why?"

"I was wondering. You asked me to come over here. I knocked on the door so many times. I've been standing at the door for over ten minutes." I felt like a little girl caught redhanded doing something that I shouldn't have been doing.

"Your eyes are swollen. Have you been crying?" he inquired. I confessed that since returning from the police station last evening I've been thinking of my father and didn't have much sleep.

"Don't look back. There are some things that you cannot change. You are educated enough to know that you have to accept life as it is. The day you accept that you'll have peace of mind. Don't punish yourself for what happened in the past. That was beyond your control. In any case too much sadness, too long and too intense can make you ugly—both inside and out," he said as he made himself comfortable on the sofa.

This was exactly how he sat, with his arms spread on the back of the sofa as if he were holding court, when he visited us in our house in Evanston and in the Hyde Park apartment. I remembered his visits; mother enjoyed them more when father was not around. Even if he dropped in for a few hours he made himself at home and wore my father's purple terry-cloth bath-robe. He had on his black socks usually. I don't think I ever remember him fully dressed at our home.

"This is my home. I don't want to be in my stiff collar," he used to say. He looked a lot like my grandfather but Uncle Henry was a lot taller. He was soft-spoken and gentle and he was more like a friend to me. His beautiful broad shoulders and his extreme good looks combined with his kindness to my mother, made my mother say that there was a halo around his head.

Uncle Henry never got along with my father and he put on an air of superiority with all my aunts. His four other sisters, all younger than my mother, respected him though he was their "baby brother." All of them had arrived in the United States under Uncle Henry's sponsorship and they were all doing well in their newly adopted country. They felt that they all owed him the world for getting them here. Uncle Henry was abrupt and was very often rude to his sisters but he loved my mother. When he visited us, mother would serve him tea in her best magenta and gold Royal Doulton tea set that she had bought at Fortrum & Mason, in Bond Street in London. Every time he drank mother's tea, he pretended he was so thirsty as if he had just stepped out of a desert. That was his way of showing his appreciation and he knew that little pretense brought a smile to my mother's pretty face.

It was almost mid-morning. Time has a way of flipping through my fingers these days. I made tea and offered Uncle Henry a mugful. He refused to eat the English muffins I served. While sipping tea, I informed Uncle Henry of the telephone conversation I had with mother's insurance agent. He listened without interrupting me and after a somewhat long pause asked, "Is this the same agent who handled Nalin's case?"

"Yes," I answered.

"She has a lot more work to do before preparing the claim forms. Let's go and see your mother now," he suggested and I agreed.

It must have been around mid-morning when we reached the hospital premises. As usual the crowds spread from the foyer along the corridors. I always found hospital crowds to be troublesome. I hated to see distorted faces, scaly rashes and bandaged limbs. I felt like getting into a shell to avoid being breathed or coughed on. We had to take the elevator to go to the Intensive Care Unit where my mother was being treated at the time. The elevator was even worse that morning. I found myself pressed against a group of medicine-smelling patients. We quickly got out of the elevator and walked towards the ICU. On the corridor we passed a few white-coated young internees coming out of the wards talking softly to each other on the conditions of their patients. The corridors seemed crowded with hospital staff trying to push their way through friends and relatives of patients waiting to get news of their loved ones.

As we approached the ICU, I realized that it represents the most critical area for patient care. It reminded me of those alien environment scenes depicted in movies. Mechanical and elctronic sounds dominate, especially the rhythmical beep of the cardiac monitors and the hiss of the respirators. I was terrified at first by the hushed sound enveloped by the absolutely silent atmosphere inside the ICU. My mother was in one of the alcoves, on a high bed with the side rails pulled up. We observed the intravenous bottles and hanging tubes and the sharp needles connecting them to her blood vessels. My mother like some of the other patients was buried in layers of bandages. When we walked in a few of the patients were awake, their eyes betraying their fear and acute pain. The first time I went in, my eyes caught the fluorescent blips racing across the front of oscilloscope screens and not being aware of the information that these instruments conveyed made me feel as helpless as the patients themselves in knowing what state they were in.

That morning when we walked into mother's ward we were surprised to see several people standing around her bed. We got excited and quickened our pace. As we reached mother's bed, we saw someone bending over and trying to communicate with mother. When we came nearer, I recognized that someone as the young doctor in the green coat who injected medicine to my mother's arm that first night.

"What's up?" Uncle Henry inquired from the doctor as we stood at the foot of the bed. The doctor looked up at Uncle Henry and me, gave us a slight smile and said, "She is coming around."

"You mean she opened her eyes? Did she say anything?" I rushed in.

"Yes. She opened her eyes. She has regained her consciousness; and today is the fifth day after the accident. This is good; there is much hope now," the doctor's words were very encouraging. I almost hugged the doctor. We were all exhilarated with so much relief. Now there was hope—even if mother could not walk she could still live. Standing around mother's bed that evening we talked into the late afternoon. Mother's eyes remained closed. Now and then she would show signs as if she wanted to open her eyes. Then her face would get agitated as if she wanted to say something. Her breathing was normal though all those tubes running inside and outside of her body were intact.

My aunts decided to stay with mother until she regained consciousness completely. Mother was on the way to recovery and her sisters were helping her to get her muscles back into action. Since I couldn't help them, Uncle Henry brought me home and left assuring me that things would work out well somehow. When he was around, I felt that problems had a way of resolving themselves. I hugged him and reminded him that there was nobody in this world I loved more. I knew at the time that my feelings would have been transferred to him for he squeezed my hand and looked into my eyes with such tenderness, that I burst into tears.

"I'll see you in the morning," he said and walked slowly out of my apartment. Once he left, I felt very lonely. I had nothing else to do but seek comfort in my thoughts. I will always remember Uncle Henry with deep gratitude. After father passed away, Uncle Henry encouraged me in my studies, talked to me for long hours on the telephone and was there for me when I needed someone to talk to. He helped me to buy this luxury apartment when I was offered the teaching position at Christchurch University. He told me that day that he was more proud of me than he was of his own daughter, Maya. Maya qualified as a lawyer from Columbia Law School a year before and was working for her father at the time.

My mother would have loved to live in my condominium. The address itself was a status symbol. The view from my sitting room was a dream—I could see the blue-green waters of Lake

Michigan spread far out into the horizon—stretching far beyond where even my eyes could see. I owed a lot of money to my bank for the tasteful furnishing of the condo—especially the sitting room and my bedroom. This was far more spacious than the two bedroom apartment that we lived in, in Hyde Park.

The Hyde Park apartment was not big enough for mother. She missed her garden back in Kandy and the stairs to climb to her bedroom. She found something in the apartment to complain about every day. Just a year after living in the apartment, I remember, there were days when my mother became increasingly restless. She walked up and down the living room in the tiny two-room apartment, a hundred and one times a day, like a lioness waiting for her prey.

"This is so tiny; there's hardly enough room for me even to turn," she would grumble as she walked. Mother loved shifting furniture. She believed that if we moved the furniture in the place where we lived, we would create movement in our lives. There were evenings when father returned home from work, and he could hardly recognize his own living room. It would have been turned upside down. Of course I was right there to help her in planning and moving. We would huff and puff, and push and pull every item of furniture and place them in locations mother thought was the most suitable.

"What madness is this?" Roshan inquired from me on several occasions when he was at home on his school vacations. His help was never sought, neither did he offer to help.

It was during this time that my parents bought the lovely little three bedroom ranchhouse in a suburb of Chicago. Having been tormented for two years by mother's moaning about living in the small apartment, father contacted a realtor and she took my parents around on several week-ends to show them houses. On a few occasions I joined my parents in their search for a house. I remember when we all got down from the realtor's well-maintained Cadillac, we were graciously shown into the house by the young looking lady realtor. She led us through a cramped kitchen into the master bedroom, the door of which led to the garden. There was the stairway with no handrail. At the top of the stairs was what we liked most—the rooftop terrace with a table and chairs and the breathtaking view of the surroundings. We could see flowers spilling out of window boxes in all directions in the neighboring houses.

"At night under a cloudless sky, you could reach up and touch the stars," my father whispered in my ear—the romantic always.

"Yes, it's beautiful here, isn't it?" I agreed. The closeness of the universe was exciting and overwhelming and there was a timeless, satisfying calm about the place.

"For reasons I can't explain, I fell in love with the place and felt right at home there," said my mother when we came back to our apartment.

"Yes, indeed, so right did the place look that it seemed natural that we should live there," father agreed and decided to go for it and made arrangements with the bank to purchase the house.

We spent a couple of happy years in that house. It was as if we were back in Kandy. Father helped mother to make a garden in the backyard. We planted horsetail along the edge of our land and placed broad, flat stones along the path leading from the kitchen door to the end of the garden dividing the garden into two. On one side we planted rose bushes and on the other tulips, daffodils, marigolds and irises at the very edge. Mother wanted to plant some purple cornflowers. She said they were so beautiful and attractive to butterflies. They weren't really purple, but they grew to about three feet tall and formed a line along the horsetails. In early Spring the scent of roses mingled with the irises would sweep across the garden and enter the house through the kitchen windows. When we opened the kitchen window in the mornings and sat by the kitchen table to have our morning coffee, a heavenly atmosphere would greet us. Butterflies of beautiful hues flocked into our garden. Mother kept a redwood bench along the bed of roses and on some evenings sat there by herself. She said it made her forget every worry and she just surrendered completely to the peace around her. Some evenings, father spent long hours sitting on the bench talking to mother. In later summer days when it was not very hot and the sun had already set behind the trees on the far away horizon, smearing the sky, red and orange, my mother would walk slowly along the edge of the garden, gently touching the horsetails and humming one of her favorite songs.

I recall in October, when days came thick with sun and falling leaves and the wind traced our shadows in the back lawn; with the smell of leaves just starting to decompose, we would smell the still warm earth. I scattered gravel with my feet, kicked loose stones free and watched them roll off the road's edge. It was this garden that made me feel like we were getting somewhere in America. Tending a garden meant having time, it meant having money to spend on plants, plant food, tools and pots. And most of all gardening was sheer enjoyment to mother.

But unfortunately owning a house in America was not as simple as my parents thought it would be. They soon realized buying was the simple part. They borrowed money for the down payment on the house from Uncle Henry and the bank signed off the loan. Furnishing the house was not a big problem as we already had some old furniture. Though every time mother saw some fancy piece of furniture for the house she talked about it until father agreed to buy it. The difficult part came in the maintenance of the house and the garden. Father had absolutely no idea either in landscaping or in looking after the house repairs. We all took turns in mowing the lawn at first; in fact mother and I fought over the lawn-mower many times. But soon the novelty faded and father was left to do it by himself. He detested the idea of pushing the lawn mower every six days or so. Especially in early Spring, he fertilized the lawn and watered the lawn when there was a slight period of rainlessness and when the grass grew he had to cut it.

"What madness is this?" he shouted many days frustrated. In the end he hired the neighbor's son, who used his father's rider mower to cut the grass. Money became an important issue. Each time the boy mowed the lawn he had to be paid thirty dollars.

"And how are you going to get that much money?" At first mother did not mind especially as father had to prepare his lectures, but gradually as the money situation got difficult, I could hear mother's angry mumblings.

"The grass is grown. We have to keep up with our neighbors and help to preserve the beauty of the neighborhood," mother would say, but father had to do it. She didn't offer to help. The deck and the fence around the house had to be stained with a water-resistant chemical to preserve the wood. Back at home in Kandy, I couldn't even remember whether we ever faced the problem of roof leakage. I remember father's parents sending workers to attend to our house repairs every year. When we lived in the apartments, before we moved into the house, if there was any problem mother phoned the maintenance office and they saw to whatever was needed to be done. Father did not have the know-how nor the will to attend to these mundane affairs.

"It's a disgrace to entertain my friends in this dining room. These lights are hideous," mother complained on numerous occasions. One day father and mother returned home after a shopping expedition carrying with them a beautiful chandelier. It was small but was made of genuine crystal. Father looked in the telephone directory and got an electrician to install the lights. The man came and fixed the chandelier in half and hour and sent a bill for two hours' work. Mother was furious.

"Men attend to little jobs around the house. They enjoy it. You are so different Nalin—if you could learn to fix these little things we could save so much money," she scolded father. These little details led to major problems. More money went into the maintenance of the house than my parents had anticipated.

The winter that we lived in our house happened to be a severe one. Sheets of ice formed on the roof and as the sun came up and the temperature went up slightly the sheets of ice began to slide down the roof. There were notices to warn pedestrians about the sliding sheets of ice. One night we heard a thunderous noise from the backyard. In the morning we discovered our neighbor's dog that had escaped from its kennel crushed to death by a fallen sheet of ice. We were responsible for the dog's death. So my parents had to get a dog for the neighbors!

"Let's sell the house and move into an apartment closer to the city center. Then we can save all this money we spend on the maintenance of the house and we don't have to drive all these distances either," father suggested one day. But the suggestion fell on deaf ears. Mother wouldn't hear of it. All her friends had large, beautiful houses and most of all her brother, our Uncle Henry, lived in a mansion-like house in a Chicago suburb.

During this time, I was very active in my high school and was preparing for college admission tests. So Sundays happened to be a luxury for me. I had plenty of time to read. Sometimes I looked out of my window for hours, thinking about everything which eventually came to nothing at all. I was restless some days—I couldn't get comfortable on my bed, I couldn't focus on anything. There was this echo of my parents' arguments thrumming in my ears. One Sunday morning I remember, I was in bed reading a book when it started to sleet. I turned over on my side and watched the sleet hitting the windowpane. A shiver went through me and I closed my eyes. The house was quiet except for the sleet hitting the windowpane. Suddenly I heard a voice, then another voice, two voices—shouting at the same time to drown one against the other. That was not a dream—I was not asleep. I could still hear the faint sound of the sleet hitting the window pane and over that my parents shouting at each other.

After about two years of peaceful living in our beautiful home, tension started developing between my parents. By then mother had become the principal breadwinner in the family. Words came out of her lips that had an echo of her own mother shrieking at her father, demanding he get off the couch and throw the newspaper away and do some work in the house. Mother could not help herself. Mother's success made father feel less of a man. Father admitted one day that he was a failure, that he was helpless and was getting to be jealous of mother. I heard them many times, arguing and crying and promising never to argue again saying that the struggle lay beyond their control. Each time they had a fight one of them would leave the house. But whenever mother left the house, father followed her immediately and both returned within an hour which seemed like eternity to me, holding hands, talking and laughing. Mother told me, one day walking back from the grocery store, on the street they had started an argument and walked off in opposite directions and ended up boarding the same bus, and sitting in the same corner.

"I am never able to escape what father calls our destiny, our *karma*," at least mother could on occasion laugh at their childish behavior. After an intense argument one day she told me that she felt worse with each successful day of her life, because she could not make father feel better. She said she couldn't find words to appease his ego. Father was so sensitive that whatever she said had been interpreted as an insult thrown at him for not being able to find an academic position in a good university.

They were arguing again. Arguing over a silly thing. I heard mother saying through sobs, "Why can't you bring my towel as well? I do everything for you. You avoid doing little things for me—you consider it beneath your dignity. You want to show that you are the boss around here. Well, you are the boss, nobody stole that position from you."

Whenever they started arguing, I locked myself in my little room. I could see the vehicles moving slowly down the Main Street through my window. On a cloudless day, even the building of the Christchurch University could be seen. On times like this, our little house on the hillock behind Grand Ma's big house appeared in my memory. I could see the butterflies and the bees, attracted by the different colors and smells of the roses, hovering beneath my parents' bedroom window. Roshan and I used to run down the hillock to Grand Ma's backyard to be welcomed by the retinue of Grand Ma's feudal workers. Hearing the cheerful sound of laughter that emanated from the backyard, Grand Ma would come out in her ever regal attire and hug both of us. We visited her every afternoon when we came back from school. Grand Ma fed us goodies and we told her about our day in school. Those happy days would never come again—they are only a distant memory.

I still hear my parents shouting at each other. They never argued like this when we lived in our pleasant little house in Kandy. Though my eyes were filled with tears, I could see my mother, in that beautiful, long red dress that father brought for her on one of his many visits to India, standing by the bedroom window, waiting for father to come home after work. She was so very beautiful then—she still is. She was happy then—happiness gave a radiant glow to her beauty. As soon as she spotted the gold Toyota station wagon around the bend in Grand Ma's backyard, she would run down the steps, calling Mary to prepare the afternoon tea, that the master was on his way. I remember how my father's eyes filled with love and contentment, how his smile full of sweetness added to the goodness around him. Whatever happened to my parents—where had all that cheer gone?

I must have been reflecting on my days back in Sri Lanka for more than two hours. Hearing no sound coming from my parents' room, I gently opened my room door and peeped into the living room. My father was there, his head buried in his knees, sobbing quietly. I gently lifted his head with both my hands and his swollen red eyes, looked into mine. I clung on to his neck and held him close.

"Why? Why?" I kept asking myself. Mother had left. We didn't know where she had gone to. She just slipped on her boots and disappeared out of the front door. It was snowing at the time and was freezing out there.

Every time this happened, I got closer to my father. I loved my mother dearly, but I hated her when I saw father in tears for something I believed that mother had said or done. I heard my parents arguing—shouting at each other—shrieking, crying and howling from my mother. They seemed to be intolerable at times, pathetic, unbearable. I couldn't bear to see their helplessness. They were in their early fifties at the time, but they looked older than their years, worn out, life strained out of them.

I think it was this stage of my parents' lives that influenced the life I chose. I remember on many occasions I stood there, murmuring to myself: I will not be like them. I shall never let myself be shouted at and made the object of so much hatred. I told myself—remember these moments, remember always, don't ever forget these. Don't be like your parents—however much they sacrificed for our sake, they are leading miserable lives, trapped by circumstances. Moments like these were not there in my childhood, but my adolescent years were full of them. I found it difficult to understand then. Now I know my mother was frustrated and felt lonely; how could she not have been, an ambitious woman married to a placid man.

XI

It's been over a week since my mother's hospitalization. The doctors told us that she was out of danger though her recovery would take a long time. I went to see her every morning and stayed with her until late in the evenings. When I drove to the hospital in the mornings, I had my hopes raised and cheer in my heart. The thought of being with my mother, now that she could recognize people and speak a word or two, brought a feeling of warmth to my heart. We've been apart for too long.

One morning, as usual, I drove slowly towards the hospital parking lot, parked my car, and looked at the main entrance to the hospital. I felt the old impressive building glaring at me through the light falling snow. In spite of the bitter cold, the sparkling snow in the bright sunlit morning set a festive mood. Snowflakes drifted to the ground in a steady breeze of icy air, but the chilly weather did not seem to affect the group of people walking with worried looks on their faces up the steps to the building.

I pushed through the revolving door and stepped inside. To the right of the entrance was the hospital gift shop. An atmosphere of cheer greeted me as I stepped inside. The shop was run by a group of gracefully aging women volunteers from the neighborhood. Dressed in black pants and blue polo neck sweaters they looked smart. With smiling faces and kind words, they looked after their customers. The windows of the shop faced one of the hospital parking lots giving the shop the appearance of a busy boutique in a market square. Its shelves were filled with snacks on one side and light fiction and daily newspapers and magazines on the other. As I entered the gift shop, I headed for the magazine section to buy the day's paper to read for mother.

Three days after mother came out of her coma she was shifted to the recovery room. To me it seemed superficially similar to the Intensive Care Unit except that it was brighter, noisier and more crowded. There were about fifteen to twenty spaces set aside for beds. Each space had a set of equipment built into the wall. Most of the spaces were occupied by high beds with the side rails pulled up. In each bed was a patient with bandages over some part of his or her body. Bottles of intravenous fluid were tied on tops of poles which looked like coconuts on leafless palms.

On some mornings when I arrived at mother's bedside, I found her sleeping. Not wanting to disturb her I would sit by her bed and watch the ward. I often observed new patients arriving. I also observed those who had recovered leaving for their private rooms. People who worked in the ward spoke to each other as if they seemed to have felt at ease in this less formal environment. I even heard some occasional laughter amidst intermittent groans. At one instance, a child's wailing drowned the laughter of the workers. Some of the beds had groups of doctors and nurses busily engaged in checking pressure and temperature of the patients, adjusting the bed sheets, valves and tubes. I noticed some stains on the green coats worn by some of the doctors. Some doctors wore long white coats starched stiff. Generally in the mornings, the recovery room seemed a busy place to me. One evening, I observed a group of doctors passing us. As they passed each patient, the patients' heads swung around to watch the group recede down the corridor. I assumed, as the patients did, that a group of doctors had been called on an emergency, and it was reassuring for me to see how earnestly the doctors responded at emergency calls.

"Some days are like this," I overheard one of the young doctors say holding the door open for the nurse as they left the recovery room.

"A cup of coffee can be considered a luxury," he said looking back and hurrying down the corridor, perhaps to answer another emergency. Chicago Methodist hospital is a caring place. It was a relief to know that my mother was in good hands.

My aunts left a few days after my mother regained her consciousness, promising to come again.

"We are just a phone call away. Don't hesitate to call us if you need help," both of them assured me before they left. Though it was just over a week, it seemed a long time to me since my mother was brought into this hospital. The fact that she was being shifted to one of the wards was a sign of recovery, the nurses told me. Yet, very often when I approached my mother to kiss her after my arrival, I heard a drugged murmur and I sensed the odor of medicine. At such moments of helplessness, when I am in despair, I stir up enough emotional energy inside myself to create in memory my father's presence. I try to create in my memory the smell of the air and the glory of the moonlit nights in our garden in Kandy, and see my father handing a glass of juice to my mother and her grateful response to the gesture. I see as in a slow-motion movie, my mother turn her head towards father, with her sweet smile. . . . Yet, suddenly I realize it's not possible—it's nonsense—I cannot face this situation alone by myself. At times, I felt like shaking my dazed mother who had once been so full of life, and shouting, "Come, mother, wake up. Help me to look after you." When I stood by her bedside, she would slowly bring her hand out and keep her hand on mine. When Uncle Henry was around, she liked to join in our conversation and when he said anything funny she smiled in response. But she could still not remember what happened to her on that December afternoon at the Exit to Washington Street from Lake Shore Drive. That scenario had been erased out of her memory. She talked of driving down Lake Shore Drive after work. She said it was early afternoon—almost past two—when she left the library; her colleagues at the library confirmed this piece of information. Gwen, one of her co-workers, said that mother was not her usual cheerful self that day; she said that she thought the Chicago weather had brought down my mother's spirits. It had been dark and gloomy—almost like night that afternoon. It had to be, for it was mid-December and a snowfall was on its way. My mother had been reluctant to work that day but the staff situation in the library had made it necessary for mother to work until half past one in the afternoon. Poor visibility would have affected mother's driving. How could mother speed at sixty or sixty five miles per hour on Lake Shore Drive? It puzzled me.

Her right leg in plaster was still hanging from a hook attached to the ceiling. Sometimes I worried about the pain mother would feel after the effects of anesthesia had waned; I worried that mother's leg might not function as before, as the doctors had promised, worried about the cast she would have to wear on her leg for several months. She could not turn; she had to lie on her back. The nurses who came to clean her up in the early mornings told me that mother had not developed bed-sores. I was there by her bed side every morning and inquired after her health from the hospital staff. I spent every evening with her. Now that mother was getting better, Uncle Henry joined me on alternate evenings.

One evening, maybe it was the eighth or the ninth day after mother's accident, I was alone with mother. We were just beginning to enjoy each other. She allowed me to pour the chocolate and to butter pieces of a croissant for her. She held the plate on her lap like a child, and for a minute, tears appeared in her eyes—she must have realized how much she missed being mothered. She looked at me with kindness. Mother scalded her lip on the hot chocolate. She returned the cup shakily to its saucer and placed it on the tray. Then, she covered her face with her palms and I noticed tears appearing through her fingers. Not knowing how to console her, I sat on the chair beside the bed and looked around to see to my great relief Uncle Henry hurrying down the corridor. No sooner had Uncle Henry arrived at mother's bedside than I noticed a woman walking towards us. I had seen this woman one evening, passing by with concerned looks—I had the feeling that she wanted to tell me something but didn't say anything as someone was with me all the time. She was a pleasant young woman with brown hair—would have been just a few years older than I. She walked to the bed and stopped in front of me and looked at my face. She held her hand and I shook it, indifferently.

"I am Irene Peters. Your mother?" she asked looking at my mother. I nodded and kept silent. She came closer to me and looked down at my face again and said, "I've been wanting to talk to you for sometime. I saw your mother's accident."

"You did?" I was awestruck. Thinking that the woman might not be forthcoming in the presence of a stranger, I quickly introduced Uncle Henry to her and she held her hand and they shook hands.

"I saw her at the traffic lights, about a half mile from the Exit to Washington Street. The time would have been around 2.30 in the afternoon. I smiled and she smiled back. That was just minutes before the accident. I remembered her face—I had seen her on the Christchurch University campus," she said.

One week and a day before this freezing December afternoon, between two thirty and four o'clock in the afternoon, on the Lake Shore Drive, driving towards home, my mother had met with this accident, which confined her to bed. We still didn't know with certainty whether she would be able to walk; whether she would be able to function like a normal person. Her beauty was gone; her glory days gone; she was lying on the hospital bed not knowing what hit her. Why didn't this nice woman come to me before? Lots of speculation had gone into this incident as mother had shut the incident out of her memory and there had been no eyewitnesses to the incident. Several anonymous calls to the Police Station had mentioned a hit-and-run car; but it had been too dark for anyone to notice even the color of the vehicle as it disappeared at great speed into the fog.

Now, here standing in front of us, beside my mother's bed was a woman who had seen what took place. She said she knew that I was a professor at Christchurch University. Her husband worked at the bursar's office at Christchurch and she had seen me on campus. She had seen a yellow taxi cab driving at breakneck speed cut in front of my mother's car. My mother had cut sharply towards the left to avoid the vehicle that jumped into her lane and her car had hit the barrier throwing her over to the opposite lane. My mother's car had turned over, crushing her with its weight.

"I called the police on my car phone. I couldn't stop because of traffic," she said with a slight embarrassment.

"How do you know it was my mother? Did you see our appeal in the local paper?" I wanted to know.

"Yes. I thought some other person would stay behind to help. Did you have any eyewitnesses? Her car was a wreck," she said and continued. "I saw a yellowish vehicle but I couldn't see its number. It drove away at an amazing speed. I cannot remember seeing other vehicles around. Is she paralyzed?" There was concern in her voice.

"No, fortunately not. But there seems to be some trouble with her right leg. She is lucky—she has three broken vertebrae in her back, but her spine is fine—so the doctors say. Her brain—she has lost her memory of that incident," as I spoke, I saw Irene Peters seeing my mother's car flying over the barrier, turning over and landing on the opposite lane. Uncle Henry stood aside and listened.

"So you drove away without stopping?" I said to myself.

Mother opened her eyes; she held Uncle Henry's hand while listening to our conversation.

"Mother, this is Irene Peters. She was there at the Exit the afternoon you got hit." Mother looked intently at her. Her mouth opened and she whispered, "You were?" I saw mother's eyes getting agitated—as though she had just heard something painful, but it had not yet fully struck her. I looked up at Irene Peters, and imagined her driving away while watching my mother's car flying over the barrier and landing on its roof. Blood rushed into my head—so it was an accident. How wrong of me to believe that it was a deliberate action on my mother's part. For a moment I was there—at the Exit to Washington Street on Lake Shore Drive on that gloomy, cold December afternoon.

"We are grateful you called the police. The paramedics arrived in time and saved my mother's life—she might have bled to death."

"Some other passer-by would have called."

"Maybe. But it would have taken time. Every minute mattered at the time."

I wanted to ask her what she saw—what she saw of my mother that evening, but I could not. I couldn't bear to hear how my mother lay there on the road, crushed inside her own car—crushed in between the steering wheel and the seat.

Irene Peters was soon joined by her husband. His face was not familiar to me at all but he addressed me by my name.

"Professor Fernandez, how are you, Ma'am?" he inquired very politely shaking my hand. Then he shook hands with Uncle Henry. His face did not carry that very serious look of most university administrators, as though work had taken away all fun from their lives, and working at the bursar's office was only work and money, which is what that matters most in one's life. He looked the jolly sort who worked to enjoy life.

"So my wife bundled up enough courage to talk to you," he said smiling.

"It's incredible. This is the first time I met someone who saw my mother getting hit," I said.

"How's your mother?" he asked.

"Getting better every day; but as you see it's a long way to go," Uncle Henry joined in. We talked of the weather and mother's slow recovery for a while. In the course of the conversation, Irene assured us that if ever we wanted, she was willing to give a statement to the police.

"Thank you very much for coming forward. You'd never even imagine how much we appreciate your kind gesture," said

Uncle Henry overwhelmed with relief. Then they shook hands with me and Uncle Henry, took leave of my mother and left. After they had disappeared from our view, Uncle Henry heaved a sigh of relief.

"I feel as if a heavy burden has been lifted off my chest. We are on to something here now. I have to go to the police station straight away. Now that we have an eyewitness I want to hire a private investigator. I know of a good man who will do the job within a few days. We have clues to go on. Police will take action if we help them," said Uncle Henry. I felt as if I was on the near end of a broken circle whose separated ends were beginning to move towards each other. Soon they would meet and help us resolve the issues we had been faced with these last three weeks. Mother had closed her eyes again, oblivious to what was happening around her. After a while we decided to let mother rest and leave without disturbing her.

While walking through the hospital corridors heading for the exit, Uncle Henry told me that he met with his friend Jeffrey Ashland, who was a personal injury lawyer and hired him to look after the legal battle that mother's accident seemed destined to become.

"Jeffrey is of the opinion that no sensible person would be naive enough to think the case might boil down to whether your mother was negligent in her driving that evening," said Uncle Henry. The lawyer was convinced that there was some hidden character involved in the accident—an unknown character, who purposely hit my mother's car. He had also brought to my uncle's notice that these days in America everybody was suing everybody—that one of these days someone would get the bright idea to sue God for letting all that snow fall!

"I am seriously thinking of suing the mayor of Chicago for not getting the streets cleared of snow," my uncle said lightheartedly.

"Let's keep all these from your mother for the time being," he asked me, and I nodded in agreement. Apart from the brief statement mother had given to the police in the hospital, all she had to do was give a deposition under oath to her lawyer.

"She need not be troubled by the fact that she has to go over the events prior to the accident several times with Jeffrey," Uncle Henry assured me.

As we stepped out of the hospital building the wind had increased and it was still snowing. A faint, quiet amber glow had fallen outside the hospital, cleaning the mushy surroundings, mantling the dirty sidewalks off the streets. From a distance, as though emanating from a neighborhood far away, came the muffled metallic clang of a snow truck quietly cleaning its way down.

Uncle Henry slipped his arm through mine. I had hoped he would just do that. This was a time I needed support more than any other time and who else would know it better than my Uncle Henry? He lifted up my coat collar to cover my ears, and looked into my face.

"You take courage, Nelu. Things will work out for the best. Your mother is getting better—it's a slow process but she is out of danger now," his words of consolation filled my eyes with tears. I shook my head. I could hardly see him in the dim light of the street lamps. "You are a very special daughter," he said, his hand still touching my coat. There was something tender and kind in the way he spoke to me. My father had shown me this kind of gentleness, but that was so long ago. He placed a palm on my cheek. We crossed the road together and entered the hospital parking lot, following the flakes of snow gathering like a swarm of distracted bees in the faint light of the street lamp, growing even more dense as I looked for my car. Uncle Henry followed me to the car and waited until I got in. I wished him good night and started the car's engine and watched him walk towards his car.

I remained there by the lamp post, trying to collect my thoughts. I wanted to get down from my car, clear the snow off one of the old wooden benches in the hospital parking lot, sit down, and simply think, disturbing nothing—not the snow tapering on the curved metal armrests of the bench or the footprints of our shoes where we had walked from the hospital just minutes ago. I pictured Irene Peters driving away watching my mother's car turn over. I pictured the paramedics pulling my mother's blood stained body out of the vehicle and placing her on the stretcher. I pictured my mother in the emergency room, ten days ago, on that bed, with her left leg hanging from the hook attached to the ceiling and tubes supplying nourishment into her body through her nose, mouth and abdomen. I wished I had stepped into something like a magic world—a world where time stops and where miracles happen. I thought how the things we want most in life are rarely given but when they are granted we seldom believe it, and without knowing, sometimes turn them down. The lamp post near where I was parked, stood upon a gleaming pool of light and seemed almost to be leaning towards my car, as though eager to help, not knowing how. I saw an empty beer can tumbling into the street from the parking lot. The familiar sea of red tail lights and the wisps of exhaust fumes could be seen as far as my eyes could observe them. I noticed the windows of cars covered with frost. I had to clean the windscreen of my car before I pressed the accelerator.

Later that night, I was awakened by the loud bang of a snowplough scraping the Lake Shore Drive and was suddenly filled with an overflowing joy. It reminded me how mother and I walked in our first snowstorm in Brunswick—how we found the college quadrangle blanketed with snow, how mother had held me by my shoulders and walked home. Now, in the dark, the memory of her arm had almost come alive on my shoulders. I got out of bed and looked out of my window and saw how peacefully the snow had settled on the roof tops of the high rise buildings. I was able again to appreciate the beauty of the spectacle.

XII

Mother and I had been so engrossed in our conversation and our thoughts that we didn't notice Uncle Henry coming towards us until he came and stood by mother's bed. He was accompanied by a man immaculately dressed in a three-piece suit. He displayed a few streaks of grey hair already showing signs of middle age. I remembered seeing him before—his face was familiar. When Uncle Henry introduced him as Paul Williams it occurred to me that I had seen him at Uncle Henry's office some time ago. Paul was Uncle Henry's friend. After inquiring about mother's health Uncle Henry told mother that he was hiring a private investigator to unravel the mystery of the yellow vehicle that hit my mother's car.

"The PI I am thinking of hiring is Paul," Uncle Henry said looking at his friend. In response Paul smiled and I noticed that my mother's eyes widened. I knew this was coming because Uncle Henry talked to me about helping to activate the police investigation by giving them a lead. Moreover, he had been talking to me about not being able to have a good night's sleep until he found out the secret behind all the turmoil.

"Now that we have an eyewitness in Irene Peters, Paul might be able to bring some more light onto this case. The police are not going to spend time and effort unless we provide them with a lead," Uncle Henry said.

"I work hard for the money," Paul said smiling.

"I know. Good PIs cost money. I want somebody good, that's why I am hiring you. Let's keep this very quiet," Uncle Henry looked at mother and continued. "Paul has been a police officer in Los Angeles and now he works in the Chicago area. He has his own investigative service. He has a way of charming information out of people who are reluctant to talk to the law."

At this Paul joined in. "People were afraid of me when I was a cop. They wouldn't talk to me. Now I have better luck. It's amazing how almost half the world is running away from the authorities—old traffic violations, not paying child support, no Green Card—it's tough to stay clean in today's society."

Uncle Henry held my mother's hand gently. "Leila, I want you to talk to Paul. Tell him whatever you can remember of that day. Tell him whatever he wants to know to help him to catch the man who did this terrible thing. We just can't let him get away with it," Uncle Henry persuaded mother. Observing mother's reaction, Paul smiled. Mother had spoken to a police officer earlier. Other than that no one had approached her on the incident, not only because she couldn't speak a few words without getting tired and it was painful for her to talk about the incident, but simply because whatever that took place there had been erased out of her mind. She remembered driving along Lake Shore Drive after work and some vehicle crashing onto hers. That's all she remembered of the accident.

"How did this happen?" Paul asked and Uncle Henry, observing mother's reluctance, responded to keep the conversation going.

"Hit and run—almost ten days ago. As you know we have an eyewitness in Mrs. Irene Peters—she spoke to us last Friday," Uncle Henry said.

"Go on," Paul encouraged settling down on the chair beside mother's bed.

"Mrs. Peters will talk to you," Uncle Henry said.

"Have you seen the police reports?" Paul wanted to know.

"Yes," answered Uncle Henry. "I can get them for you. I'll come with you and introduce you to the officer-in-charge. I know him well enough now."

"Did you have any enemies, Mrs. Fernandez?" Paul directed the question at my mother.

"Well—not that I know of—certainly not anyone who hated me enough to want to kill me!" my mother said, a little shaken at the unexpected question.

"As you know the roads were covered with snow that afternoon and the police records note that the investigation was obstructed by weather conditions," Uncle Henry informed Paul.

"So, no trace of the vehicle? Was Mrs. Peters able to describe the vehicle at all?" Paul wanted to know.

"She said she tried to get the license plate number, but she herself was driving at the time and by the time she looked ahead the vehicle was disappearing out of sight. She said it appeared to be a yellow vehicle. Though the time was around half past two in the afternoon it was dark there and the street lights were too dim for her to see much at a distance," I joined in.

"You've talked to her yourself?"

"Of course. She has talked to the police since then. Her statement should be in the police file. You can talk to her," I gave him Irene Peters' telephone number and her address.

"No trace of the vehicle, hmm. . . ." Paul repeated, this time to himself.

"Permanently disappeared into somebody's garage or driven to some outlandish place and sold for parts, but not repaired in the vicinity. Whoever drove that vehicle seemed to have done a thorough job, so the officer informed me," Uncle Henry said with some certainty.

"Sometimes the vehicle disappears but leaves tell-tale traces on the damaged vehicle," Paul said showing his investigative strategies.

"Paint chips—you mean?" Uncle Henry wanted to know.

"Yes. As I see it, even though the police couldn't find the vehicle or the driver, they have not yet ruled out the accident as a hit-and-run. They will ultimately do so once they get enough information from the eyewitness to satisfy themselves. What we are looking for is premeditation. Anyway it's just a couple of days since the eyewitness came forward. Sometimes the guy responsible might be picked up on an unrelated charge and would confess to the crime. No skid marks . . . the driver wouldn't stop even if he hit the car accidentally. For the purpose of our investigation we have to start with the idea that it was deliberately done. Your sister had no enemies. There is always the possibility of a psycho somewhere obsessed with your sister—you know the feeling? If I couldn't have her, nobody should!" Paul said quite seriously. At this Uncle Henry got agitated and there was urgency in his voice when he asked Paul to begin work on the case immediately.

"Paul, I would like you to start the investigation soon. It's not revenge that I am looking for—we want some peace of mind. I just cannot understand why anybody should do this to my sister!" There was a trace of emotion in Uncle Henry's voice.

"OK. I am in," Paul said, getting up to go.

"Fine, you have a free hand. Contact me or Nelu if you want to talk to my sister again," Uncle Henry said, shaking Paul's hand.

XIII

Paul Williams did not waste any time on his new assignment. He had spent two days double-checking the week-long police work. The local repair shops had turned up nothing—all vehicles that had been brought in for accident related repairs had checked out clear. The tow-truck companies and junk yards and police departments for miles in and around the Chicago area had been advised to report vehicles disposed of over cliffs or in water or for junk—nothing had come out of the effort. Paul did not have a good description of the vehicle. Irene Peters, our only eyewitness, had said she vaguely recollected the color of the vehicle as yellow. Yet Paul remained hopeful.

The Spring semester at the university was due to begin in a week's time. I had not yet completed the paper I was preparing for the Annual Shakespeare Conference. I was well aware that once the teaching began my students would demand most of my time. They would want to talk to me about their assignments and I would need time to prepare my lectures. In spite of my very heavy workload I went to see my mother every evening. I spent time with her talking and reminiscing about our days in Kandy, Brunswick and Chicago. We talked about father and my brother Roshan. How could we leave father and brother out of our conversations—they were a part of our lives. But I was careful not to step deep into controversial topics. Some subjects are impossible to set aside, yet they are too delicate to handle, especially when I was trying to rebuild our lost bonds with my mother.

My mother's leg was still wrapped in plaster and when I pinched her toes she still didn't show any response. But it was heartening to hear the doctors say she would recover and would be walking along the hospital corridor some day soon. Very often in the evenings I met Aunty Rani, my mother's best friend, seated by her bed. She proved to be a loyal and good friend to mother during these difficult days when mother longed for company. I had not liked Aunty Rani much because I thought she was too loud and talked ill of other people. But during this time as I got to know her better, I began to like her. She took delight in amusing and being amused. She adored gossip and I think that was one reason why mother was attracted to her. I remember in our early days in Chicago mother visited Aunty Rani during weekends and she would return home in the late evenings full of juicy stories about Sri Lankans living in the vicinity of Hyde Park. She brought news about diets of Sri Lankan women, who was the sexiest doctor, who was rich and influential, who so and so was reputed to be. I remember mother telling us that Aunty Rani liked watching macho television shows such as Starsky and Hutch and Hill Street Blues and my mother also began to watch these until one day when Roshan questioned why mother was watching violence on televison.

Aunty Rani gave me the impression of a wild woman clamoring to be let out. She must be missing the high life she led in Sri Lanka. She worked as a clerk in a Social Service office down La Salle Street though she liked to be referred to as the Administrative Officer there. Before going home after work she came to see mother in the hospital almost daily. I appreciated Aunty Rani's visits to mother not only because she brought laughter to mother's bedside, but also mother felt happy to speak to someone from back home, especially to speak in her native tongue. Mother told me that she could talk about her pains and troubles more effectively, she could release her emotions and felt relieved when she spoke in Sinhala. We all feel the same in a crisis, for that is natural. However, my native tongue seems foreign to me now. I find it more comfortable to think and speak in English and I speak to mother in English.

One evening I set aside the books, the magazines and the tapes I brought for mother and stood by Aunty Rani and listened to their conversation. Then I noticed Uncle Henry's tall, slim figure appearing briskly behind the pillars at the entrance to the ward. I was worried. Why should Uncle Henry hurry in at this time of the evening unless there was some urgent news—bad news? But the smile on his face erased the fears from my mind. He hurried towards us smiling all the way. He kissed me and held my hand briefly before bending down to kiss my mother's forehead. Mother was recovering slowly and was happy to have those whom she loved most gathered around her.

"What's up, Henry? You are in an unusually happy mood!" mother inquired, smiling and holding Uncle Henry's hand. Mother was as curious as were the two of us—Aunty Rani and I.

"Well, why wouldn't I be? My favorite sister is getting better and we will be taking her home soon!" said Uncle Henry.

"Don't keep us in suspense. Come out with it, please," pleaded Aunty Rani.

"Well, I've found answers to some of the questions we've been looking for," announced Uncle Henry.

"What answers? The suspense is killing me," mother blurted out.

"You remember we hired Paul Williams as our private investigator to help the police to trace the driver who ran into you? Working with Irene's account and from the paint chips found on Leila's Toyota, Paul has traced the vehicle to the Chicago Yellow Cab Company. Paul has met with the manager who had given him the name of a driver who had parked a vehicle one evening and not reported for work for over ten days. He found something to work on. Well, soon after, the rascal was caught!" he said with a triumphant ring in his voice. "Paul has tracked him down to some place in Baltimore and now he is in police custody in Baltimore—now isn't that great news? Can you believe that the guy was yet again driving a taxi when he was caught?"

"At last some relief! But why? Why did he do this to me?" mother started to cry and Uncle Henry sat by her bed and stroked her cheeks, now damp with her warm tears. Meanwhile, a million thoughts poured into my mind. Why did I have to cast suspicions on mother? All those nasty, wicked thoughts that have been flashing across my mind for days after I learned about the accident—of my mother committing suicide, not being able to stand it any longer because the hopes and dreams she had built around her family had gone up in flames. She is not as desperate as I feared. It's my wicked mind playing wicked tricks on me and now I am repenting. Good thing I didn't open my heart to anybody at the time, not even to Uncle Henry.

Uncle Henry had learned from Paul that the cab driver had cashed his last pay check from the Chicago Yellow Cab Company somewhere in Baltimore area, and Paul had tracked him down to a taxi company in downtown Baltimore. Since he had run away out of state after the accident without informing the authorities, he had not been granted bail and was being held in police custody in Baltimore. The driver had confessed to the police that he was the one who was involved in the accident.

"Well, that's not all," said Uncle Henry reminding me of my father's actions, when he brought presents to surprise us at the most unexpected moments. "Now be prepared for the real surprise!" Uncle Henry said arousing our curiosity to still higher levels. He held my mother's right hand with both his hands and announced, "Paul had found out from him that he knew the lady in the car! The guy is a Sri Lankan. He is a Sinhalese, and, would you believe this? He claims to be a student of yours, Leila!" At this my mother's eyes opened wide and her lips though parted failed to say anything. She was shocked and so were we. We remained silent for a moment.

"He has given his name to the police as Senaka Salgado. Does the name ring a bell, Leila? I think it must be a false name!" Uncle Henry inquired of mother. Mother turned pale.

Her eyes remained opened wide in amazement. Her lips quivered. There was a period of long silence.

"With his experience in detective work Paul sensed that the guy had planned the whole episode. That was not an accident, Paul told me—it was an intentional attempt to cause you harm," Uncle Henry said pensively, still holding my mother's hand. We all waited for Uncle Henry to tell us more about the man who had created all this misery.

"When we left Sri Lanka, I thought I was leaving that wicked world behind us for good, but no, they keep chasing us. I don't know! I can't remember anybody by that name," mother's eyes were filled with tears of anger. Little bits of memories lingered back into my head. Could this Salgado guy have been one of father's students at the University in Sri Lanka? During the insurgency days, father had reported to the police a student who attempted to bomb the university waterworks. The house where we lived at the time was situated about a quarter mile from the waterworks. One evening while walking in the front yard, father had observed a student walking past our house several times carrying a brown paper bag. Father said he was certain that the student noticed father looking at him suspiciously. There was a rumor during that time those who carried brown paper bags carried bombs inside them. Father had promptly telephoned the police. The police had attempted to track him down but had failed. Could he have found out that father phoned the police? But why should he try to kill my mother? Could this be that student? But how did he appear in Chicago? All these questions rushed to my mind with no answers.

"Paul gave me a photograph of the driver. I have it here." Uncle Henry put his hand into his coat pocket, took out an envelope and pulled out the photograph. He held it in front of mother. Both Aunty Rani and I strained our necks to take a good look at it and saw the picture of a handsome guy in his late thirties, with curly hair and a fair complexion.

"A good-looking young man! What the devil got into him?" Aunty Rani shouted in anger. She had suffered enough during the dark days when the rebels in Sri Lanka had almost got hold of the country. Mother held the photograph and continued gazing at it for sometime.

"I think I know him, the rascal," she mumbled, biting her teeth. "Sure, he was one of my students and a good one at that. I remember him as Sena Salgado. Both his father and mother were clerks at the hospital in Kandy. Nalin knew the father well. I actually liked this guy, he was a JVPer and was an activist. As I recall he was a leader in the school." Mother didn't talk for some time, she kept her thoughts to herself. After a moment of silence, she raised her head and asked Uncle Henry, "Why should he do this to me?"

"We'll find the answer, Leila. Don't you worry," he assured mother. "Paul has not finished his investigation yet. He told me he was going to find out the guy's motive next. I'm going to the police station tomorrow morning. Nelu, if you can find the time, would you like to join me?" Uncle Henry addressed me. I agreed.

"OK, then, I'll come and pick you up around nine in the morning. Now I have to go. Leila, you keep the photograph if it's going to help you bring back any hidden stories of those days. If as you remember, the guy held leftist views that might throw some light into the whole affair," said Uncle Henry while giving a gentle peck on mother's cheek before taking her leave.

XIV

"Leila, I know you too well! You must have done something to provoke this guy. What have you been up to? Did you give him any encouragement?"

No sooner had Uncle Henry left us that evening, Aunty Rani directed a barrage of questions at mother. Receiving no answers, she began to talk about the terrible life she had had to live in Sri Lanka during the time the rebels who were fighting the government brought the whole country to a standstill. After a while, getting tired of hearing her own angry voice, Aunty Rani turned to mother again. What's mother's relationship with the young man? Aunty Rani wanted to know. Seeing no escape, mother came up with numerous stories that went back to the days when the JVP used terror tactics to keep the people under them. (JVP was the abbreviation used for the political organization known as the Peoples Liberation Front that fought the government to overthrow the capitalist establishment and share equally the wealth of the country with everybody.)

"Oh! God, that was an awful time, awful, awful. How did we live through it?" mother questioned.

As I stood watching and listening to my mother and Aunty Rani, our past in Kandy surged up in my mind, vivid and clear, bringing back a life which had ended forever, when our parents decided to leave Sri Lanka to find a safe haven for them and their children. How often I had thought of those events. They changed my parents' lives and set the course of mine and my brother's in directions we never anticipated. Revolts shape futures, even of those who are in the margins. Even though my mother longed to leave Sri Lanka, on the day we left, she wept at the airport—she didn't let go of my grandmother's hand for a long time. My father's eyes were wet too, but he put his arms around my mother's shoulders and said, "Now, come on, Leila. We are getting late," and turned her away from the tear-filled eyes of my grandmother and of my cousins and uncles and aunts. It was such a painful experience to leave them and come to start a completely new life in a foreign land.

Aunty Rani had also left Sri Lanka because of the harassments she and her family had faced at the hands of the JVP rebels. Her younger sister had refused to put up a poster as ordered by the rebels in the neighborhood. The poster had announced another day of work stoppage in protest against the dictatorial government. She and her husband had been punished in the most cruel fashion. Her husband, who was a journalist and a newspaper reporter, though with very liberal views sympathetic to JVP ideas, had been forced to carry his wife and stand at the junction in the middle of Kandy town at the busiest and the hottest time of the day. He had stood there carrying his wife in his arms for four long hours—this was to ridicule the couple.

"We—my sister and I—were so devastated by the humiliation we suffered at the hands of those rascals that we almost begged of Alex to sponsor our entry to the United States," said Aunty Rani through tears. Alex, their brother, was a doctor who worked in a hospital in the neighborhood of Chicago.

"Once we arrived here we never wanted to go back—even to visit our friends and relations," Aunty Rani showed nothing but hatred and contempt in her eyes when she talked about the JVP rebels and what they did to them and the country. I now understand why she was so bitter—though she laughed and made fun of serious situations. As I heard her stories of survival during those difficult times in Sri Lanka, I understood she was trying hard to put aside those painful events that had ruined her life.

The next few days when I went to see my mother, she would talk of nothing else but the JVP and its horrendous actions and how the Sri Lankan government failed to do its duty by its citizens and how we were all chased out of the country that most of us still love to go back to. It was during these few days, more than at any other time, that I got to know Aunty Rani. Three of us sat for long hours in the evenings talking about the JVP and our arrival in the United States. Aunty Rani kept digging into my mother—pleading her to look deep into her memory.

"Leila, this rascal must have been an active JVP rebel. Maybe you said something in class that offended the JVPers there."

One evening, in response to Aunty Rani's prodding and to our great surprise mother came out with an amazing story. The guy who caused the accident, Sena Salgado, had fallen in love with my mother, jealously, hungrily. "You can say even angrily, with a degree of anger that meant a man was in conflict within himself," explained mother. "He was only eighteen at the time for God's sake and I was a married woman with two little children and was his teacher." Sena had been so young and confused, so immature in his beliefs—my mother had showered kindness and affection over him in those difficult days and mother said Sena took it the wrong way. Did he? or did my mother use her beauty to have a little fun at the expense of a good looking confused young man? My mother, I knew, had flirted with most good looking males that she had met—did she flirt with Sena and fill his young mind with dreams that he would never be able to realize? As Paul Williams said, did Sena want to destroy something that he couldn't get? The questions that came to my mind intrigued me.

Mother told us Sena had been one of seven children, the third, of parents both government clerks. He had to walk two miles to school as his parents couldn't afford to pay his daily bus fare. The parents could scarcely provide the seven children with food and clothing to wear to school. Sena had become a JVP believer when he was sixteen, like most of his schoolmates. He was a strong JVPer, for whom the party was his home, a family, the future. When my mother started teaching him, his closest friends in his class had all finished attending the Five Lectures of the JVP and were looking forward to establishing a just society where everybody would be equal in possession of wealth. They had been made to stand in the eyes of the rest of the country as traitors and enemies of the established order. When the government crushed the JVP rebellion, Sena's parents and siblings had all sacrificed their lives because of the sins of their son, Sena. They had all faced the army's wrath. For Sena though, a great believer in JVP ideas it had been as if the very foundations of the world had collapsed.

Sena's story was indeed intriguing. By some miraculous effort on the part of his uncle who lived and worked in Canada at the time—he had been able to escape death and take refuge in Canada. Sena had arrived in Toronto and had somehow forged his travel documents and managed to enter the United States. He had obtained a Social Security number by giving somebody a large sum of money borrowed from his uncle in Canada and had managed to find a job as a driver in the Chicago Yellow Cab Co. If he had stayed in Sri Lanka he would have faced the same fate as his siblings and parents but fate had it—he managed to escape.

Aunty Rani had no sympathy for the escaped JVPers. How could she? She and her family had suffered tremendously at their hands.

"Back in Sri Lanka we had all the comforts that money could buy. We didn't want to come here and live this hard life, but we were forced to," Aunty Rani had said this many times. She talked about the football sized rocks that crashed through the window into their living room one evening when they were having dinner. The tea-factory that her father owned in the hills had been fire-bombed. A few days earlier the government had torn down a wooden hut that was near the tea-factory because it had been used as a secret meeting place for JVP activists; it had been found complete with booklets of JVP propaganda and khaki uniforms worn by the fighters. Not surprisingly Aunty Rani's father had concluded that these young men were arming to destroy those who they thought were rich. The rebels argued that the rich became rich by exploiting the poor so they did not deserve to live, their wealth should be distributed among the poor who worked to make the riches. Aunty Rani's father was not alone in this analysis. Across the country politicians, university professors and businessmen sensed the spoiled hopes of the younger generation. They said the youth were styling themselves as 'freedom fighters' in the tradition of leftist guerrilla warfare and were trying to establish what they called 'a movement for national liberation.' They drew their tactics from a five-lesson manifesto that was taught to all young recruits—recruited forcefully by the party. "We must create a space for ourselves to form a just society—punish deviants and enemies, support comrades in the struggle, help fellow citizens who are oppressed, marginalized and persecuted," their manifesto declared.

"A majority of those so-called freedom fighters lived among the rural people and terrorized the poor souls to keep them silent. Few infiltrated the urban businesses and government offices and spied on their activities. None was safe in that atmosphere," Aunty Rani continued with her agonized tale.

My mother listened quietly, watching Aunty Rani's quick moving lips, as if she was not aware of the situation that existed in Sri Lanka at the time. What was my mother thinking? Why did Sena attempt to harm my mother? Have they met, since his arrival in Chicago?

I was well aware of the causes that ignited the youth rebellion. Predominantly in their teens, the young men used violent methods to achieve their goal. After more than five hundred and fifty years of foreign domination and four decades of governments that the people thought didn't do anything to uplift the conditions of the masses, they wanted to create a sense of nationalistic vision of superiority, especially against India, that translated into violence. They took over government offices and police stations in rural areas and converted them into JVP activists meeting places. Aunty Rani's experiences illustrated the support the JVP enjoyed among the government officials.

"When our home was set on fire, police did not even turn up at the scene to investigate the incident," she said. It was not that the rural people supported the rebels—people were afraid to talk. They felt the government was not doing anything to protect them from the terror. Then there spread the rumor—compilation by the JVP of lists of unwanted people. The first time we heard of it was when the list was linked to the death of a young university professor. The government newspapers carried daily reports of horrific killings by the JVP and rumors abut who was on the lists made many people live in fear. "Please keep my name secret. There are others at home who would suffer," they were supposed to have said when divulging names on a JVP hit list. Those whose names appeared on the list had spent every two or three nights sleeping in different places.

"When my brother Greg, heard that he was on their list he kept away from us, so he would not endanger the family," said Aunty Rani in a voice filled with sorrow and hatred. "It was then that we eventually decided to run away from our own country. One of my brothers disappeared and Greg was eventually beaten up by the army. We were sandwiched, in between the rebels and the army." Angry tears flowed down Aunty Rani's cheeks as mother and I listened to her.

Listening to Aunty Rani brought back bitter memories of those days in Sri Lanka to me. I remembered the boy standing on a chair beside the busy intersection in front of Queen's Hotel in Kandy. He would have been twelve or thirteen years old and he was weeping. Along with him was his mother on another chair. They had been punished by the JVP for failing to put up a poster on their front door prohibiting anybody from going to work the next day. Their punishment was to stand in humiliation for hours in the hot sun, their faces covered with their sweat. The police were there, people were walking past them, but nobody even raised their heads to look at them. Everyone was frightened—if you said something against them or sympathized with the plight of the victims, then the very next day either you would be the one to stand there on the chair or you would not be around in this world at all.

I still vividly remember when those JVP posters were put up and there were 'strikes'. We had to go without water and electricity for days. There was a time when our taps ran dry for ten days at a stretch, we opened our umbrellas when it rained, placed them upside down in our garden and collected rain water to wash ourselves. When we wanted to bathe, Roshan and I stood in the rain. The JVPers bombed the waterworks one night—we heard the bomb go off. We heard that the JVP had announced that the island is blessed with rivers and streams within every mile and people should go and bathe in the open—we did not need water services provided in our houses. The colonizers had exploited the indigenous people and built these things because they were lazy to go out into the open. I remember mother using banana leaves as plates as we didn't have water to wash the plates. "It's not the 1970s, it's 1500," had become a common wisecrack among the educated, but it was spoken only out of earshot of the ruffian young men of the JVP with their rifles and bombs. Such scenes had become part of life under the JVP. The harshness of the way the JVP enforced punishments on those who didn't obey their laws, had spread an atmosphere of terror among the people, who were afraid they would be among the next to be victimized by JVP roundups. By ordering such punishments, the JVP without realizing it brought on themselves widespread unpopularity which contributed to their fall—but the fall came much later. By the time the government took serious action people who had the means and friends to sponsor them had already left the country. We belonged to that category.

Six months after we left the country, we received the news that the rebel leader had been captured by the government and the uprising had been crushed. That happened after thousands had died on both the rebel side and the government side.

I remember back in Kandy those days, on occasions, when my parents entertained friends, they would draw their chairs to the round table in the kitchen and talk in hushed voices that faded into silence as we children approached. My brother Roshan and I spoke of these hushed talks. In the town in front of restaurants and littered alleys men huddled around bicycles or leaned against walls in whispering groups. The villagers from deep in the hinterland of Kandy had left the village, not caring one way or the other, whether the sun rose or set to escape from the terror. I remember them squatting in my grandmother's backyard eating rice and curry and relating stories of what had happened the night before. They talked of the horrors that had befallen their villages in the way of peasants—repeating the dialogue, presenting each detail of expression and movement, sending the listeners back to the scene.

XV

A couple of days later I found a letter from Irene Peters in the mail. "I am sorry that I didn't provide the information earlier regarding the accident," it read. She better be sorry, at least. Angrily, I pictured her driving away, looking at the overturned car with the corners of her eyes, while my mother lay crushed beneath the overturned vehicle. I handed over the letter to Uncle Henry.

"Jeffrey will find it useful," Uncle Henry said while folding the letter and placing it inside his coat pocket. Jeffrey Ashland was our lawyer. As a personal injury lawyer he would gleefully use it to prove to the insurance company that the accident obviously was a hit and run, rather than, as the police had suspected, one caused by negligence in driving. "The damages caused to Mrs. Fernandez, both physically and mentally, and her inability to go back to work in the library would be worth over a million dollars," Ashland had told Uncle Henry. I pictured my mother's broken cheek bones, her cracked lips and her pale face. I mulled over the expertise of Jeffrey Ashland able to quantify the cost of pain and heartbreak in terms of dollars. But then, don't most of us believe that money can heal almost anything?

Maybe because it's the heart of winter and the Chicago air is so cold that it hurts to breathe. So much that came easily in the fall has become a struggle this winter. But knowing that mother was well on the way to recovery and knowing that the mystery man behind the accident would be brought to trial soon brought some relief to my mind. Yet the mystery of the mystery man bothered me. I wanted to find out from mother more about this young man—Sena Salgado—but every time the idea surged in my mind, I held back, sensing there was something more, something that my mother was trying to hide from all of us. There was a murky feeling in the back of my mind that, that something more would have led Sena to take such a drastic action. Time will tell, I told myself and suppressed my urge to talk to mother on the subject. Instead, I walked into the hospital that afternoon with two *New York Times* best seller fiction books in my handbag, thinking that she would welcome reading romances again. When I entered the ward I did not see my mother. Usually I walked right into the ward and stopped at the bed where my mother lay with her right leg hanging. That was how I recognized her bed from afar, her right leg wrapped in white plaster of Paris hanging from a hook in the ceiling. That afternoon I did not see this rigging. I got nervous. Blood rushed into my head and my heart began to beat at such great speed that I felt palpitation setting in. Where is she? Have they taken her back to the Emergency Ward or to the Intensive Care Unit? What has happened?

Fear gripped me as I rushed towards my mother's bed. I remembered overhearing one of my mother's friends telling about a nurse taking her to the operating theater for surgery and suddenly realising that her shift was over, had left her in the corridor and vanished. Nobody had been around to take her to the theater until the doctor who was in charge had raised the alarm and discovered her in the corridor. Mother's friend had been under heavy sedatives and did not have the strength to appeal to anyone passing by. The nurse had been reprimanded, but mother's friend had a terrifying experience! Through my tear-filled eyes and to my great relief I saw my mother lying on her bed, her right leg stretched alongside the other on the bed. The white blanket that covered my mother's body was rolled to one side exposing mother's fragile body, now covered only with her flimsy cotton night dress.

I could hardly see her because my eyes were a pool of tears. She was sound asleep. It was so quiet that I could hear her soft breathing. I wanted to wake her up and tell her how relieved I was to see her getting better. "Old bones take a longer time to heal," the nurse told me once when I asked her how long mother would have to remain in bed with one leg hanging from the hook. I watched her sleeping peacefully; yet her face seemed as if she was in some kind of pain. I stood by her bed and watched her and listened to her soft breathing. Though it was late in the afternoon, Aunty Rani, who usually dropped in to have a chat with her before going home after work, had not come to see her. In a way, I was thankful that I was alone with her, for I could let myself be dragged into my private world of thinking of the past. My mother looked so helpless resting on the narrow hospital bed that I regretted deserting her eight years ago. How did I let myself be so distanced from my mother? When did the strained mother-daughter relationship begin? Was it since our Brunswick days?

Memories of the days when I began not to like my mother rushed into my mind. It all started because I thought she favored my brother Roshan over me, and she also ill-treated my father. I hated her fiercely during most of my adolescence. I kept my distance whenever possible. I did not offer kindness when it might have helped. I did not console her when it might have held back her tears. I tormented her whenever I got the opportunity just as I thought she tormented my father. She had borne my childish tantrums, my wild fury. I hated her beautiful face and saw it as arrogant. I hated the way she took disappointments and sometimes thrived on them as though they brought her relief from pain. I thought she envied my youth and hated me for it. She stood behind me like a long, dark shadow that I couldn't escape from. There were times when I hated her so much I wished she would die. I despised the sweet smile she reserved only for her friends and Roshan.

And now watching her lying helplessly on the narrow hospital bed, her arms calmly folded across her stomach, I turned my face towards the window in shame. It was so quiet that evening I could almost hear the trees rustle with snow in their branches. I blamed myself for the rift that had developed between me and my mother. My eyes were filled with tears; I could hardly see the moving traffic on the road below.

My mother sighed. Perhaps it was not a sigh after all—merely the sound of snow falling outside. I turned to look at her. I had not really looked at her with a daughter's love for a mother, for years. She had grown so much older. I had forgotten how much time had passed since I moved away from her. Her long, blue-black hair was now short with streaks of grey. There was a time when she pulled out the grey hairs—one by one—very carefully, but now . . . the grey hairs softened the lines of her middle-aged face. I hesitated to touch it, but I gathered enough courage (or was it the daughter's love?) to touch it. She lay on the bed almost like a lifeless life-size doll. I never knew she could be so pale. She was breathing softly. Her closed eyes had bags under them. Her face, with marks of pain though long forgotten still visible, was still beautiful to me. Her once beautifully set nose was drawn slightly to one side, and her full sensitive lips were cracked and looked almost purplish in color. Ear lobes were pierced but her earrings were no longer on her ears. Her hands were small. I gently touched her small wrists. She sighed and opened her eyes. I did not know they contained such sorrow. The lines around them were from thinking too deeply and not able to find solutions to her problems and failing to find hope in a world that she thought had been cruel to her.

How could I have thought she was my enemy? I hated her at times yet she did not deserve to be abandoned, especially by me—her only daughter. She looked so sad. I did not know how to beg for forgiveness. I wanted to hold her hand and say, "Mom, I love you. I want us to be the closest of friends," but at the time I could not gather enough courage to do that. Instead I touched her cheek and I felt my hand shiver. I put my lips on her forehead—it was hot as fire. Shyly I held her and she opened her eyes and touched my cheeks with both her palms. They were frail, cold and yet soft. I thought I heard her heart beat and suddenly I realized it was my heart.

The intimate and emotional moment I enjoyed with mother was cut short by the sound of the door to the ward being opened. Two doctors in long white coats came inside, continuing their conversation. One of the doctors looked agitated, but on seeing me, they turned their attention to mother.

"Good afternoon, doctors," I greeted them. They acknowledged me and gave their full attention to my mother, their patient. The younger of the two doctors stood by and placed the tips of his fingers together and lifted the charts attached on the foot of my mother's bed. The other doctor, who seemed the senior of the two, examined my mother. He took her pressure, her temperature, opened her eye lids and looked into her eyes—he was satisfied.

"She's coming through nicely," the senior doctor said looking at me. Once they were gone, "Mom," I whispered. "You are getting better!" She did not say anything. Her eyes were filled with tears—I was at a loss to understand whether the tears were tears of joy at getting back her long-lost daughter or because of the pain she must be going through with the fading effects of the anesthesia injected into her body when her leg was removed from the hook. We remained silent for a minute or two; it seemed like a long time to me. I could not say anything. I was overwhelmed at seeing my mother normal again, or almost normal, her leg was in plaster from hip to ankle. The plaster would take another four to five weeks to come out, but at least for now I need not identify my mother's bed by the leg hanging from the hook attached to the ceiling.

Mother was tired. She kept her eyes closed and tears seeped through her eye-lids. She smoothed her eye-brows as if to ease her pain.

"There is some kind of pain somewhere in my body all the time," she said. I wished I could help her but I was as helpless as she was. I wiped the tears on her cheeks with my fingers and sat by her until late into the evening. The nurses tip-toed in the surrounding area so as not to disturb the already tired out patients. I wanted to talk to them but I did not see any of the familiar faces; the night staff seemed all new to me. I stayed for another hour or so, left the books on my mother's bedside table and quietly walked out of the ward.

XVI

"I was just this minute thinking about you," she said flashing her magical smile. Mother was in an unusually good mood that Sunday morning.

"What's up, Mom?" I questioned as I put the *Chicago Tribune* on her bedside table and sat on the edge of her bed. I held her hand and kissed her forehead.

"You will never guess who was here this morning!" she said.

"The head physician, of course. You can go home!" I said jokingly. My curiosity was overwhelming.

"You are way off," mother said smiling. After a short pause which really aroused my curiosity still more, she said, "Uncle Les was here!"

"Oh!" Mother's eyes still twinkled and her face brightened up when she talked about Uncle Les. As I remember from what little I gathered from heated arguments I overheard between my father and mother, Uncle Les was one reason why mother wanted to come to America. I was actually waiting for an opportune moment to ask mother about Uncle Les. My parents had drifted away from Uncle Les since our days in Brunswick but why they drifted away from him remained a secret to me. Uncle Les was father's good friend from their school days. After his university career in Sri Lanka he had come to the United States to work on his Ph.D. He had been a good student and had created a good impression on his professors, that the university where he had studied had offered him a position immediately after his graduation. He had gone back to Sri Lanka, married his village girl friend and had started his life here in a new country. He visited Sri Lanka almost every year during the summer vacation, to gather data for a book that he was working on, and made it a point to see father whenever he was there. They were such good friends then. Sometimes he stayed at home with us in Kandy. My brother and I liked him because he played *Monopoly* with us. I remember him as a fun loving, kind person.

Mother's face brightened as she spoke of Uncle Les. Last Sunday's *New York Times* book review section was lying on the side of her bed. She had been reading a review of a book on males where a male selfish gene had been identified. She read the relevant section out for me and added her comments. "That doesn't give the men permission to sleep around," mother insisted. "A woman is programmed to find one good man and remain true to him. She has to choose the best father to her child and provider for herself. In my opinion this does not give the woman any feeling of lust. And listen to this, Nelu. The English Common Law centuries ago enshrined a man's legal right to beat his wife with a stick as fat as his thumb!" she read with disgust and impatience.

"I tell you Nelu, when you are married and when you have an affair, it gives you confidence; an enhanced sense of well-being and you enjoy life more. I am talking through experience." She was proud to talk about her frivolities—and to justify her behavior.

"When at work a woman has to suppress her femininity to show off her professionalism. It's a sacrifice we women have to make. So an illicit affair gives one a vehicle to air one's desires—it's a delight. When Uncle Les came to see me those days back in Kandy, I felt I was walking on air!" My mother was happy to talk about her admirers.

Listening to mother reminded me of an incident that took place at home in Kandy. It was raining heavily one afternoon when we saw Uncle Les parking his golden colored Toyota station wagon on our porch and walking into the house. From the top of the stairs I remember seeing my mother running to greet him.

"I've been waiting for you since six in the morning," she said smiling, her face more beautiful than ever.

"When you smile, the sun seems to shine brighter. Flowers bloom and I can even hear the birds chirp," he said. He flirted with mother and my mother enjoyed every minute of it.

"What happened? I was worried." He smiled back at her. He sat on the sitting room couch stretching his long legs placing his well-polished shoes on the coffee table. He always dressed smartly.

"Good to know that you are an early bird! They get to catch the worms, don't they?" Flattering words came to him easily. He could laugh his way out of a difficult situation making a lark of life. It was evident from my mother's radiant face that Uncle Les brought joy into my mother's life.

"So, are you ready with your story for Nalin? Tell him that I said America is a paradise. I am hoping to see you there next year, Leila. Talk to Nalin tonight. Don't postpone—this is very important for me—for us." I heard Uncle Les telling mother.

"I'll make it happen this time. Don't worry. We'll be there next year." Mother assured him.

To be sure, handsome men have appeared in my mother's life, in the most mysterious way. For me all these men who have swept in and out of my mother's life could in no way replace my good, warm father.

After we came to America, Uncle Les visited us several times in Brunswick. At first my father was very friendly and treated Uncle Les as if he was his own brother. When the visits became frequent and phone calls to mother became too long, my father's attitude towards Uncle Les became hostile and cold. The long, tense hours after Uncle Les's visits flashed across my mind like pictures on a movie screen. I could almost see my father seated at the round table in the kitchen with his hands folded in front of him. He moved his lips as if he was talking but no sound came out of his mouth. Busy preparing dinner, mother ignored him. Mother placed a pan on the stove and poured oil into it. I stood there with spoon in hand to help fry the *papadam*—one of father's favorites.

Father spoke with Roshan in a hushed voice, one hand outstretched, palm moving away from his body. The smell of frying *papadam* filled the kitchen air and slowly spread into the living room. Suddenly there was absolute silence—the hissing sound of the boiling oil could be heard louder in the kitchen.

"Damn him," my father uttered under his breath. "I am sick of seeing him around here." Father opened the door leading out of the kitchen, down the steps he rushed, climbed into his car and roared out of the driveway. That's what he did when he got angry. He ran away from what bothered him. He did not return until late that night. The next morning, I saw him having a cup of coffee and rushing out of the door before mother was up. He returned at lunch time. There was tension in the air. We all sat down to eat, no one saying a word. Half way through lunch father began to draw attention to himself by dropping his food on the carpet, gulping water noisily and making ugly noises while eating knowing only too well that mother hated such behavior. Receiving no response from mother, father shouted.

"I don't want to see that man around here again!"

"But Les is your friend, Nalin! He comes to see you," mother said very innocently; her voice hardly audible.

"He is not my friend any more. He is your friend. He comes to see you, not me," father shouted her down. Mother remained calm.

"Why do you invite him here so often? Are you in love with him?" Father blurted out. The ball of rice he held in his hand suddenly was thrown on the table. Roshan and I gasped. We had never seen our parents behave this way before.

"I don't want that parasite hanging around you. I don't want to see him again here!" All was quiet after that outburst. Uncle Les stopped visiting us and I hadn't seen him for over fifteen years.

"Les brings back memories of my youth, which your father never spoke about," mother said breaking the silence.

"So you've broken so many hearts in your youth, Mom," I said flippantly. I wanted to get mother to talk about her glorious past—her flirtations with Uncle Les, her love life before she married my father. This was as good an opportunity as any—she had just had a visit from one of her admirers.

"Well, I've had my heart broken once really badly you know," she started. I've heard these stories before but I wanted to listen for that made mother happy. I wanted to get closer to her and never let that closeness disappear again.

"Well, I have seen this young man flirting and taking walks with all the pretty and rich girls on campus. This was back in Kandy during our university days. He was very good looking." Mother's face lit up and I could almost see her gathering up the scattered details of her story.

"It was the final semester of my final year—I and my friends were gathered in front of the library discussing what books to read before we held a group discussion when I noticed this young man, tennis racket in his hand walking past us. He looked back at us and smiled. I thought he was smiling with one of my rich friends as he was known to be snooty and, as I told you, he went around with pretty rich girls only. Everyone knew that I did not come from a wealthy family. Sure, I was pretty those days. On several occasions I noticed he made it a habit to pass by us whenever I was in a group discussion with my friends. One day he walked up to me, took me aside which stunned my friends and me and announced that he loved me. I wanted to tell him that he was out of his mind and ask him to go away and leave me alone, but I was too shocked and embarrassed because it happened in front of my friends and at the same time I was so flattered, I kept quiet. The very next day he approached me and made the same announcement again. Then, he kept coming almost everyday for the first few weeks of the semester until I finally agreed to walk with him from the library to my hall of residence." She paused for a moment and I took the opportunity to remind her that she did not tell me his name. She brushed aside my inquiry and continued. "It didn't take long for me to fall madly in love with him. Kapila was his name and he was the most polite, handsome and interesting young man I've ever met." I had heard this story before but every time I heard it, the story sounded better than before.

"Anyway," she sighed, "I never got to marry him and I never got over him."

"What happened, Mom?" I egged her on.

"We were inseparable those last few weeks of his university days. We walked to the library in the mornings, we walked under the same umbrella in the sun and rain and when there was no sun and rain also we walked under my umbrella. I held the umbrella while he had one hand wrapped around my waist. We sat side by side in the library and attended to our studies. He studied while I day-dreamed. Kapila came from a very wealthy family of lawyers. His father had a lucrative legal practice in Colombo and was an influential member of the Colombo elite. Kapila told me that he was going to join his father's law firm when he completed his law degree. I pictured myself married into an aristocratic family, having no financial worries and wearing the finest of clothes and jewelry. As the examination days came closer I saw my friends burying their heads in books and so did Kapila. As for me, when I opened my books to study I saw only Kapila's smiling face there. Every time I turned a page, there he was, smiling up at me and looking at me adoringly. I couldn't study. I couldn't sleep. I failed the exams while all my friends got through and Kapila passed with flying colors.

As planned, he went to work in his father's law firm. I was upset but in a way I liked what happened to me, because Kapila arranged for me to stay with the parents of one of his friends and sit the exam again. I was contented, for now, I could stay closer to the campus and use the library facilities and also follow a lecture or two if I really wanted to. During this time, Kapila came up to see me almost every weekend. I stopped day dreaming and concentrated on my studies. One weekend, when I received word from Kapila that he could not make the trip to Kandy, I went to the library. There I met a friend who whispered some disturbing news in my ear. There had been a marriage proposal and Kapila had gone to see the daughter of a wealthy businessman in Colombo. My friend informed me that Kapila had agreed to the marriage proposal and was to be engaged to be married soon. I was shaken up but didn't give it much weight; in fact, I didn't even mention this to Kapila when he came to see me the next weekend because people spread stories through jealousy. It was foolish of me not to have been more cautious and alert because before long I got the news from Kapila's friend, whose parents I was staying with, that he had been invited for the engagement party! I was devastated, I couldn't believe what I was hearing. I was completely heartbroken and lost faith in mankind.

I managed to finish the exams anyway, got a teaching job about forty miles from Kandy, stayed at a boarding house and tried to get on with my life. I felt very lonely and miserable during this time. I don't know what would have happened to me if I hadn't had the teaching job to take my mind away from what Kapila did to me. It was during this time that your father walked into my life. He came to see me in the boarding house several times. We were good friends. His visits gradually increased and I suspected that he was falling in love with me. I was taken aback one evening when he told me, "I was like a madman those days. I was madly in love with you but was afraid to tell you that. I thought you would laugh at my face because I felt I was not good enough for you. When Kapila came home and took you away in the evenings, I walked all over the town trying to grasp something that I thought was disappearing from my life." Nalin couldn't keep away from me—he visited me whenever he could get away from work. He was very gentlemanly, shy and soft spoken, so soft spoken that at times I didn't hear what he was saying. It didn't take long for me to realize that he was deeply in love with me. When he proposed to me a couple of months later, I just couldn't refuse him, for if I did at that moment, I would have broken his heart completely and I was fully aware what a broken heart feeling was like.

"So you finally decided to marry him?" I asked.

"You know, Nelu, I was never in love with your father. I was so madly in love with Kapila that when Kapila abandoned me I fell for Nalin on the rebound. They say that boys chase girls but girls catch the boys. It's very true of your father and me."

"Mother! I don't get it. Why did you marry my father if you didn't love him?"

"I wasn't in love with him, but I thought I could grow to love him. It never happened—there was no romance ever in my marriage. Nalin was good-looking and kind and I somehow knew that he would take good care of me. For Sri Lankan girls that's what marriage was about back then."

On many occasions mother told me that she should never have married my father.

"It's only now that I realize that one cannot live with a saint; that's how the outside world saw your father. He couldn't do any wrong and it came to a point that I could do no right. On innumerable occasions he did what I had suggested and got the credit for it. Nobody even dreamed that they were my ideas. I was not smart enough to think of bright ideas. Even you questioned one day whether I was smart. I remember when you were around ten you turned your face to me one night and asked, 'Mommy, are you smart?' You were comparing my accomplishments to those of your father who spent most of his time at home in his study reading or writing. While I was there to see to the needs of my husband and children, the starry-eyed admiration of my children went to the father not to their mother who raised them. It was painful when the part I played in his life to make his life successful was completely forgotten or ignored."

Mother got agitated as she related story after story of my father's selfishness in ignoring her contribution; she continued with her lamentations. I realized then that it was painful for mother to talk about her own talents which had been wasted, withering and unused, and she had always had to be a shadow besides father.

"For a while, just before your father passed away, I hated him. That was because I knew I treated him badly. I am not saying he behaved well towards me, he did not, but that isn't the point. I think he stopped looking for a reasonably respectable academic position to spite me. If he was not making an effort why should I stay with him? In the latter stages of his life, what I liked best about myself, what I held fast and dear in my life, your father showed he liked least. I felt betrayed and he became more sentimental and tearful, and I got more cold and matter-of-fact. It seemed we were under a curse that made me look at him with hate. It was as if I did not know him at all. I felt that we had reached the end of our marriage. We never even had time to think of sex. It would be dishonest of me to say that I was not interested in sex. Sex flourished in my dreams—but not with your father—not during that period of time."

She wiped her eyes with the kleenex and looked at me as if she was begging for compassion and understanding.

"Some say that dreams belong to men, and women are expected to marry their dreams. No, Nelu, that's not so. A woman could have anything—interesting lives in exciting places." Mother touched her heart with both her hands.

"A woman should not need to give up anything. The idea that a woman just serves a man, that you just stand in the background and be the supporting actress, the caretaker and the man's helper as head of the household? Well, as a young woman I did believe in that. Not any more. Experience has taught me that a woman can stand on her own. When I came to America where I could have made my dreams come true, unfortunately it was too late. Dreams have always been my friends and they helped me to forget reality. But during this time even my dreams went against me. No sooner than my head hit the pillow I would start to dream about staircases falling apart under me or sitting for examinations for which I had not studied. I believed that dreams gave me warnings. For a period of time I had a recurring dream of flying. Climbing a tree, I would hold out my arms to the sky, and with a little bit of help from the blowing wind, lift off. Just like that, like a bird with no care in this world. And then my dream always ended up with my falling onto a rock and hitting my head on it. I would get up crying, holding my head with both hands. Now that was the sign that I was heading for disaster."

I was getting worried for instead of making my mother happy by encouraging her to talk about her past love life, I was making her unhappy, yet I had to ask her one more question.

"Did you ever think of a divorce?" I asked her, gulping mother's left-over coffee from breakfast.

"Divorce? Oh! no. Even though I knew that I should never have married your father because I was ambitious and he was not, I didn't want to put my children in difficulty. I was like a bull, pulling the cart. I was too full of life. I sacrificed love and passion. I chose life with a family. That happened to be the Sri Lankan tradition." Mother paused to catch her breath. "I had two wonderful children, I had a job and I had lots of good friends and enjoyed a full social life back in Sri Lanka. Yet, at times I felt lonesome and felt as if I was wasting my life there," she said with a sigh. My mother's sadness made me think how the few dark days of our lives and the miseries we have experienced last longer than the good times. Why is that? I have wondered on many occasions. Instead of thinking of the many good times and making one's life happy we tend to dwell on the few bad times and make ourselves miserable. Is there something inherent in human beings that attracts us to grief and memories of grief? Do we recall days or even weeks of good times less than a single day of pain?

During the first year or so after we made Chicago our permanent home, my mother transformed herself to a completely different person. I began to hate the affectations she put on when she went out with her friends at work. I found her pretensions, the pitiful air she wore of being a certain sort of upper class Sri Lankan person now adapting to American way of life, intensely irritating. I remember commenting to Roshan one evening, listening to mother talking to her friends, that mother shines from a distance as long as she doesn't open her mouth, but the moment you get closer to her she ceased to shine. Now I am seeing a different person—a humble woman pouring out her painful memories. She continued talking about father and his love for her. She said she was upset sometimes at the way father brought flowers to her every time he received his pay check. He used to put them in the vase next to her side of the bed where he slept with her every night.

"It was his care for me that drove me to despair—that loving ceaseless care that I understood, and could not return. I did not want that loving care and I did not know how to tell him. He was a good man. He loved me with a love that very few men could give. But we wanted different things from our marriage. That's where we failed." Mother's eyes were filled with tears. She was truly hurting. I listened to her without uttering a word, for I realized she was pouring out her suppressed feelings. She had suffered all these years not having the opportunity to talk about her suppressed feelings. She needed someone to listen to her—never mind if that someone happened to be the daughter she had with the man she never really loved. I was hurt by the way mother talked about my father, but I kept quiet.

I cannot lie about my mother's love for her children—she always did the best as she saw it. She was a good sort, a good sport. I cannot remember her ever hitting or slapping me or my brother, though she shouted at us very often. There was a time when I had nightmares of my mother shouting at me—those nightmares are as clear in my mind now as they were then though the emotion, the anger had long gone away. "I have sacrificed myself for my family—for my children," was a common theme in our house. She talked about how much she was unappreciated; what a burden her children were to her; how none but a mother knows how much she had to give of herself to children.

As we grew up she didn't show any affection towards me, but my brother became her object of affection. She was all tender and loving kindness where he was concerned. She worried and fussed over him and overfed him that at the end he got sick of eating mother's food. My father was my ally, my support, my rock of strength to whom I ran to when I needed comforting. He was all that's affectionate but he was not open in showing his affection. He was a shy man.

During those long weeks in hospital, I realized as never before how wide the gulf between me and my mother had been, how completely far apart the two of us had stood. Yet looking at mother's ageing face, I was struck afresh by her beauty, a beauty that seemed to have survived the years, to have risen triumphant over time and grief. And now as in the days of my childhood, mother's beauty filled me with a kind of wonder, so calm and so assured, a beauty that I thought she had made use of to climb the social ladder. My heart suddenly tightened a little, a sense of not understanding just what I had lost all this time or why I had lost it. While she continued talking, I kept looking at my mother's face not knowing what else to say.

XVII

"There you are! I don't want you to come in the cold, yet I want to see your smiling face every day," said my mother as I bent down to kiss her. She touched my cheeks with both her palms.

"Nelu, your cheeks are cold," she said tenderly.

"It's warm in here. I'll be all right, Mom," I responded, taking my seat at the edge of her bed. The air outside was still cold that evening and the ward was a little quieter than usual. Mother talked about her past a lot these days. Whenever Aunty Rani was around our conversation drifted towards the JVP uprising. Then mother pulled herself into a shell and kept herself out of the conversation as much as possible. With me around she appeared to be at ease, releasing her bottled-up disappointments. I brushed and combed her hair. A few more grey streaks had appeared behind her ears and her hair felt soft to my touch. I was thinking of how mother after her bath used the hair dryer on rainy days and sat in the sun during weekends. The image came to my mind, of the way she touched her hair with the palms of her hands, feeling for the places that were still damp and turning in her chair towards the sun, so that her hair would dry evenly. I held her feeble hand and kissed her forehead. I felt a faint sensation passing through us as if a light breeze was touching our bodies and uniting us again. The joy that shone on my mother's face at that time brought tears to my eyes. This was not how I wanted us to get close to my mother, but I was thankful we were getting close, somehow, as mother and daughter.

Her comfortable life had fallen apart with their arrival in the United States. I remember one evening, after a heated argument with my father, mother walked into my room in our Hyde Park apartment. She sat on the chair at my computer desk and related the story of their coming to the United States. As she talked the tip of her nose turned red and her eyes filled with tears. The force of the memory pushed mother forward in the chair and she clasped her hands.

"Believe me Nelu," she said. "There were times when I've thought about leaving. But I couldn't for the shame it will bring on my family. That's why I have to work hard to make the situation work." I remember the way she stopped and looked at me straight on the face. "And it's more difficult than I ever imagined. So I've tried to be more assertive—about work. Who will bring in the money if I don't continue to work the way I do?"

That evening, sitting on the edge of her hospital bed, I wanted to take mother back to her happy days in Kandy. I wanted her to talk about the good days she spent with my father there. I thought just talking to me about her happier times would bring some cheer into her monotonous life, now entrapped in this narrow hospital bed. So I opened the conversation.

"Mom, you had such an easy life there, in Kandy. What a pity you had to leave it all behind."

Her eyes brightened; a sign that she loved to talk about her past—her past with both good and bad times. A dream—that's what Sri Lanka was to my mother now. As I watched her carefully working at her fingers, stroking them gently—one by one—I was reminded of the belief that those struggling to come to America held—America was the land of dreams, and that was why my mother came here. They are her shattered dreams now.

"Don't ever think that I didn't want to go back. But when your father never managed to get a permanent position in a good university, how could I even think of going back? Remember we came here to better ourselves—everyone does." Mother's face tightened with anguish as she recalled that a friend visiting Sri Lanka had the audacity to tell father's family about the difficult times we were experiencing in America.

"Why did she have to talk about us?" she questioned.

"I told your father, when we left Cambridge for Sri Lanka after he received his Ph.D. from there, that he took me to the top of the mountain, showed me the rich green valley below and brought me back to the desert," she said. "I wanted to go back to England. I loved it there. I am not talking about the materialistic life. I loved the cultural and intellectual life there and most of all as a woman, I enjoyed the freedom." Mother was happy to continue with the story and I was ever so ready to listen. I had been waiting for this too long. She told me of the many arguments she had with Grand Ma, when Grand Ma asked mother not to take her son away to a far away country. "We belong to the Kandy elite. We are the elite here. Why do you want to go away?" Grand Ma had asked. Mother had always justified her going away by giving the reason as the children's education. Mother told me that evening, that there lurked in her mind a deep sense of guilt: a guilt of not listening to her husband's mother, of not fulfilling the duties and obligations she owed her as her daughter-in-law.

"Sometimes I think that my sufferings, my family not achieving success, came because I didn't listen to Grand Ma, because I wasn't good to her," mother said showing repentance. Mother lived after her marriage to my father in a suffocating upper-middle class community where what the neighbors said mattered. She was taught by her parents to believe that the traditional manners of the high society women, properly acquired, would give a certain dignity which would protect her from embarrassment.

"I knew I was not going to stay in that life," mother continued. "I screamed and wept at times. I knew I was too ambitious and the environment around me was not what I had in mind. I felt that Kandy was a backward place for a smart woman like me. Sometimes when I went to the Kandy market, the beggars there would trail me. Instead of giving them a few coins, I shouted at them. I had no sympathy for them. They were able-bodied men, surely they could find work. I just refused to see their side of the story. Surely they would have worked if they could find something to do! Anyway, I had nothing in my mind at the time as serious as a plan or a program. Maybe I wanted to get out of the poverty around me; maybe I merely dreamed of a life with a free spirit in London or New York. I said to myself that I did not belong in Kandy. I felt as if my wrists were tightened by handcuffs and my feet bound together by chains. But I was a great actress; I smiled and chattered. I was friendly, affectionate and competent and Grand Ma and my friends were deceived. They thought I enjoyed teaching at the high school and was happy to be a part of the social life in Kandy. I was beautiful, bright, full of humor, and an attractive young woman then."

"You still are, Mom. You are very attractive," I said, squeezing her fragile hand. She looked at me with a smile that I had seen a long time ago—a smile that she had reserved only for Roshan. She got into a pensive mood for sometime and kept staring at the ceiling. Perhaps I had broken her trend of thought or perhaps she was thinking of her youth—happier days when she was floating carefree like a butterfly. Then she smoothed her slightly lined face with both her hands and continued.

"But inside my heart I felt an intense boredom. There is no boredom like that of an intelligent young woman who had to spend the whole day teaching some adolescent boys who were not interested in learning about a war that was fought a hundred years ago in a far away country which had not affected their lives or mine. And then I got pregnant with you. When your brother was born in England I said to myself I was not going to bring another baby into this world. Grand Ma was waiting for a girl and so was your father. All my friends and my sisters were having second babies and five years had passed since Roshan was born. So I changed my mind and thought it was my time too.

Your father was excited. He was so overjoyed when you were born he presented me with a necklace studded with deep blue sapphires. I don't know where he got the money to buy that piece of expensive jewelry but I have it with me to this day. You will inherit it one day." Mother paused, drank the hot cup of tea that I made for her and continued with her story.

"You know that Uncle Henry wanted us to join him here. Coming to the United States was glorified as a prestigious option then. Those days I received letters from him almost every other week to persuade your father to immigrate to America. Whenever I mentioned this to your father, he would smile and quietly walk out to avoid a possible argument; an argument he knew was not possible for him to win easily. Your father said that Uncle Henry boasted of his success in the United States. Henry makes it sound more impressive than it really is, he warned me. He said he was frightened for the two of you. He feared that Roshan like any other teenager in the United States would get addicted to drugs. He feared that you would be sexually defiled. I thought at the time that he was trying to discourage me. But I was never happy in Kandy." Listening to mother even now I fail to understand why anybody would want to walk away from all the comforts that Grand Ma's house provided and the love that Grand Ma showered on us. There were servants at our beck and call, plenty of room for us to play, delicious food at any time of the day and most of all no responsibility. Grand Ma's retinue of servants looked after everything. But my mother was not satisfied; she had longed for something more which even she had not figured out.

It was the JVP uprising that compelled my father to make the ultimate decision to leave Sri Lanka. The unruly situation in Sri Lanka had destroyed the educational system and my brother Roshan and I had had no schooling. Added to the chaos were reports of young boys disappearing—they were wedged in between the JVP recruiters and the government forces trying to crush the rebels. My mother got so frightened that she wouldn't even let Roshan out of her sight.

"I still remember the morning when your father opened his mail and read a letter he had received from his friend in Brunswick. I had no idea that he had been looking for any opportunity to get out of the country at the time. He read the letter loud for me to hear. 'We would be happy to offer you a Visiting Professor's position for the coming year . . .' the letter began. It was from his good friend John. He made it possible for us to get away from the troubled country. 'Let's go out for a year. Hopefully the chaotic situation here will clear up in a year's time,' he said. I was so thrilled to hear him say these words, I felt like an entrapped tortoise let loose into the flowing stream. I wanted your father to apply for permanent resident status in the United States straight away, but it was not easy. He had to swear out affidavits, go through police checks, bribe clerks whose job it was to move files from desk to desk. Even if he had put together documents which itself was a long and tiresome process, the clerk had said the process would take two years. We did not have much time. Your father got the offer in April and we were to leave in August and in any case he was not going to stay in America for more than a year. He came for a year but I had other plans. For your father life in Kandy had been lighthearted, and his intellectual life almost fulfilling. When I think of those nights, when after dinner your father and I would walk across to your Grand Ma's garden and watch the necklace of lights down Trincomalee Street, I feel so guilty I don't ever think I can die in peace. His life was full back in Kandy—he died a lonely man in Chicago." Mother's eyes were filled with tears; her lips began to quiver; I felt her hands shaking and she couldn't talk for sometime.

Instead, I filled in and began to talk of the day when father took all of us to the American Consulate in Colombo to get the visas to enter the United States. I reminded mother how shocked we were to see the long line of people waiting outside the Consulate, standing in the sun on the pavement along Galle Road. "These lines are formed in the early morning. People come at four o'clock in the morning to get a place in the front, because only forty applicants are taken in each day," father said.

"Remember Mom, those scruffy-looking touts wearing sarongs squatting on the pavement amidst the well-dressed people in their Sunday best standing in the line? You remember father said that those fellows in sarongs stay there all night and sell their spots to late arrivals? It's only now it occurs to me how privileged we were back in Sri Lanka; difficult things were reached easily for us there." I helped mother to continue to look back on the days when we were getting ready to leave for America.

An influential friend of father had made special arrangements and we walked right into the air-conditioned building from the sweltering humidity outdoors. The spotless, air-conditioned antechamber of the Consulate, with the American flag, its blue carpets and its photograph of Jimmy Carter smiling down at the visitors, was very impressive. It turned out that our visit was only a formality. Since father had an invitation from an American university and as he had been in the United States several times before, they granted us visas to enter and live in the United States for a year. But there were others applying for tourist visas who had to prove that they planned to return to Sri Lanka. They had with them surety bonds, land deeds, bank statements and anything else that showed that they possessed wealth in Sri Lanka, as proof that they were not going to the United States to better themselves and not forget about Sri Lanka. Families often transferred their assets to an applicant for twenty-four hours so that the applicant could be rich just for a day until he obtained the precious visa. Of course despite all the wealth shown most applications were turned down. The officers knew in spite of all the pledges to return, the applicants had no intention of returning. The situation in the country was so bad at the time that anyone with some means and someone abroad willing to sponsor them tried to get out.

XVIII

"Mom, leaving Grandma was the most difficult thing for me," I said after a short period of silence. "When I went down on my knees to worship her she lifted me up and held me for a long time. Then I felt her warm tears flowing down my neck. I think Grandma loved me more than she loved any of my cousins. I promised Grandma that day that I will write to her every day. I still write to her, not everyday, but at least once a month." I said holding back my tears.

Mother started to talk about our plane trip.

"Boarding an aircraft brings the worst fears into my life," she said. "All I had to do was to look at the nose of the plane, and imagine it thousands of feet above the earth, and I begin to feel the first ripple of panic. The takeoffs were the worst. On my very first flight, that was way before you and Roshan were born, I remember as the jet gathered speed and rose heavily skyward, I was certain that the plane would lose momentum and crash. So, as the plane ascended, I broke out in a sweat, my chest felt tight and even keeping my feet on the floor of the aircraft seemed difficult to me. Worst of all I had lost control of my emotions; terror and discomfort engulfed me. This was increased by the slightest change in engine sound. 'What's that?' I would ask your father, my fingers digging into his arm, as I heard a high, whining sound in the belly of the jet. Getting no answer from your father, 'Why is the plane doing that?' I would demand an answer from the stewardess, who very calmly explained that those minor fits and starts I felt during takeoff were caused by the wind. Even the announcements that summoned the air hostesses were enough to make me nearly jump out of my seat, convinced every time that it was an alarm to signal impending loss of cabin air pressure. Once the aircraft reached its cruising altitude, my fears subsided somewhat. Landings were tolerable because I figured that we were close enough to the ground that the plane ought to be able to get down safely. Your father adored flying. He said he sleeps like a baby during flights, whereas I couldn't even have a wink because of the roar of the engines. Oh! it's so terrifying—I could never get used to flying."

I cannot say I enjoyed the plane ride. I was excited but at the same time once we boarded the aircraft it seemed like an eternity to me. We sat in the crowded plane. Across the aisle, I could see mother's misty eyes. She stretched her hand towards my father and they held hands as the plane rose above the clouds.

The flight was full. Roshan and I were first timers aboard. We marveled at the baby pillows and blankets, the cakes of soap in the lavatory. We marveled at the way the toilets flushed, the sheen of the stainless steel and all those paper products neatly fitted in separate compartments. I remember once the aircraft reached the desired altitude, and when the stewardess took her place before us to demonstrate the safety features of the aircraft, all eyes turned on her. She donned the orange life vest and pulled the white tabs and the tube above each breast to fill the life vest with air. Then she put away the vest, donned an apron, and became an airline hostess—presenting a tray for each passenger, that held as many different food items as one would serve at a five course meal.

We stopped in London to spend a couple of days with some friends of my parents. After the stop-over we were crossing the Atlantic when we felt the plane drop out of the sky. The aircraft lost altitude so suddenly that all the passengers gave a loud gasp. Gripped with terror and her face contorted with a mask of fear mother held on to father with one hand and she put the other arm around me. Roshan remained cool as usual. The pilot in the same cozy drawl he had used before when welcoming the passengers announced, 'Remain seated. We have fallen into an air bubble.' "I was convinced that we were all going to fall on to the ocean that very instant. I told your father we would all simply drop out of the sky. He was also frightened at the time and got so angry with me when I shouted that I couldn't go with this terror anymore, he snapped at me, 'You are being silly. Think of something to get over your fright. I can't help you!' That helped to quieten me a little. The flames rising from the burnt aircraft appeared in front of me," mother related the incident still showing signs of terror in her mind. Of course after thirty seconds which seemed like an hour the plane leveled off.

Looking back at those days I can say now that neither of them could have known what lay ahead. For my mother it began as an adventure and turned out to have more twists and turns than she expected or knew how to handle. My father never even dreamed of staying in America for good. As for Roshan and me, we didn't remain for long as the children who left Sri Lanka—it did not take long to create completely different persons out of the two of us.

Sri Lanka has not been my home for a long time. Though I was born in Kandy, I lived there only through my pre-teens. I left at twelve when my parents emigrated to the United States during the JVP uprising. When I left I never knew that I'd never go back, but here I am settled in Chicago now for almost twenty years. Since I left, I have made only three short trips to Sri Lanka; all to connect myself with my roots—so my father told me. I remember Sri Lanka as a country where I was happy—where I remember my mother and father were the happiest people on earth. But when they decided to leave Sri Lanka, I did not hide my excitement because I wanted to go to school in America. The JVP had made us all prisoners in our own homes

Now I think of those bad days under the JVP siege as a distant bad memory, but a trip to Sri Lanka is like a sudden trip back in time. The minute I board the plane, fear takes hold of my whole body: the past is like a volcano waiting to burn me in its lava. As soon as everyone is settled in the Air Lanka plane from Heathrow, London, Sinhalese, Tamil and English announcements welcoming us to the flight remind me of the polite language I was taught as a child. The seats are mostly occupied by Sinhala brown-skinned people and I get a strange feeling sitting among them. They look darker to me now, perhaps after moving among fair skinned people for so many years. They are louder and more vociferous than those one would encounter in a British Airways flight. In the crowded cabin, the beautiful, polite stewardess dressed glamorously in sarees float toward us like a pleasant mist. But actually this politeness seems to me like a steel net hauling us into the country where nothing had been done to wipe away the poverty and accompanying violence which drove most of us away to distant lands. Even before we left Heathrow, I felt as if I have landed in some place where I am terrified of what I say or ask what I want to know. I hear these fears are illusions and they are not there anymore, but those hard times we went through lingers in my mind. I hear the chief steward's announcement of the meal time and trolleys of food rolling down the aisle, immediately followed by a strong smell of curry that fill the cabin. Plates of *kiribath* (milk rice) and *ambul thiyal* (fish curry) are handed over, accompanied by cups of the best Ceylon tea to wash it down with. Did I enjoy all this? No! I relish the pizzas and the burgers and the French fries! Mother laughs and agrees with me.

XIX

"I thank my lucky stars we can now speak of the joy as well as the pain in our hearts," my mother said one morning as I bent down to kiss her. "I've been waiting for you for over an hour. I felt very lonely suddenly. I wanted to talk to you." Her eyes were red. Had she been crying?

"Memories of good and bad days keep rushing back. It's not possible not to feel nostalgic," she said wiping her tears. A little color has appeared on her cheeks. Over the weeks, both physically and mentally she has been slowly improving. And, over the weeks our bond—bond between mother and daughter—had become strong. That strength is not the result of just listening on my part. I have grown to tolerate and respect mother's point of view. Out of respect for my mother, I did not interrupt her when she spoke. The days when I used to jump at her or make fun of her whenever she opened her mouth to say something, seemed to be in the past. As I listened to my mother, I thought I understood the pain she had gone through—some of it, I believed she had created for herself. But then that's my mother.

"Like a lot of families, ours was not a perfect picture of love and kindness. I've reached the period in my life where the mistakes I have made with Nalin and you and Roshan glare at me like the mid-day sun. Not enough attention here, too much criticism there. I put my work above family needs. I figure that your father withheld himself at times and drew inward when he should have opened up. That was what led to Roshan's misfortune. We touched the sky back home in Sri Lanka and hit rock bottom when we came here. But in a world which I now think is so cruel to other's feelings, love shared with one's family is the closest thing to heaven I know." She said all of this in a soft voice, with just a touch of urgency in the last phrase. As she proceeded her eyes filled with tears and she wiped her cheeks with both hands and seemed to shrink even further into her shell. Age brings with it a desire to review one's life and, perhaps more important, to make sense of it. I listened—she had to get these thoughts off her chest and so she needed to tell me.

"When Roshan went away to college and you started high school, I knew my life would be lonely. When a mother is left on her own she feels like the lone hub of a wheel with no other lives revolving around her. It's very hard to get back to normal life. It takes time to find a meaning for living. Life without children, living for oneself—the words themselves ring a hollow sound to me." Mother started to cry. She was missing her family. I sat on her bed and held her hand. I stroked her head and talked to her. I tried to comfort her. It's not easy to be away from one's own loved ones, especially when you are in distress.

I think because of the receptiveness of Americans to immigrants we managed to survive among strangers. I grew up possessing an unnervingly clear view of both worlds—white American and Asian, yet feeling at home in neither. I feel uncomfortable with the aspect of life my mother's friends observe, but equally at odds with much about the cheerful, self-satisfied American culture in which I have lived since our Brunswick days in Maine. At the beginning I was anxious to show my American friends how much a Sri Lankan girl could accomplish—but now that I've grown up and fully understand the significance of one's roots, I feel that a life spent outside the company of my Sri Lankan friends and family seems barren. Since childhood I had been schooled in the traditions and beliefs of an obedient Sri Lankan girl. I now realize that confidence comes to us from the family bonds rather than from one's own deeds alone. At the present moment, without Uncle Henry to lean on, where would my life be?

As mother seemed far from being happy, I tried to shift our conversation to something that would remind her of happier days of our lives in Brunswick.

"Mom, remember the fir tree in the front yard of our house in Brunswick? I wonder if anybody fixes light bulbs on it for Christmas. I often think of the way Daddy used to stand the ladder against the tree and fixed all those colorful bulbs. Remember how carefully he chose the different colored lights to match each branch which he said would give that special festive look? We laughed at him secretly because the tree didn't look all that great, but we three danced and clapped and announced that that was the most gorgeous Christmas tree in the neighborhood! The lights remained there on the tree until well into the New Year." Mother's eyes brightened like a little girl's.

"It's funny we don't even think of the Vesak Day now," I continued trying to get mother out of her pensive mood. "We used to light lamps and lanterns and candles in Sri Lanka. The whole country looked heavenly for three days. We don't even go to the temple now. There is a Thai temple in the outskirts of Chicago—let's go there when you get better," I suggested. Mother pretended to listen to me. I could feel that her mind was somewhere else. She bit her lower lip to keep her emotions under control and slowly turned the pages of the *Time* magazine she was holding on her lap and said in a soft, gentle voice, "Though your father didn't go to the temple on *poya* days he remained a true Sri Lankan Buddhist in his heart. He believed in what's called 'outward assimilation.'" I listened without intruding into her thoughts. "Not only was your father proud of his Sri Lankan heritage; he did his best to inculcate those ideas into his children's minds. He was also planning to return to his motherland one day." I nodded in agreement.

"You will find this hard to believe, Nelu, and it seems strange to me too, that on the day we became US citizens I was excited but somehow that feeling of excitement was tinged by a feeling that I had somehow betrayed my native country. I love both countries. In spite of the fact that we were almost chased out of our country, that did not stop me from longing to go back. Circumstances stopped me from doing so. That day I felt like I had been asked to choose between my mother and father," my mother said, slowly turning the pages of the *Time* magazine. She pointed to an article in the magazine, which she had been reading, on recent immigrants applying for US citizenship having to wait for over two years to get their papers through. Foreign born people living in this country have applied for American citizenship in record numbers in the last few years, largely prompted by concerns over Federal laws that cut off benefits for legal immigrants.

"I was prompted by the ease in traveling and somehow I managed to convince your father to apply for citizenship. With the Sri Lankan passports we had to get visas to almost every country we visited and that's a lot of money. More important than that was, with the reputation that Sri Lanka has earned in the international community as a country where terrorists operate, we were searched at every airport we landed, and sometimes though we fully appreciated the need for it, it proved to be humiliating and left a bitter feeling in us against the country," mother gave me her justification for becoming a US citizen and seemed happy to continue.

"The day we took the oath of allegiance in which we had to swear to. . . ." She stopped in mid-sentence and started reading from an article in the *Time* magazine on recent immigrants to the US, "absolutely and entirely renounce and abjure all allegiance and fidelity to any foreign prince, potentate, state or sovereignty," she paused and looked at my face and said, "Your father was very upset. He did it because I urged him on. 'I want to keep my family together, so I'll go along with you,' he said when I pleaded with him to apply for US citizenship after six years of our arrival in the US. 'When I gave up my Sri Lankan nationality, I felt like a lost person. You lose your roots, your history,' he told me later. He said that there is something wrong in the oath that we took that day. The oath is very strong in its wording I agree. Your father thought that it's ridiculous to require new citizens to renounce all 'allegiance and fidelity' to their native land which put them in a position to commit perjury in their very first action as citizens. Sri Lankan law forces anyone who becomes a citizen of another country to give up their Sri Lankan nationality," mother stroked her face and remained silent for a few minutes.

Uncle Henry is an American citizen. He was the one who convinced mother that it was to our advantage to become American citizens. "Nalin would never agree to that idea," my mother said at the time. But she managed to change father's beliefs.

Mother talked about attending the party held at Aunty Rani's when she and her sister and brother obtained their citizenship.

"It was different with Rani. From the day I met her, Rani talked anxiously about the day when she and her sister and brother would be entitled to an American passport. She told me how important it was to get US citizenship. She said it would open doors all over the world for them. 'We'll have a special celebration when we get our citizenship papers, because then we would have a definite identification with the most powerful and prosperous country in the world. The golden eagle would be stamped on the cover of our passports!' Rani was so eager. And did you know Nelu that as American citizens we have the right to political asylum at any local American Embassy and the American Ambassador himself would be at our service? That's what it says here—read this article," mother handed me the *Time* magazine.

I took the magazine and put it in my bag. I glanced at my watch and noticed that it was almost mid-morning. The ward seemed a different place now from the usual commotion and chaos that exist during lunch hour and the evenings. It was very quiet and peaceful. The only sound that disturbed the peace around us was the humming of the power polisher that came from the far end of the room. One of the janitors was using it on the vinyl floor.

Realizing that after all the talking she did, mother would appreciate a hot drink, I poured the chocolate from the thermos flask I brought and handed the mug full of lukewarm liquid to mother.

"Hmm, it tastes delicious!" she said looking up at me. Her eyes had a pleading quality like an abandoned child's.

"You know what I'd like to have for lunch today?" she asked me still looking at me with that same look in her eyes.

"What, Mom?"

"I'd like to have a really hot spicy chicken curry and yellow rice. I was thinking of asking Rani but she didn't come yesterday," mother said smiling.

"I'll make a hot chicken curry for tomorrow's lunch, Mom," I offered, eager to satisfy her longing for Sri Lankan food. My mother was feeling homesick for Sri Lanka. Trying to distract her trend of thought, I reminded her of the day we made hot-dogs at home in Brunswick and offered one to a Sri Lankan friend who was visiting the United States for the first time.

"Remember, Mom? 'Hot? Are they spicy or are they warm?' he asked, made a funny face and ate first and then said 'it didn't taste like dog meat at all?' Remember? how you laughed and asked how would he know, has he eaten the stuff before back in Sri Lanka!" Mother laughed out loud, the chocolate spilling out through her lips on to the bed sheet making brown patches on the pure white linen. Seeing her enjoying the story, I continued.

"Once you left the kitchen, he threw the hot-dog into the garbage bin, Mom. Then Daddy told him that hot dogs are really pork sausages put inside a long bun and served with ketchup and mustard sauce! He was so embarrassed." Mother had been laughing so much that tears oozed from her eyes.

"'Why are they named so?' he wanted to know," I continued.

"I still don't know the answer!" mother said. I was happy that morning. A little story from our past had made mother happy.

"I'll bring a packet of delicious rice and curry for you for tomorrow's lunch—all wrapped in a real banana leaf, just like they used to do it at Fountain Cafe in Colombo."

"Yumm, my mouth is already watering!" she said.

The door to the ward opened slowly and a hospital attendant pushed the drinks cart inside. She handed the drinks to the patients as she pushed the cart along the narrow path in between the beds. She looked at mother with a bright smile on her face.

"You've been well taken care of, I see" she said as she stopped by mother's bed. "Your mother is a fine lady," she said addressing me. "You are fortunate to have a mother like her. She is very proud of you."

"This is Ruth, you know her, don't you?" mother said looking at me and reaching for Ruth's hand. "Ruth is like my own family now. The hospital staff—they all helped to make me get better. They came to my help when I was in pain and despair. Their friendly, kind gestures helped me to be what I am now." Ruth freed her hand gently and arranged the books on to a neat pile on mother's bedside table, touched mother's cheek gently with the palm of her right hand and turned to the drinks cart. She was gone. We observed her serving drinks to the other patients. Mother was extremely polite to the hospital staff. She didn't fail to say please and thank you whenever she wanted to get something attended to. She knew she depended on them to take care of her. My aunts have gone and I spend only a few hours with her now.

I looked at my watch. "Mom, I have to go now. I want to go to Devon Street and buy the spices to make you that delicious chicken curry!" I said in a lighter spirit getting down from the bed. She held my hand and I felt her grip tighten around mine. When I leave after each visit with my mother (anxious to get out of the door because I didn't want to hear her cry) I hear a sob that drops into low moan, and this held-back cry draws me back to her. I put my arms around her shoulders and I hold my mother just for a second. I have never done this before, not since I entered college, and now I feel she belongs to me and I know I can hold her until the end of her life. I held her so tightly that she—so frail and weak—almost bent backwards. I see in her eyes the loving trust she has now resolved to put in me. Her lips quivered and she did not smile for fear the tears of joy she had been holding back would overflow. At that moment I thought my dreams were fulfilled, though mother's would remain forever shattered.

XX

I drove back to the apartment planning my treat for mother and found to my pleasant surprise that Lindy was waiting for me in the foyer of the building. "I am so happy to see you!" I said hugging her affectionately. Lindy has remained my best friend since high school days. I find her company so invigorating and especially during the past two months when I needed someone to talk to she was there for me. Talking to her helped me to see the brighter side of life.

"I've got a special assignment for tomorrow!" I told her light heartedly, giving her news about my mother. Instead of waiting for the elevator we climbed the stairs to my apartment.

"Let me come with you to get the ingredients to prepare the special meal for tomorrow," Lindy offered as I opened the door to my apartment. I was glad to accept her offer. We talked and laughed not realising that time was passing swiftly until Lindy said she was feeling hungry. It was already late afternoon! Lindy made chicken sandwiches for us while I made a list of what I wanted to buy from Devon Street. I opened my kitchen cupboards to see what I had and saw them bare. I was embarrassed at Lindy's seeing my empty cupboards.

"I don't bring much food for fear that I might start eating and put on weight and lose my waistline. You know we have to remain slim to wear fashionable clothes when going to work," I said and Lindy nodded in agreement.

"Mine is not much different from yours," she said seeking to ease my discomfort.

"In our kitchen in Brunswick, Mom used to fill the kitchen cabinets and the refrigerator with food. During the first few weeks after our arrival in Brunswick, she almost turned our kitchen into a mini-grocery store! Daddy laughed at her then and said that maybe Mom still thought of being prepared for closure of stores for long periods of time, as had happened during those troubled days back in Sri Lanka. She found it difficult to forget the two difficult years we went through in Sri Lanka," I told Lindy looking for the Sri Lankan cookery book which I had borrowed from Aunty Rani sometime back.

"Those early days in Brunswick, mother cooked every meal for us. Though Daddy did not ask for it, mother knew that he enjoyed rice and curry and every day she prepared a delicious Sri Lankan meal for dinner. When Mom's workload at the library increased, she did not have time to prepare meals every evening. She cooked during weekends and stacked the food in the freezer and with the help of the microwave she managed to have a warm meal appear on the table within minutes." I continued talking while Lindy enjoyed the sandwiches. Lindy knew our family well, so she understood every word that I said.

"Evenings, when mother was late, because she had to work overtime or attend a meeting, Daddy, Roshan and I would sit on the front door steps leading to our house in Brunswick and crane our necks to spot mother appearing at the bend. Mom walked faster when she saw us, laughing to hide her tiredness. 'So you are hungry for rice?' she would ask us knowing that we were all hungry. Daddy would take the bag from her hand and Roshan and I would hold her hands while walking through the front door. I often think of those days, when we were young. We were so happy together. Mom used to wait for Daddy to come home to have meals together. Back at home in Sri Lanka he was the one who got to come home late. As months went by and pressure of work kept her at work for longer hours, Mom just gulped the food that we had prepared, and left for bed after the evening meal leaving me to clear the table. Roshan and I sat with Daddy and enjoyed the meal. Daddy made balls of rice and curry and gently pushed the ball into his mouth while talking to us about his day."

While talking to Lindy of those days back in Brunswick, I listed what I wanted to buy from the Indian Store. Unlike in Brunswick where they did not have a single Asian Store, Chicago has one whole street—Devon Street, part of it renamed Jawaharlal Nehru Marg—full of Indian grocery stores. I rarely go there because I had given up cooking and in any case I cannot let my lovely condominium get polluted with curry smell! But today was a special day, I must prepare a chicken curry, a lentil curry, and Basmati rice all wrapped up in a banana leaf. Oh! I can visualise the delight in my mother's face when she opens the parcel and inhales the aroma of Basmati rice.

Lindy and I drove down Sheridan Avenue towards Devon Street. On the way I continued with my reminiscences of the days when we first arrived in the United States and I joined mother on her grocery shopping in Brunswick. Lindy was ever willing to listen. So I kept on talking.

"Mom never went grocery shopping alone. She couldn't do anything by herself then."

"I remember those days in Brunswick, Leila took you and Roshan along for grocery shopping," joined in Lindy.

"If Mom wanted to buy some groceries before the week-end and if Daddy had no time to take her, she would ask Roshan to walk with her after school to the grocery store. She insisted that Roshan walked with her and me. Roshan loathed it—he said he missed out on TV programs or school work or meeting friends at school. Roshan was taken to speak up for Mom—it was not that Mom couldn't speak English, she said she was afraid to ask for things. She had never done this before in her life and was not going to learn it either. One day Mom had invited some faculty friends of father and was planning a special meal. Do you remember that special butcher's shop in town?" I asked Lindy keeping my eyes on the crowded street. She nodded.

"We didn't have much money then. Mom used to stand in front of its window. It was always lined with hams, roasts and ropes of plump handmade sausages. Mom used to smack her lips and admire the bounty there. Roshan and I would try to persuade her to go in but she resisted and walked past it because she said she could not afford them. She would instead buy packaged links at the Shop'n'save supermarket, where she felt comfortable looking over the items, touching each with her fingers, poking into them and noting the prices without having to talk to anybody.

But that particular day she was different; she was buying for a special meal. The store was crowded and as we stepped inside the doorbell jingled our arrival. No one noticed us. We waited for some time, and the people who entered after us were being served. Finally, a woman nudged my mother and waved a little ticket which we had not taken. We patiently waited again until one of the big men behind the counter shouted our number. Mom dragged the two of us and went forward but what she wanted to buy was nowhere to be found. There was a line of people waiting behind us. The big man got impatient at Mom and shouted, 'Com'on lady, what d'ya want?' The shout unnerved Mom and she didn't say anything. The man looked at the three of us as if we had come from another planet; he dismissed us right then, looked at the lighted board and called the next number. Before I could realize, Mom had rushed us outside and back on the road. She was furious, almost vibrating with shame and grief and we noticed a little red patch appear on the tip of her nose—a sure signal that she was about to cry! None of us said a word. So much for the special meat for the guests that night. We ended up buying chicken breasts at the supermarket. Those first days at Brunswick proved to be hilarious at times. Mom refused to adapt herself to the new conditions and depended on Daddy or Roshan to act on her behalf."

"Isn't it surprising how quickly she overcame her difficulties and adapted to the new conditions? I still remember the first day you took me home when she served us lunch. You want to know what she served, Nelu? I think Pearl also came with us that day. She served us each a fresh green salad, a beef brisket with oven-roasted potatoes, carrots and onions and coconut creme pie for dessert. We all enjoyed it very much." Lindy who had known my mother from our early days in Brunswick responded to my little story with her own.

We stopped at several food stores in downtown Chicago. Until then I had not realized that finding the ingredients would prove to be such an awesome task. It was easy to get the chicken, lentils and the basmati rice, but the spices, the curry powder and various kinds of dried leaves like lemon grass which give the curries the special flavor were nowhere to be found. Most important, I had to find real coconut milk to prepare the chicken curry. The Sri Lankan cook book said to use coconut milk. I had no idea that canned coconut milk imported from Thailand was available in Indian grocery stores. Before going to Devon Street, Lindy accompanied me to almost every food store in downtown Chicago but everywhere we went the shopkeepers gave us the same blank look, canned coconut milk? For cooking chicken curry? Why not use cow's milk? It's not the same—nobody would understand—that special flavor of chicken curry made of real coconut milk. They had never heard of such a thing. Finally, I called Nedra, an Indian friend of mine who used to prepare curries and who I thought might give me an idea where to find coconut milk. "Oh! Yes," she said. "Go to Devon Street. You can find canned coconut milk in any of the Indian stores there. You can find real coconuts too if you can scrape the flesh from the nuts and squeeze the milk out!" So we found the canned coconut milk but it proved to be more like jelly—it didn't have that special coconut milk flavor; but this was better than using cow's milk. I was determined to make a picture-perfect Sri Lankan chicken curry for mother!

It happened to be a weekend and Lindy stayed with me that night.

"Let's get up early tomorrow and prepare the special lunch then both of us can visit Mom in hospital," I suggested and to my delight Lindy agreed.

That night we talked of our days back in Brunswick; we talked of our school friends, of Lindy's parents and of my parents and my brother.

Lindy listened carefully when I told her about the delightful experience my parents and my brother and I enjoyed at our first Thanksgiving dinner at Storers. They were our host family when father was a Visiting Professor at St. Peter's College. Lindy was amused when she heard that when the Storers invited us we didn't know what to expect and how to behave at such an occasion.

"Daddy took it very seriously. He made Roshan and me go to that little public library down Maine Street and read about Thanksgiving day! Lindy, you want to know what we found out? Well, Mom wanted to know every detail about the dinner so that she could join in the conversation. Dinner was at two o'clock in the afternoon. Mom said that was an awkward time—neither lunch nor dinner. There was a huge snowstorm around noon that day and when the four of us arrived at Storers we saw them removing piles of snow so that guests could park their vehicles on their drive-way. Daddy whispered that we should quickly get out of the car, take the snow-ploughs from their hands and clean the driveway which Roshan and I did. They appreciated that gesture very much and that made it easy for us to make ourselves feel at home.

I remember Roshan and I looked at each other because as we entered their beautiful house we got the smell of brown sugar and allspice. These smells merged and then drifted from the kitchen into the sitting room where we sat while being introduced to the other guests. We had just read about these sumptuous Thanksgiving dinners but even Daddy who had visited the United States many times before had not tasted them.

So we waited impatiently to be led to the dining room where Marjorie had set the table for the twenty or so guests. It was very formal but somehow we felt at ease in the presence of the Storers. Roshan and I couldn't sit together because Marjorie had placed name-tags in front of each plate making us get acquainted with newly introduced friends. Once all the guests took their seats Jim led the Thanksgiving prayer, and then got up to carve the turkey. While carving the turkey Jim asked Roshan whether he knew that turkey, the main meat dish served at Thanksgiving, was called *nahenan* by the Wampanoag Indians? At this Mom jumped in.

'At the first Thanksgiving dinner the Pilgrims fed 140 people. So can you imagine how many birds they would have brought?' Daddy was pleased at Mom's desire to join in the conversation, but Roshan and I were taken aback. Roshan threw a glance at me as if to say Mom just learned about this yesterday from us and now she is showing off!

'They also brought corn,' said Marjorie smiling and passing the Indian corn and blueberry pudding she had made. Later in the meal came pumpkin pie.

'Indians called the pumpkins, *pompion*,' said Jim. 'I am sure at the time pumpkin pie would have been stewed because the Pilgrims had no ovens for baking.' He served us the pumpkin pie. We all appreciated the meal and thanked the Storers for their very generous gesture. I remember after dinner Mom and I helped to clear the table. It was a memorable evening."

After listening to me Lindy said that her grandmother took great pains in preparing the Easter meal. "My grandparents spent every Easter with us and our house smelled of food for a couple of days. The centerpiece of our feast was ham. Granny would shape the rolls before going to Mass. After church she washed and seasoned the greens, just after breakfast, but before Grandpa could start washing the dishes. They were a very loving pair. Grandpa was the slow, steady type and Granny didn't want him getting in the way. When Grandpa did the dishes, Granny entertained his conversation with a few nods of the head and a gentle, 'Yes, dear,' every now and again. Granny didn't hear what Grandpa said. She cared but she didn't have time to truly listen to him. She was too busy minding the yams that bounced about in the huge pot of boiling water or carefully mixing the ingredients for the sour-cream coffee cake or chocolate rum cake." I thought Lindy paused for a while and I waited to hear her continue the beautiful story. But instead, in the darkness of my bedroom I heard Lindy's faint sob.

"What's the matter Lindy? Talking of your Granny and Grandpa makes you sad? I know the feeling! They were such dear people, I knew them so well." I tried to console her. Lindy didn't want to talk any more. After a period of silence, "Let's go to sleep. It's late now," she suggested and I agreed.

The next morning when we got up we found the sun's rays piercing through the window panes. They carried a springlike atmosphere, but the bright sun was deceptive. It was mid-March and the air outside was still cool.

"Before we begin our cooking session let's open the kitchen window slightly and switch on the fan," I said gently pushing the window panes sideways. My kitchen is small and hardly used, so it stays spotlessly clean. No Sri Lankan cooking smells emanate from my kitchen window to pollute the fresh air above Lake Michigan. But today, it is a different story.

"Please Lindy, see that all the closets are closed," I asked her.

"You are afraid of the curry smell, Nelu? I know, it's awful once the smells settle on your clothes." Lindy said laughing and went out of the kitchen to check. Once she entered the kitchen, I closed the door and started on the most important task for the day.

"What can I do? Shall I clean the chicken?" Lindy had already opened the refrigerator and taken the meat out. I looked at her for a moment. She's very kind and was offering to help. But I couldn't trust anyone, not even Lindy to remove the skin and all the fat from the chicken. Mother wouldn't like it if the meat was not cleaned properly. It will show; there will be a layer of fat formed on the curry. I must not hurt Lindy's feelings but I must refuse her kind offer.

"No, Lindy. That's too much work for you. Would you clean the onions and the garlic and wash the *dhal*? You have to wash the *dhal* several times if not it gives an odd smell when cooked."

"*Dhal*?" she inquired with her eyebrows raised.

"Yes, the *dhal*. I put some in the pan over there," I said pointing to the pan.

"There's lentils here."

"Oh! I am sorry. *Dhal* is the Indian name for lentils. We are so used to calling lentils *dhal*." Once Lindy started attending to her little things, I cleaned, washed and cut the chicken into sizeable pieces. Then I rubbed the chicken in the curry paste I had prepared—the curry paste consisting of chili powder, roasted coriander, cumin and saffron powder and pepper. I also added a piece of the lemon grass that I managed to find in the Indian Store together with slightly crushed cardamon and cloves. All the directions given in the Sri Lankan cookery book were followed to the very letter. Last of all I put salt to taste.

"Adding salt to a curry is the most difficult of all things, Mom told me once," I said as I added a little salt to the chicken. Just the right amount of salt makes all the difference in the taste of the chicken curry. I mixed all the ingredients again, rubbed the mixture well into the meat and left it to marinate for one hour.

During the one hour that I had, I washed the basmati rice and put the washed rice in the rice cooker.

"It's very important to see that the right amount of water is poured into the rice cooker. Do you know how much water you should add to the rice so that it won't become a rice pudding instead?" I asked Lindy.

"No. How?"

"Well you pour the water and measure the water level with your right hand fingers. If the water level reaches up to the first knuckle then that's the correct amount," I showed her the way I did it and switched on the rice cooker. The rice would be ready in twenty minutes. Then I turned to the lentils. Preparation of the lentil curry was not difficult. Lindy had already washed the lentils and the lentils were ready in a cooking pot. I put a little of the chopped onions over the lentils and added half a tea spoonful of saffron and chili powder. Then I poured a cup of water into the pot, mixed everything together and placed the pot on the stove. It took only about four to five minutes for the lentils to cook. Once the lentils were cooked I added two tablespoons full of coconut milk and let it boil thoroughly. Then I added salt to taste.

"Mom won't like it if she finds out I used canned coconut milk. Lindy, don't tell her—I can't scrape the coconut and squeeze the milk out. Aunty Rani has a scraper and she has the patience and the time too!" I said laughing.

"Canned milk won't give the same flavor?" Lindy wanted to know.

"Yes, and also this stuff must be years old. Sri Lankan food preparations are time consuming and labor intensive. That's why back in Sri Lanka we had a woman living in our house whose only job was to prepare our meals. Meals meant breakfast, mid-morning tea, lunch which was our big meal for the day, afternoon tea and dinner. Imagine how we had got over those habits or were they luxuries? Some days I forget to eat—I exist only on coffee!"

The lentils were cooked in five minutes. I removed the pot of lentils off the stove and put another pan there. I reminded myself that today's cooking was for a special event. The past and present, love and disappointments hissed like the oil in the pan in which the chopped onions and a little garlic were being transferred into golden colored flakes. Suddenly the delicious aroma of the frying onions filled the kitchen. The cooked lentil curry, I gently poured into the pan. And it was ready!

"Yummy! What a delicious smell!" I heard Lindy's appreciation.

While cooking the lentil curry that mother loved so much, I told Lindy of the day I cooked milk rice and made chili sauce for my friends in the university on the Sri Lankan New Year's day which we celebrate on the thirteenth and fourteenth of April.

"I wanted to give my friends a taste of Sri Lankan food that we enjoy on our New Year's Day. This was the one holiday in my family that we were all together, we showed respect to our parents and we exchanged gifts. I think when we were in Brunswick, you were with us on one such occasion," I reminded Lindy.

"Yes," she said. "We had milk rice for lunch."

"During the first couple of years even after Roshan went to college Mom made certain that Roshan came home. But after three years or so in America the family occasion became Christmas and the traditions we observed on New Year's day became a thing of the past. I never realized how much Mom cared about our New Year celebrations until I offered to make milk rice for my friends. I explained to my friends that we celebrate New Year after the harvesting season was over and offer gods who helped farmers in providing them with plenty of sun and rain for the crops to ripen and share with others what we had been blessed with. This was something similar to what the Americans celebrate as the Thanksgiving Day.

They were fascinated by the milk rice and the jaggery pudding I made. They treated them like an exotic delicacy from a far away land. 'Everyone has to have both kinds,' I insisted. Some found the chili sauce too hot and ate the milk rice with white sugar instead. I remember at the end of the meal, they hugged their sides, saying they had eaten for a whole week. Lindy, here in America, you guys don't need much persuasion when it comes to eating. Everyone had second servings that day." Lindy laughed and reminded me that the meat must be ready for cooking.

"The longer you keep the chicken to marinate the tastier the meat will be," I said placing a large pot on the stove. I fried chopped onions, garlic and two small pieces of cinnamon in hot oil until all the ingredients turned golden brown. I put the chicken into the pan, lowered the heat a little and turned the chicken pieces several times until all the sides were fried. Then I added a cupful of water, covered the pan and cooked for fifteen minutes. Once the meat was soft, I added enough coconut milk and let it boil. Oh! it really looked wonderful.

While clearing up the kitchen table we returned to our conversation regarding the food habits of some of my American friends.

"Lindy, you must have noticed that Americans are generally fatter than Europeans, certainly more so than Asians? What is served in Sri Lankan restaurants is paltry when compared to the heaping plates of burgers and fries which we get here. When we first arrived in the United States, I remember we looked anemic and dreary. In fact we were embarrassed by our 'pigmy look' among the big Americans and by our accents which sounded sing-song British as a Mainer once remarked to Mom." Lindy listened to me while enjoying a slice of bread with a little of the lentil curry I had served for her on to a plate. It was already mid-morning. The cooking smells made my stomach rumble as well.

I told Lindy how over time I had got accustomed to American ways. Now that I am nearing thirty, and moved around with those of my age, I find that 'gluttony' or overeating—the American vice is in danger of losing its flavor. I am actually surprised at the way some people talk about food these days. "You drink whole milk?" a friend of mine asked me recently, with her eyes wide open almost as big as saucers, as if I had inhaled marijuana or something. Another day when I found out that the Faculty Club candy machine had run out of my favorite candy bar, Kit Kat, and I was standing there lost in thought as to what I was going to have during my break, "When that happens to me," I heard a lady professor's voice passing by, "I feel saved." Despite my occasional candy bar and the milk that I prefer with two percent fat—the milk that I can't see through—I do believe in healthy diet.

"I am going to show you a little secret now—a secret that my Mom showed but I never used before," I said taking out the banana leaves out from the refrigerator.

"In fact I wondered why you bought banana leaves from the Indian store. I wanted to ask you but it escaped my mind. What are you going to do with that? I thought the cooking was over," Lindy looked at me with a look of surprise. Without saying a word I demonstrated to her my secret. I spread a large piece of foil on a plate and over the foil I placed a banana leaf which was about one square foot in size. Then I served three big full spoonfuls of basmati rice on to the leaf. On to a side of the heap of rice I served chicken pieces and over it the curry. On to the opposite side was served the lentil curry and a little of the onion pickles and chili sauce that I had bought from the Indian store. Then I carefully wrapped the rice and curry first in the banana leaf and then around it the foil. The foil helped to keep the food warm.

"Won't it be a good idea to take two extra packets so that Mom can share the delicacy with her friends—the hospital staff?" inquired Lindy.

I agreed and made five packets to take.

"Why so many?"

"Both of us are going to enjoy our meal with Mom! Let's turn Mom's bedside into a small picnic site," I said, laughing.

Mother must be waiting for me without eating the meal provided by the hospital. I made certain that she was going to enjoy what I had made for her. I remember at the beginning when we arrived in Chicago and when she made friends with Aunty Rani, she went to Aunty Rani's during weekends to learn to cook the "real Sri Lankan way". She looked forward to the weekends because she said she met other Sri Lankans there and they exchanged news about Sri Lanka and sometimes listened to gossip about the Sri Lankans living in and around Chicago. Mother said she learned a lot about the way the small Sri Lankan community lived. She didn't want to make too many friends for fear that they would take back news of our family to Sri Lanka.

Mother regarded father's underemployment as an embarrassment and she said she made up stories to say that father did not want the job at Harvard because of the excellent position mother held here in Chicago and also because of my school. I was getting along fine and excelling in my studies that father and she didn't want me to change school. Sometimes she brought home what she cooked there and it tasted delicious father said, though Roshan and I by this time had lost the taste for Sri Lankan food. We preferred the burgers and fries. On weekends when mother was busy and couldn't go to Aunty Rani's, Aunty Rani sent us food. "It's delicious to eat food prepared by someone else," mother used to say while sitting at table and mixing the food with the fingers of her right hand. I imagined her doing the same again.

XXI

My telephone rang late one evening and when I answered it, I heard Uncle Henry's voice on the other end.

"Nelu, get ready to go to court. The police case against that Salgado guy is coming up next month," he said. I could almost see Uncle Henry's smiling face with the telephone pressed against his cheeks. He had done everything possible to find the man who caused the accident to put my mother just seconds away from certain death. But he was not satisfied with that. He wanted to find out the man's intentions in causing the accident. "It will take just half a day, but you better have the whole day set aside for the case. Don't you know, court cases tend to drag on for periods longer than one anticipates."

A cold shiver ran down my spine. My hand holding the receiver began to shake and I felt my heart pounding. Would I want to see my mother's tormentor? My brain stopped working. No word would come out of my mouth. I felt as if my tongue was stuck to the roof of my mouth. Getting no response from me, I heard him say. "You needn't attend if you don't want to. It's difficult, I know. But I intend to be there. I am very keen to see the guy and to find out what he had to achieve from all this."

"I want to come, Uncle Henry." I heard my voice say and was surprised how calm it sounded. "But, I don't know if I can hold my emotions down when I see him and hear him speak."

"I know it's not easy, but don't forget I'll be there to hold your hand," he assured me. He gave me the time and day and said he will take me to the court house. I placed the receiver gently on its hook and walked back to my work. The news of the impending case disquieted me terribly. The events involved in my mother's horrifying story and my reaction to it, stirred echoes in my ears, drawing forth my fears and my empathy. Is there anything else more terrible than being the victim of an attempted murder? Just finding out the man's intentions to harm my mother, the man who my mother says had fallen madly in love with her, bothered me tremendously. Had she given him false hopes? Had she, by her flirtatious looks, raised his hopes so high that he came looking for her and then what happened? What had my mother been up to? I could get the answers to these questions if only I could bundle up enough courage to talk to mother. How could I? The bond between my mother and me was getting firm, but it was still fragile. I didn't want to unsettle it by a quest for answers which would make her to dig into her not so glorious past. I was certain, that it was a past she wanted to get away from. I better tell Uncle Henry not to mention the impending case to my mother until it was all over. Why should we bring back painful memories of the accident—her physical wounds are just beginning to heal and she is enjoying our presence around her.

On the day of the hearing, Uncle Henry took me to the court house. Normally, I would have been chatting with him on anything that I thought would catch his interest. But that morning, seated on the passenger seat of Uncle Henry's car I found I couldn't talk. I cannot explain what got over me, I was in tears most of the time. As we drove past the police station, and observing my unusual silence he said, breaking the silence, "This has become a familiar sight to me now. I've come here half a dozen times." I knew he sensed my fear, my nervousness and most of all my emotions mixed with anger and sadness—anger at the man who did this horrible thing and sadness at mother's plight, being confined to a hospital bed for well over eight weeks now.

Once we passed the police station it didn't take long for us to reach our destination. The courthouse was located just ten minutes from the police station. Uncle Henry drove the car towards the courthouse parking lot. It was early and we had no difficulty in finding a place. Walking towards the white-gray building we noticed the columns along its front. Its heavy urn like light fixture hanging from chains above its ornamented doors appeared in front of our eyes.

"I think this courthouse must have been built at the turn of the century," said Uncle Henry. "This looks like one of the Greek houses of the University of Chicago," he said looking at me trying to get me to say something.

"Maybe both buildings were designed by the same architect," I said agreeing with him. We walked past the small houses around the courthouse which were occupied by lawyers and title companies. We climbed the twenty or so steps leading to the building. Once inside the courthouse we observed many courtrooms which had long, narrow windows and fine furniture, and wood paneling around the bench, on the jury box and along the walls. The ceilings were high giving the rooms a more spacious look than they really had. Uncle Henry pointed out to me the significance of the seating arrangements that showed the symmetry of justice.

"See, the placement of the judge's seat above everybody else; the jury to one side of the judge looking on, waiting to pass judgement." I listened to him making no comment, struck by the awe-inspiring atmosphere that surrounded us. Few people walked along the corridors with us, with grave looks on their faces, silently. The silence around us was broken only by the sound of our footsteps.

We looked around for our lawyer or for Paul Williams, our PI. Seeing neither, we entered the room assigned for our case, and found it almost empty, rightly so; who else would be interested in the case but Uncle Henry and me and those that helped to administer justice?

"That's him—Salgado—in front, seated beside the court appointed lawyer who is going to defend him," Uncle Henry whispered in my ear as we stepped inside. Seeing him, my body went limp, my knees wobbled and my palms felt wet with instant sweat. I felt my heart pumping blood into my head so fast that I felt dizzy. Realizing my difficulty Uncle Henry tightened his hand around mine. How could I sit here and listen to this man tell the court why he wanted to kill my mother? We could see only the profile of his face and his face looked so very familiar. Oh! of course—I'd seen his photograph—the police photograph Uncle Henry showed mother. The real face looked so very different. He was stunningly good looking. He sat there straight-backed and dressed in a grey suit. His face well-shaven and his curly hair combed back, he looked pathetically timid.

"How could a guy like this commit a horrendous act and get himself in deep trouble?" I heard Uncle Henry's voice whispering into Paul Williams' ear, who had just joined us. Paul was immaculately dressed in his three-piece suit.

"Well, desperate people behave horrendously when they are in desperate situations," Paul responded.

The defence lawyer was in coat and tie, his narrow lips pressed together over slightly protruding teeth. He was in a pensive mood. His hair was ruffled. I saw him running his hand through his hair. Maybe he is thinking how to get his defendant out of trouble.

We took our seats behind the state prosecutor James Goodwin. As we were bending to sit, I saw with the corner of my eyes the defendant turning his head and looking back at us. Imagine his audacity, his arrogance, to look at us! Paul Williams took his seat next to Uncle Henry's.

"The eyewitness, Mrs. Peters, is under subpoena, though she is a willing witness. She and her husband are waiting outside in the corridor until they are called in," he told Uncle Henry, releasing his coat button and making himself comfortable on the chair.

"All rise! Justice William Harper." No sooner had we taken our seats we heard the shout of the bailiff. The sound of his loud words still echoes in my ears. There was absolute silence for a second. We all sat down once the judge took his seat.

"People versus Senanka Salgado," the judge announced in a pleasant tone. A pin drop could be heard in the silence when we all listened to the judge giving his standard speech about the purpose of the hearing. Then he adjusted his black robe and while looking at the state prosecutor, James Goodwin said in a firm voice, "I understand that your client is charged with negligent driving with the intention of causing bodily harm to Mrs. Leila Fernandez." A court reporter was taking down every word that came out of the judge's mouth.

"How do you plead, Mr Goodwin?" the judge directed the question at the defence lawyer, still looking at him.

"We plead guilty, Your Honor!"

The defence decision to plead guilty did not come as a surprise to us. The public defender had advised Salgado to cooperate with the state to get a lighter sentence. The state prosecutor and the defendant's court-appointed lawyer approached the bench immediately after the pleading. They conferred with the judge for about five minutes or so and took their seats.

"The court will announce the punishment in two weeks' time," the judge said and stood up to leave the courtroom. We all stood up with him and dispersed once the judge left the room.

"There will be a hearing before the sentencing," Paul said. "There's a defence story that I had not heard yet. Goodwin after speaking with Salgado had arrived at a theory that provocation on Mrs. Fernandez's part had led to the action taken by his defendant. He wants to present this to court to get a lighter sentence for his client. We were taken by surprise at this news. "Don't worry, I'll find out from the state prosecutor," Paul said and walked out of the court room with the state prosecutor.

"It took about three days for Paul to bring the information to Uncle Henry. The news was so astonishing that it opened for Uncle Henry and me a new facet to mother's life in her youth.

"Did you know that your mother had sent Salgado money for an air ticket to come to the United States?" Uncle Henry asked me, the day he broke the shocking news to me. Innocently I responded, "Mother didn't have money and in any case she couldn't have done it without father finding out."

"She borrowed money from me. She said it was for her tuition at library school. This was about a month or so after your arrival in the US. Leila persuaded me to keep it a secret from your father. She never returned the money and I didn't ask her to return the money either," Uncle Henry said. Salgado had given his side of the story to the court-appointed lawyer to prepare his defence briefs.

"Salgado had not been able to make use of the money that Leila sent him because he had been caught by the army for JVP activities and had spent five years in prison. The guy had said that he had written to Leila from his prison cell. He thinks that the army never mailed the letters to her," Uncle Henry continued as I listened with increasing amazement.

"Mrs. Fernandez gave me some contacts in Toronto. I stayed with them for a while and with their help bought fake travel documents and arrived in Chicago," Salgado had said.

"Leila's friends in Toronto had given Salgado Leila's address. On the evening of the day of his arrival in Chicago, the guy had gathered enough courage and had gone to see Leila in her apartment. 'I went unannounced to surprise her. I knocked on her door and when she opened the door, I introduced myself. You should have seen her face then. She was so shocked at seeing me that she almost fainted. We talked till late into the night. I told her of my imprisonment and my escape.' According to Salgado, Leila had been very happy to see him." Every word that came out of Uncle Henry's lips shocked me. At times I didn't know whether to believe him or not. I stopped him and questioned him many times whether he believed the guy's story or whether he was making this up. No, he said, it actually happened, but he reminded me that he was relating to me Salgado's story as told by him to the defence lawyer. Within a few days of his arrival in Chicago, Salgado had found himself a job at the Yellow Cab Company and had been a regular visitor at my mother's apartment. He knew that since he was an illegal visitor to the country he would be deported as soon as the authorities found out about him. So the only way for him overcome that barrier was to marry an American citizen. 'So, I asked her to marry me. It was the easiest and the surest way I could stay in this country,' Salgado had told the police investigator. My mother, at first thinking it was a joke had laughed in Salgado's face. Later, when he persisted and begged her to marry him, not only had she refused but had got angry and thrown him out of her apartment and had asked him never to visit her again. 'She sent me my air fare, provided me with useful contacts in Canada and encouraged me to come to the United States and then she refused to help me. I am stranded. I was furious with her. I think she treated me badly. I was after her money, she said, that I was making use of her—she would have to support me financially. She said she was alone here; her daughter, the only surviving member of her family, had abandoned her. She asked me, if I was not after her money, why a young man like me would want to marry an old woman like her. She just refused to see the picture from my angle. When she closed the door on me, I decided to frighten her and make her change her mind. A few days later I saw her driving back from work. I followed her for some distance and waited until there was no other vehicle in sight. I overtook her on Lake Shore Drive at the exit to Washington Street and just cut my cab in front of her car. She was driving at a considerable speed, maybe sixty miles or so. Though it was around two in the afternoon it was foggy and dark. To avoid my cab she cut towards the center of the road, hit the cement barrier and the vehicle slid and went out of control. I saw her car toppling and landing on its roof. I had absolutely no intention of killing her—I just wanted to scare her.' Salgado had cried while giving the lengthy confession. Seeing no other vehicle in the vicinity he had driven away immediately. He had been afraid that if he was caught he would be deported immediately and deportation he wanted to avoid at any cost. At the police inquiry, Salgado had been reluctant to plead guilty for fear that he would be sent back to Canada from where he sneaked his way to the United States. In the end, however, in exchange for a lighter sentence, he had been persuaded by the court-appointed lawyer to plead guilty for driving dangerously with the intent of causing harm to another driver.

As planned, neither Uncle Henry nor I spoke about the courtroom proceedings, the events that had led to the accident as told by Salgado or their outcome with mother. We decided at the time that mother was in no physical or emotional condition to hear what we had discovered. She was going through enough turmoil in her life that we didn't want to add any more pain to her suffering. As time went on though, we were mystified by her constant silence about the outcome of the police case. She never even inquired after the fate of the young man who caused the accident. Thinking it was for the best, both Uncle Henry and I remained silent on the whole episode.

We did not attend the sentencing hearing which we were informed was held three weeks later. We learned from Paul that Salgado had been sentenced to six years' imprisonment without parole. He was an illegal immigrant serving a prison sentence—now the Immigration and Naturalization Department would hound him.

XXII

It's not the oceans and the continents that distance us from the people we love and care for. It's the restlessness in the mind; the desert waste of secrets and deceptions. These last three months my mother and I had come as close as a mother and a daughter could ever be. But there lurked in my mind—and in my mother's—a secret; a forbidden topic that we both knew had distanced us just a little but enough to question the sincerity of our love. Surely my mother knew that the man who caused the accident had to be tried and convicted? Then why didn't she ever ask us about it? Although Uncle Henry and I had decided not to talk about it with mother, for fear that Salgado's version of the story could upset her, on that morning walking along the hospital corridor I found I couldn't hold out any longer. "I will tell Mom about the trial today," I said to myself. But when I approached her bedside I changed my mind. Fear of losing what I did not yet possess wholly made me suddenly timid.

As I entered the ward I saw the physiotherapists already at work. Two therapists came every morning and evening and helped mother to get her muscles back into action. They made her walk gradually from a half hour to two hours each day until they said she was able to walk without help. Their visits continued for a long time (even after she left the hospital) and mother was tired each time they came and went.

"We'll do it slowly and gently. We don't want to tire you, Leila," I heard the comforting words of one of the therapists as I walked towards mother's bed. "Therapy will take time. But you will be able to walk one day soon," the therapist assured mother.

That morning mother was overly exhausted. Streaks of sweat glistened on her forehead and her cheeks were red. I helped her sit on the bed, legs stretched and her back resting on the pillows. Once she settled comfortably on the bed she gave me that look—the look which I have got accustomed to by now—the look of a pleading child, pleading for love and compassion. I sat beside her trying to think of something to say to distract her from the physical pain she was going through. My mother then pressed her palms against her eyes.

"Oh! I give up! I hate to see them coming through that door," she whispered to me, as they left. But I knew secretly she appreciated what they were doing. We could see the improvement in her movements as she recovered gradually. Mother had gone through most of the long process of recuperation and the doctors were ready to release her. They warned us though that she needed care and that she needed to continue with the physiotherapy.

"Dr. Reynolds told me in the morning that I could go home next Monday and today is still Wednesday! I can't wait here for another week," she said in an almost inaudible voice. I wiped the sweat off her forehead and gently brushed her soft hair. It seemed to me that the few streaks of grey hair I noticed on my first visit to her in the hospital had multiplied tenfold.

"I know, Mom. But then you were here for almost four months. What's another week? It's for your own good, besides I'll come every day."

Just three and a half months ago this hospital atmosphere had been so alien and threatening. Now, it seemed comforting to me. We had grown to appreciate the hospital staff. The young interns who stopped by mother's bedside in the mornings were always cheerful and the nurses were so caring that mother now felt somewhat at home in their presence.

"Last evening, the therapist walked me to the window over there," mother said, pointing toward the far end of the corridor.

"Through that window I saw a glistening line of traffic flowing down the street. That sight reminded me of my apartment. I've been counting the hours since then." I could almost feel mother's eagerness to go out into the world again.

"I am thirsty. Can you hand me that orange, Nelu?" My mother peeled the orange and neatly piled the peels on one side of the plate I placed beside her. Then she offered me some, and ate the rest slowly, putting pieces one by one into her mouth. I watched her enjoying the orange and we both remained silent for a while. There was something I wanted to ask her but that could wait. Mother wiped her lips with the kleenex and placed the plateful of orange peel on the sidetable. Then stroking my hand gently and slowly she said, "Nelu, I thought about this for a long time last night. I think I'll stay with Henry for some time. He's already hired a nurse and a therapist on a daily basis."

I wanted very much to keep her with me but there was no way I could have given her the care she needed. So I was relieved when Uncle Henry had suggested, that she live with him and Aunt Viva, and mother agreed. Mother was not very fond of Aunt Viva. I had always thought mother was jealous of Aunt Viva because Uncle Henry was rich and he provided his wife with all the luxuries that money could buy. She lived in a mansion like house, like a real lady. I admired Aunt Viva. She had a knack of getting Uncle Henry to do things her way while making him think it was his idea. I sometimes wanted to do things just like her. My mother envied her for the same reason. My mother didn't like Aunt Viva's sense of style, she called it the killer style sense. On her few visits to the hospital she had her lips painted blood red and her cheeks rouged in pale rose. My mother must have wondered as I often did, whether she could live with Aunt Viva. But then she was so fond of Uncle Henry and Uncle Henry loved my mother very much. Mother would be well looked after.

XXIII

The bitterness that I had built up towards mother during my adolescence and my young adulthood seemed a thing of the past. What I believed to be the discriminatory attitude of my mother towards my father and me had driven me out of her life. That attitude of mother had fractured our lives to such an unimaginable degree that I never thought I would get closer to my mother ever again. But sometimes, fortunately, the unthinkable suddenly becomes real.

Now here I was by my mother's hospital bed, early on Monday morning, waiting impatiently until the formalities were over to take her home; to take her home to Uncle Henry's. Mother was happy to walk out of the ward yet found it difficult to bid farewell to the hospital staff who took care of her during the last four months, who eventually made it possible for her to walk out of the hospital. They were all there that morning. Far more than any words, the tears of joy in her eyes and the smile on her lips expressed her gratitude.

Uncle Henry pushed the wheel chair while I carried the bag containing mother's few belongings. Uncle Henry lived in a large beautiful house in one of the best residential areas of one of Chicago suburbs. As we entered the development, we noticed some children skating in cul-de-sacs. It looked like an affluent neighborhood but at the same time it appeared to be a friendly community. We saw two women talking over their backyard fence. Uncle Henry drove into the driveway which led to a four car garage. The huge trees surrounding the house were putting out their leaves as if in preparation to shelter the beautiful house from the scorching summer sun. They also gave an atmosphere of the house being located in the middle of a large woody area.

"This seems like an earthly paradise," mother said, stepping into the house holding Uncle Henry's hand. Uncle Henry's house had features that I thought were only found in southern plantation mansions. Its columned entrance and two-story foyer with marble floors and the dramatic curving staircase were unbelievably beautiful.

Aunt Viva stood at the main door to greet mother. She opened another door leading to the large sitting room and stood at the entrance, holding the door open, until we all walked in. A faint smell of roses greeted us as we stepped in. The sitting room was extravagantly furnished making it picture perfect. A grand piano gleamed in one corner.

"Mom can play the piano again," I said, walking behind Uncle Henry, holding mother's hand. Uncle Henry carried mother's bag and walked through the sitting room and the corridor to the large room prepared for mother. It was beautifully furnished and spotlessly clean.

"I ordered yellow roses to decorate Leila's room," Aunty Viva said, gently caressing the vase of flowers that was placed on the dressing table. Mother commented that Aunt Viva had gone out of her way to make the room beautiful for her.

"I wanted Leila to feel happy here. I feel I am in charge of Leila's happiness. Remember you are not our guest, you are family." Aunt Viva smiled with pride as she stepped onto the balcony. A tall rubber plant stood between the room and the corridor that led to the balcony. We walked towards the bedroom window and stood there for awhile. It had a glorious view of the golf course on one side and a slow flowing stream on the other.

"This house has been empty for too long," Uncle Henry said. He led me to the adjoining room. In between the two rooms was the bathroom. "Mom, this is like a spa. You are going to enjoy the whirlpool and the steam shower!" I said admiring the large tub.

"This is yours, Nelu," Uncle Henry said as we walked to the adjoining room. Its walls were painted in pink. A beautiful rug was spread at the foot of the queen-sized bed, over the smoothly polished hardwood floor. Aunt Viva had been so thoughtful she had lined a few bottles of expensive perfume on the dresser as well. A chair near the window that overlooked the golf course was filled with stuffed animals.

"Uncle Henry, this is very kind of Aunt Viva," I said picking up one of the teddy bears.

"We know you'll spend more time here now than at Lake Shore Drive!" he said, his eyes glowing with happiness.

"It's been lonely here since Shiran and Maya left. We will be looking forward to see Nelu moving in here anytime soon!" Aunt Viva joined. I liked Aunt Viva and I hoped that mother would get along with her. Just then we heard the telephone ring and Aunt Viva went out to answer the phone. Uncle Henry looked at his watch.

"It's almost noon. Leila must be hungry. Have lunch and take a nap, Leila. Don't tire yourself out. It's been an exciting morning for you—for all of us!" he said rubbing his palms together, and leading us to the kitchen. We walked through the TV room in which one wall was covered with a large screen. Aunt Viva was still talking to someone on the phone. She listened and murmured something and put the receiver down and headed into the kitchen where a Sri Lankan maid was preparing the mid-day meal. Next to the kitchen, in the family dining room, the table was laid for lunch.

"This reminds me of the days in Kandy. A true Sri Lankan lunch—yellow rice and *seeni sambol*!" mother said sitting down at table. It was a luxury to have a live-in-maid attending to your needs and washing the dishes after the meal.

After lunch Uncle Henry said he had to attend to some work and went to his office. After he had gone, I helped mother to get into bed and arranged her things in the room. By the time I'd finished hanging her clothes in the closet, she had gone to sleep. She was either exhausted or contented, or both.

I walked out of the room quietly to have a chat with Aunt Viva, but she too had gone to her room to rest. So I walked aimlessly into the luxurious sitting room. I thought of the first time we came to Uncle Henry's house. That was almost eighteen years ago. Roshan and I were shocked at the riches of our cousins, Shiran and Maya. Shiran was tall and dark and very good-looking at the time. Maya was pretty, lively, with a quick sense of humor and the air and manner of someone who was used to having her own way all the time. I liked Shiran better but I thought at the time that Maya was more fun. Aunt Viva was not beautiful but she made an effort to look attractive. I was stuck by the amount of jewelry Aunt Viva wore. A jingling charm bracelet adorned her left wrist and there were an abundance of gold chains around her neck. Many tiny diamonds shone on her ear lobes and the colorful rings on her fingers gave her an ancient, almost Turkish look, as if some Sultan had showered her with expensive gifts. When I remarked this to mother later, she laughed enviously and said, "Well, the Sultan is Uncle Henry!"

I remember Maya took me to her room that day. I'd never seen that kind of extravagance before. I was afraid that if I touched anything I would stain or break or in some way contaminate the fragrant atmosphere in her lovely room. It was not only the size of the room but the luxury and the elegant furnishings that went with the size that made my mouth open with surprise. "Wow!" I exclaimed, I couldn't help myself. She had her own stereo system and a stack full of CDs. There were dozens of cassettes lying on the floor. As soon as we entered the room, she switched on her CD player and lay on her large bed, with her hands on her chest and her eyes fixed on the ceiling. I remember telling Roshan and laughing on our way back home, at the way Maya spoke English that day. She used 'American teen-girl speech,' with its fixations on reported speech, 'so she gives' and 'I am like,' and 'he goes' and its stock vocabulary of accompanying grimaces and gestures. She was using less language than gestures to communicate. After almost every sentence she said, 'this was really cool'. She also did the teen thing of climbing half an octave at the end of every sentence. She dragged out vowels for emphasis. Maya is changed now. She went to Law School, married a young man of Dutch descent, whom she met in Law School and both are now working for a law firm in Los Angeles. Shiran is the doctor in the family. Shiran is the son my mother would have liked to have. He married his Caucasian girl friend from high school days and now lives in New York.

Thinking of my cousins whom I hadn't seen for years, I walked towards the basement where Uncle Henry entertained his guests after dinner. A pool table was there in the center of the large area, and there was a bar with row after row of bottles of liquor bearing fancy names, neatly arranged on a shelf fixed on one wall.

A sliding door from the basement led to the tennis court and the swimming pool. I walked out into the open backyard. There the freshly mowed lawn, covered with soft green grass added to the peaceful and beautiful atmosphere of the surroundings. This was ideal for mother. Walking here can be therapeutic. The mind stops worrying when one's senses take over the nature, beautifying all that's around you. I was overwhelmed by the smell of apple blossoms that drifted my way from a pair of trees in the backyard. The purple-blue wisteria flowers amidst the maple trees created a picture that appeared to have been touched by a magic brush. Here mother could sit and read, and listen to Mozart piano music that she loves so much. I must get her a Walkman; she'd like that.

While admiring the peaceful surroundings that afternoon I thought of my brother. We were two young hopefuls when we first visited Uncle Henry. "If Uncle Henry can make it in America and have all these riches, so can I!" Roshan said that day. That made mother's eyes shine with hope. "I will study and be a doctor and doctors mint money," he said. "But then what about me?" when I asked Roshan, I thought he was teasing me when he said, "You are only a girl Nelu ! You'll have to marry a doctor or a developer to enjoy these luxuries. Girls are not supposed to work to get rich. They just marry into riches!" He then looked at me with a twinkle in his eyes. What has happened since yesterday when we were young?

'Could my mother live happily in this manor-house with Aunt Viva?' the thought crossed my mind many times. My mother would have to cultivate a complete new style of living. We, Roshan and I, were raised both in Brunswick and in Evanston in a three bedroom ranch house. The garage was detached from the house. I remember early mornings in winter months, my father had to walk on two feet of freshly fallen snow to open the garage door manually. The only luxury my brother and I had enjoyed was the ancient pool table left behind by the previous occupants in the basement that was cluttered with all the heating and water storage equipment. I saw no alternative, for my mother couldn't live by herself as she needed constant care.

XXIV

"Ever since Shiran and Maya left for college this big house seemed empty," Aunt Viva told mother and me one evening. "Now I look forward to Nelu's visits. I wish you would come more often," she said as she smiled with me.

"More often? I am here every weekend Aunt Viva! In fact I wait for Fridays to head in this direction," I said showing my appreciation of her kindness. She spent her time alone in the big house, occasionally going out with her few American friends but most of the time entertaining Uncle Henry's clients at home.

"When I talk with you, I feel I am with Maya again," she said, flattering me. I knew she liked talking to me, especially about my friends and my students at the university. I liked Aunt Viva and got along well with her. It's been almost a year since my mother moved in with them and I have heard no complaints from mother so far. We all enjoyed each other's company and we had a good time. I visited my mother almost every weekend which gave me the opportunity to be with family again.

Due to her neck injury, mother still had difficulty in keeping her head erect for more than an hour or so. She spoke of an occasional sharp, stabbing pain in her back and frequent headaches. The doctors prescribed medication for a long period of time. The therapist continued to come; she came once in two days or so and worked with mother.

Some days, when mother wished to go out into the sun, I walked with her along the stream by the golf links behind Uncle Henry's house and sat with her under the shade of the pine tree.

"This is a good place to contemplate life. It's soothing to watch the running water," my mother said that evening. It was October and it was a fall evening. We felt a chill nudging through the last traces of summer's warmth, and the leaves hinted of changing color.

"The signs can't be missed," mother said pointing at the maple leaves turning their color. "I've seen this spectacle for over two decades and I still like it."

There was no one else on the stretch of land around us. The maple trees, the elms and the white pines hung thickly over the path of the stream. There were frogs on damp logs enjoying the cool of the fall evening. Occasionally, we heard the sound of a fish jump, though we rarely saw one. There were birds, including several red-winged birds and a couple of cardinals. Except for the occasional bird song and the gurgling of the running stream, it was absolutely quiet around us.

There were wild flowers along the bank of the stream, nourished by the natural compost made of the fallen maple leaves. The soft wind made the flowers sway and also kept the insects away. We sat on the soft ground and watched the slow flowing water. I leaned back against the maple tree and looked at mother. In the fading sunlight her face appeared almost golden and her grey hair let loose on her shoulders shone like a patch of silvery cloud. My palms felt the warmth of the earth. Was it because of the sunlight pouring into the clearing where we sat? My mother still not saying a word, looked at me, her dark brown eyes softly laughing and put her hand on my shoulder and sighed. We both looked at the squirrel that darted down from one of the white pines that lined the stream.

My mother looked at me again, a question in her eyes? I held her hand and said, "I love you Mom. You are the best Mom in the world." I wanted to say this to my father so many times when he needed comforting, but I could not summon up enough courage those days. The words, 'I love you, Dad,' never came out of my lips. It seems strange, I could still remember the times when I sat on my father's lap and pulled hairs off his chest, stroked his unshaven rough cheeks in the early mornings. As I grew up and became a teenager I kept a respectful distance from him. Nobody asked me to but I did it anyway. Why do we go apart as we grow older—when we most need our parents? Is it because we get so cocky with the independence we feel that we think we can, by ourselves, handle life's problems that come our way?

XXV

"Let's go and see our old house today," mother suggested when I went to see her one day.

"It's been a long time, Mom! I've almost forgotten how to get there." Aunt Viva came to our help. She drew a map of the area and showed me the shortest route to get to Evanston. After driving for about half an hour we reached Evanston. From there on it was not difficult to find Sheridan, our former street. "There it is—the iron address sign 280 Sheridan," mother said pointing to a large house.

"That's not our house," I said and drove looking for traces of the old simple ranch house—but all we could see was a big new house rising on the site. What was left of our house was the iron address sign that Roshan nailed on to the oak tree in the front yard.

"Isn't it sad, Mom, all that's left of the house that we owned in America is the old oak tree?" We were sad and shocked. Like all the other simple houses along Sheridan Lane our house has become a tear-down. Deemed out-of-date, our three bedroom ranch house with a neat brick front is valued not for the house but for the land where it stood.

"We would have made a million dollars, Mom, if only we had held on to the property!" I told mother.

I reminded mother how she and I used to walk along the tree-lined streets in the area, while father followed us on his bicycle.

"During one summer evening, when the temperature was 90 degrees for the sixth day in a row and when everybody complained of humidity, your father rode his bicycle down this avenue," mother said as we drove along Sheridan Lane. "His face turned purple from the heat and his shirt was soaked with perspiration. He must have really enjoyed those cycle rides."

"We can hardly recognise our old street," mother remarked. We saw the new houses that had been built with two and three car garages, and courtyards with ceremonial entrances.

Our house had low ceilings, and small rooms in an L-shaped construction on the land of suburban Chicago. It was warm and intimate as our family seemed then. We had great times there. My parents bought it a year after we moved into Chicago for fifty-eight thousand dollars. My mother liked the fireplace in the living room and father liked the wooded vacant lot next door, where every thicket seemed full of mystery and where tall horsetails grew. The woods, at once inviting and forbidden for us as children, are all gone replaced by mansion-like houses. The apple tree planted in the front yard had been high enough for me to climb and grass covered the entire lot. The oak tree in the back was so tall it gave shade to the back of the house in the afternoons. Those trees are gone now. Tall trees grew along the road leading to our housing development. During spring and summer, these trees flowered and the flowers glistened in the morning sun and hung in clusters like golden grapes. The cherry blossoms took one's breath away.

When we sold our house and moved into the condominium in Hyde Park, I had felt a great loss. I felt secure at the time by small rooms but I missed the alleys, ravines and the stream behind our house. We had enjoyed rural life close to big city Chicago. Now looking at the big houses on either side of Sheridan, my mother said, "Small isn't beautiful any more, if it ever was." I agreed.

When we returned home that evening, to our surprise we saw Uncle Henry seated on the patio with mother's lawyer, Jeffrey Ashland.

"Oh! No. No more lawyers please!" I said helping mother to get out of the car. About six months ago Uncle Henry talked to me about how the litigation with the insurance company was progressing or rather not progressing. It's almost two years since the accident and nothing seemed to have happened. I had almost forgotten about it. On the advice of Ashland we filed a negligence action against the Yellow Cab Company whose driver was convicted of causing the accident. Mother was seeking damages for her injuries and the loss of her job.

"How was the drive?" Uncle Henry inquired getting up from his seat and walking towards us.

"Nelu took me to see our old house. The whole area is unrecognizable. If we had our house now, it would have given us a million dollars!" mother said, laughing.

"Jeffrey here will get you that million dollars," Uncle Henry said, looking at Ashland. We all sat on the patio that evening and over a nice hot cup of tea, Ashland talked about the case he had filed on mother's behalf against the Yellow Cab Company and the insurance company that represented them.

"The case is coming up next month and we have some preparation to do," Ashland said looking at mother. "We have to convince the jury that Mrs. Fernandez is still suffering from the injuries caused by the auto accident. We also have to show that the loss of your job at the library was due to the accident. I need to give convincing medical evidence to the jury to give a verdict in our favor. To do this I need not only your most recent medical records but also I have to prepare your testimony. I have to see that the way you present your story and answer the questions put to you by the defence, would capture the sympathy of the jury."

Hearing this, my mother became extremely nervous. She looked at Uncle Henry and remained silent.

"Don't worry Leila, Jeffrey will come here to coach you. And in any case I will be around when Jeffrey is preparing you on your testimony. It's to our advantage to do a thorough job of this," Uncle Henry assured mother.

A week after the meeting, Ashland came for a few days and sat with mother, coaching her how best to answer the questions put to her by the counsel representing the Yellow Cab Company and their insurance company. Sitting with them one evening, listening to mother's weak voice answering questions put to her by Ashland, I imagined the picture of the courthouse. First we would have to go through the metal detectors, then past the guards at the door and then take the slow elevator rides with witnesses, criminals, lawyers, jurors and victims and their relatives. Do we need to do this again? It's hard to think of a logical reason to go to courts other than the huge sum of money that the lawyer was asking which would equate mother's agony. I saw the picture of a young woman judge walking to the podium of the courtroom and taking the grand chair. I saw my mother at the witness stand, old and feeble, grown older during the last two years, showing more than her sixty years. She was answering questions put to her by the lawyers, with confidence but in a very soft voice, that the judge had to ask her several times to speak a little louder.

"Mrs. Fernandez, are you able to enjoy the same quality of life now, as you enjoyed before the accident?" I thought I heard Ashland ask. Mother in response looked down at her hands and remained silent.

"When you were released from hospital, the doctors ordered you to continue with the physical therapy and the medication. If you can't afford to pay for them, that pain in your back is going to continue indefinitely, isn't it?" I saw my mother's eyes getting filled with tears.

"No more questions, Your Honor!" Ashland walked to his seat. It was the defence counsel's turn to question mother.

"Mrs. Fernandez, it's been over two years after the accident. You still experience disorientation and dizziness?"

"Yes, I do," was the meek answer.

"You are still subject to uncontrollable pains in the back?"

"Yes, especially when I am tired," my mother's voice was barely audible.

The practice sessions went on for a few days. The day before the case was to be heard I was at Uncle Henry's. Uncle Henry came home early from work that evening.

"I've had the best news for a long time," he said entering the patio where mother, Aunt Viva and I were seated. He took his seat next to Aunt Viva and announced, "There's no case tomorrow!"

"What?" I heard my voice.

"Well, the insurance company has offered to pay the amount of money Jeffrey had asked rather than contest the case. You are richer by almost half a million dollars, Leila!"

My mother's eyes widened in surprise. "Why did he put me through all those practice sessions?" was the first question she asked.

Silence engulfed us for a moment. I didn't know whether to rejoice or be cynical and dampen the high spirits of Uncle Henry. This certainly was not the way I wanted mother to get rich for her to settle down to a comfortable retiring life. The immense physical as well as emotional pain she went through still lingers fresh in my mind. How can we measure in dollars the burning tears that oozed out of her eyes when she was in pain? I watched my mother, her eyes were fixed on the white pines at the far end of the front yard. The pines swayed gently with the evening breeze and we all felt the cool air around us. My mother turned her face towards Uncle Henry, her eyes and lips together expressing a grateful smile.

"Most things one wants in life, come when they are no longer needed," she said softly.

XXVI

"There are communities in this country that one can retire into—quite comfortably—if one has the means," mother said one day when we were getting ready to drive into Chicago.

What was I hearing? I looked at mother with a questioning look. She had turned her face away from me and didn't say anything more.

During the last few months whenever I visited my mother, I drove her to Chicago to do some sightseeing, shopping or to the theater. Chicago remained as my mother's favorite American city. It was to Chicago that my parents first arrived in the United States back in the seventies and maybe, the first impression of the Windy City had left a memorable impression on my mother's mind. She had lived there for almost half her lifetime.

She loved it when I drove through Chicago during Christmas time when the city glowed with lights, and the shops filled with music. My mother and I understood what it was to be in Chicago in Christmas time.

"It's cold—bitter cold—that cold wind blowing from the lake, but who would think of the cold when our eyes are filled with the magnificent lights on Michigan Avenue—the golden mile of America! Oh! I love to watch the dim yellow street lamps behind the gently falling snowflakes," mother said as we drove down Michigan Avenue. When spring came we drove down Lake Shore Drive up to the aquarium, parked the car in a nearby lot, walked to the lake shore and watched the joggers. Or we would sit on the steps leading to the aquarium and marvel at the Chicago skyline and the constant flow of traffic along Lake Shore Drive, both ways. We would have done this many, many times, but both of us never got tired of sitting there—sometimes we spent the time talking, sometimes we just sat there contemplating on life.

"Chicago is at play in summer," my mother would say and laugh watching the sunbathers on Oak Street beach and sail boats on Lake Michigan. On days when there was a baseball game at Wrigley Field, the roads would be crowded. On a hot summer day we sipped iced-tea at a Cedar Street outdoor cafe.

"It is so gratifying to sit out and enjoy the Chicago summer," mother told me, her face beaming with happiness.

"It seems like one long celebration." I agreed. It seemed like a happy time for survivors of brutally cold winters to cherish the loveliness of the city.

One summer day, I walked with mother along the sidewalks just northwest of downtown where the Gold Coast Art Fair was held, featuring the works of over three hundred artists—mostly painting and sculpture. She loved these walks and enjoyed herself looking at the exhibits on display, giving me the satisfaction of seeing my mother living without a care in this world. We listened to the Chicago Symphony Orchestra when they presented their open air performances at Ravinia, in suburban Highland Park. My mother loved to listen to the music of the great masters. She never let me buy tickets to these concerts for they were expensive and she had money.

"It is my treat," she would say handing over the money for the tickets.

I also took mother to the Art Museum many times for that was and still remains as one of my favorite places. We spent hours watching the museum's collection of Impressionist art. Once there was an exhibition of a collection of sculpture from India, the Himalayas and Southeast Asia. The sculpture were chiseled from sandstone as well as delicately crafted in bronze, copper, silver and gold. My mother stood there for an unusually long time and admired the images of the gods Shiva and Vishnu and the elegant seated Indra.

"The first time we came here, it was on my forty-fifth birthday. That visit was your father's gift for me. He spent the whole morning explaining the Southeast Asia collection that was on loan from the British Museum." Mother's voice sounded faint. Her eyes get filled with tears easily these days when she talked of father.

We went to the museum cafeteria to rest our feet and to find ourselves a drink. My mother liked hot chocolate, I got myself a lemon tea and an English muffin. Halfway through the drink my mother's mood changed, she became quiet and pensive. Thinking that she was tired and that memories of father were weighing over her head, I remained silent. I broke the muffin in two, left a piece on mother's plate and ate mine slowly. After a period of eight minutes or so a smile lighted my mother's face again.

"I've been thinking for some time now, Nelu. I will be independent. I'll have health care as long as I want it, when I need it. You and Henry and Viva are doing so much for me. If I stay like this I am going to continue to be spoiled for the rest of my life." I noticed that my mother had been struggling to tell me her plans of moving into a retirement community. She had hinted at this on several occasions before and she had chosen to tell me her wish when we were away from Uncle Henry's house.

"I am not talking of living alone," she told me. "And I didn't make this decision lightly. I know I still need the therapy and the pain in my back and the headaches continue to trouble me. But I am ready to move on. I have the means now. I do need my own place. I do need to do my own thing, some time to read and some time to think."

Who would understand the desire of an elderly parent to have both independence and security? What's my mother talking about now? She has four siblings living in this country and a daughter with her feet firmly on the ground. Why should mother want to move into a retirement community and spend her last few years there? My mother never ceases to amaze me! With tact, so as not to let mother feel that I had dismissed her suggestion without giving it serious thought, I reminded mother that back in Sri Lanka we used to call these retirement communities 'Homes for the Aged' and those Homes managed either by the government or the Catholic Church were meant only for the poor. No child with any self-respect would let a parent go to a Home for that would be a stigma, not only on the family but on the future generations as well. "Oh! He is a doctor but his grandmother spent the last few years of her life in a Home for the Aged!" that's what people would say.

"Nelu, you should read this article," my mother told me one day handing me a magazine, "There is a good write-up about a retirement community that had come up in the outskirts of Springhill." My mother was persistent. She, very gently, was presenting her case to me. She had to win me over first. Uncle Henry . . . ? she would manage him with my assistance. I read the article. It all sounded very logical and practical but I could not let my mother move into a retirement community. In America, old age is regarded as a raw deal, not as a universal fate—not as something that everybody has to face whether rich or poor. It's a narcissistic attitude. I think that's why the Americans do not want the elderly around, they embarrass them, like cripples or the terminally ill. Banished to the margins, they perpetuate the illusion that our lives are permanent and not just transient things. I had shut the idea out of my mind until one day I happened to talk to my friend Lindy about it.

"True, it would be the culmination of Americanization of your family, but then when you have the means why should you be a burden on others? Why shouldn't you let your mother have her wishes in the last few years of her life? If she feels comfortable living in a senior community why should you let her pass her days alone? She can make friends. Everybody is new there looking out for companionship—just like the American immigrants of old days looking out for friends." Lindy sounded very logical. Her views somehow convinced me that living in a retirement community might be good for mother. The more I thought about it, the more appealing the idea seemed to me. So I did some research on the subject and came up with a few addresses and information on several communities in and around Michigan, Illinois and Indiana. I somehow managed not to utter a word of this to Uncle Henry for fear of offending him.

I persuaded Lindy to join me on a fine summer day just to go and see one of these places. We were heading for Kendal, a continuing-care retirement community, in a suburb of Springfield. Lindy's grandfather had spent his last few years there.

"Mom will be sixty one years old this October," I told Lindy as we drove along the highway towards Springfield. "She's already in a fragile state of health. She needs constant care which I think a retirement community would be able to provide better than any of us," I was trying to justify my efforts to help mother. It was mother's idea to move into a retirement community.

After passing the Springfield airport, we drove up to the main building along a winding road past semi-detached cottages, much like the condominiums we see at ski resorts. The only detail that gave us a clue about the building's purpose was a row of electric carts and wheelchairs at the front entrance.

I let Lindy talk with the manager of Kendal, a man named Jonathan Kemper who outlined for us the financial structure of the community. We had to pay what was called an entrance fee which was fairly steep, in the range of 80,000 to 300,000 dollars depending on the number of rooms one desired—and then a monthly maintenance that was somewhere between 1500 and 2500 dollars. The entrance fee was non-refundable, so there was no resale value, but to compensate for that one received an all-inclusive life-care contract, medical care for the rest of your life, no matter what one's needs would be.

"This looks very reasonable to me," I told Lindy after examining the financial implications.

"I think the management takes a gamble. The longer the seniors live, the larger the management's losses," Lindy said thoughtfully.

I looked around me and thought that mother would fit right into this setting without difficulty. As in the rest of America, everyone there used first names—we heard them talking of recent happenings in the world around them as well as on the international scene.

"Nelu, I think I see Jeanne Westlake over there," Lindy had spotted one of our teachers from Brunswick High School enjoying hot dogs and baked beans with another retiree. We knew her as a lively, white-haired disciplinarian; authoritative, outspoken and brisk. As if recognizing us, she stared at us with curious eyes. We quickly turned away, shaken—how quickly she had aged! The seniors looked healthy and happy as if they were enjoying themselves. They went around the premises as if they had no care in this world and I told myself, 'Why not? They had earned this!' If it weren't for their shaky hands and the tremor in their voices, they wouldn't even seem old.

I told Lindy about the old Sri Lankan custom by which parents live with the eldest or the youngest son's family. That was one reason why the parents' property was handed over to the eldest or the youngest son, so that the parents could continue living in their familiar surroundings. Young ones would bring the old parents into their circle and would make them feel wanted by seeking their advice.

The manager took us around the complex. Kendal seemed like an elderly paradise to me. The visiting areas were light and sunny. There was a wood-working shop, a crafts room, an art studio for those who were interested. There was a cafe too. The bulletin board near the cafe listed numerous group activities, barbecues, movies, lectures by visiting celebrity scholars, and Saturday-night concerts by the resident pianist. It looked more like a summer camp to us.

"These communal activities offer the seniors a whole new life," our guide reminded us. As we thanked the guide and left

Kendal, I shared with Lindy something that I read in the promotional brochure issued by Kendal. It was the reply an elderly woman had given, when asked how she felt about moving into the 'last place'.

"It's a new chapter in life, like reading the last chapter in an exciting book. You don't want to end it."

XXVII

"It's a cliche to say that when you are at peace with yourself, you look beautiful, whatever your age is. That's what I am right now," my mother told me one evening as I walked out with her on to the gardens behind Kendal. It's inspirational enough just to hear her views on aging.

"As I get older," she said, "I hope that mentally I can gracefully replace what I cannot see in the mirror."

"You mean replace your beautiful face with peaceful thoughts? Is that possible, Mom?" I asked.

"Of course, that's what I am trying to do. I am trying not to bemoan the loss of my beauty to age. Life approaching seventy is going to be the best part of my life. I'll be sixty-six this year." It must be difficult though to look back on so many of the bad things that happened to her. She shook her head thoughtfully, "I am really happy now," she said and held my hand. Despite the glimpses of so many disappointments, she was philosophical about getting older. The gold necklace around her neck which had been there ever since I can remember, didn't hide the lines there; it actually highlighted them. The crow's feet at the outer corners of her eyes were very noticeable, in spite of the creams she applied faithfully every morning and night.

It's been five years since my mother moved into Kendal. At the beginning, almost every weekend I visited my mother there. I know she looked forward to my visits. She is happy there she says, but she misses our intimate talks.

Everything happens for the best they say. The best thing that happened because of mother's accident was the way mother and I gravitated towards each other—in a way it had never happened before. We laugh together now—not just a polite chuckle or an insincere smile as we did before—but loud laughter which sound happy and free of tension. There were times during my adolescent days when I could not recognize mother's laughter if I did not see it coming out of her lips. When we laugh now, it's a symbol of our togetherness; a sign that I had made it this far in America and that, all of our dreams are not shattered. We have suffered together; the blemishes are there; the hidden bruises that wounded our hearts which nobody else but the two of us can see.

"How come you know so much about me?" Mother asked me, on one of my frequent visits there. Under the dim light, in her bedroom, her narrow brown eyes looked amused as if she knew the answer and were testing me to see if I did.

"I find you fascinating, Mom," I said. "I've been listening to your stories these last few years and now I think I know more of you than you think. Do you realize that you are the most incredible person I've known?"

She smiled tenderly and we sat quietly for a moment, holding hands and smiling at each other. Was she trying to see how much of her was in me? We had been so far apart during the last few years in our lives that each of us needed time to get to know one another. Your mother looks wonderful, everyone said. Except for those horrible years we spent in Chicago—our lives had been wonderful. During my childhood days back in Sri Lanka I cannot remember a day when mother complained. My mother lived a life of style, full of activity and she possessed a will of iron but after the accident and the series of operations that followed, she now unfortunately lacked calcium in her bones and was diagnosed as having calcium deficiency leading to osteoporosis. Arthritis followed with a vengeance along with hypertension, heart murmurs and little blackouts here and there. She seemed shorter by six inches and is now slightly hunched.

"Your hair is greying and is thinning out," she said studying me. The look in her eyes when she speaks is tender.

"Mom, I came to take you to the Tibetan temple. Let's go and walk in the temple garden," I suggested wishing to shift the conversation from where it was heading. Mother liked the visits to the temple. She said walking there in the garden which in her mind was like walking in a circular path of a labyrinth, brought a peaceful state of mind to her. It helped her to concentrate on prayers for meditation.

"I find it very healing," she said. "I seem to have a need to move along. Do you remember the times when we moved furniture in our Hyde Park apartment, Nelu?" she laughed reminding me of those crazy days. "Moving is a form of relaxation for me. I can't sit in one place and meditate." I also think walking helps to focus the mind and slows breathing, which can induce a peaceful state of mind. I appreciate it too and took mother to the temple.

During one of my visits, on a peaceful spring evening my mother and I talked into the late evening. I sat on her bed rather than on the chair by the window overlooking the golf course. The conversation inevitably turned to my brother. Despite all the things we have worked out, how we relate to my brother remains the one thing that still draws a rift between us. Mothers love their sons more and get daughters to do the house work, I have heard. This was true when it came to my mother. When mother got pregnant and had Roshan, the longed-for baby boy, she told me, she fell in love with her son straightaway.

"Mothers do fall in love with their sons," she said. "I've seen it happen to my friends too," she told me. Once the baby boy is born the husband is left out, abandoned in the cold! Thinking back as to what happened those days, I think my mother was in love with Roshan until he said, "No," and walked away from her. It's easy for me to say—but this was what devastated my mother. Mother's overflowing passions had found an outlet in her adoration for Roshan. The unfulfilled dreams and desires of parents affect their children, I have read some psychologist say somewhere. I was certain my mother's frustrations of not finding her expectations in my father affected Roshan, in that she expected the world of Roshan in return for all the love she gave him. So my mother let Roshan walk all over her ever since he was a child and she disciplined me. I am grateful to her for that discipline made me what I am today. Did my mother spoil and then destroy my brother's life? I ask the question many times but I fail to come up with an answer. I decided that I was not going to challenge my mother's views and waste the happy, short time we enjoy with each other. I want to believe that I have made peace with my mother and my past. I never stop feeling that I want to make things up to my mother, make up for Roshan's failures and the loss of my father. Perhaps this is how I am easing my own guilt of enjoying the life that my parents made possible for me in the country I have come to call my own.

My father is only a distant memory to me now. Sometimes, I cannot remember what his face looked like. When mother talked of him, I tried to picture him. I could only see a faded photograph—sadness has taken away the sharp features off his face. I remember he could never say, "No," to my mother—no matter how expensive her requests were. If mother wanted to spend money on face creams, perfumes, shoes, it was fine with him. He was always eager to please her; to see her pleased gave him satisfaction. Like most men—I remember father couldn't do anything without mother's help. He could barely find his own socks in his own dresser drawer without her help or find a tie to match the shirt he was wearing. I think of those painful days when mother and father argued a lot, but then those who fought a lot often loved each other very much—if not why should they fight if they didn't care? I always thought my father loved mother more than anyone else in the world. The women in the family were smarter than him, he observed on several occasions. They were cheerful, outgoing, seemed more American somehow. Mother read hints about fashion in women's magazines and applied them to her person with seriousness and appeared formidable. After our arrival in Chicago my mother became headstrong and independent and at times I thought she frightened my father.

I often think that my father must have wondered what had happened to her baby girl; his young daughter now changed into a very American woman. I think my father did not always approve of the things I did in my growing-up days. Back in Sri Lanka, I was sent for *Bharat Natyam* lessons and piano lessons to turn me into an elegant and an accomplished young lady. I gave up dancing and music and instead, father heard me sing Celine Dion and Richard Marx. I was by no means as womanly or tender as my father's sisters had been at my age in the wistful days of his adolescence. I wished to be able to help him and mother financially—since I was a good student—I was certainly brighter than most of my class mates in school. But I am certain that my father would have regretted that I was not the daughter of his dreams. I still recall when talking with my friends over the phone when I used trendy phrases like, 'it's neat,' and, 'Oh yeah, cool' and raised our voices and if father happened to walk past me, he would look at me with a funny smile on his face and bend his head down and quicken his pace.

"Femininity isn't what I thought it meant to be," said father one day listening to a conversation I had with a friend of mine. He failed to understand that that was my way of surviving high school in a city that was both native and alien to me.

"Women now-a-days shout, spit, smoke and sit with their legs apart," father uttered in a disgusted mood after my friend left. Mother lay stretched on the couch and didn't even bother to move. I have often heard him blaming mother for the kind of woman I have become.

XXVIII

"When my day comes let me go in peace, knowing that you are in good hands," my mother told me one morning as we sat watching the couples holding hands and passing us by the fountain in Grant Park. There would not have passed a single day, without my mother reminding me that it was time to get married and settle down. This was one of her dearest wishes she wanted to see fulfilled before she died, she told me on numerous occasions. I listened to her without interrupting her thoughts and could never gather up enough courage to tell her of the disappointment I had in love.

My mother, like most Sri Lankan mothers I knew, wanted us to make friends with white American children.

"If we wanted you to mix with Sri Lankan children we didn't have to bring you all this way. This is America—so adapt yourselves to the American way of life—the best way to do that is to make friends with your classmates," she advised Roshan and me during our high school days. She encouraged us not only to be friends with white American children, she even encouraged us to marry white Americans.

"It's very important that you marry a white American for that's the path that will lead you to where power is. Integration is marrying into the powerful majority community. Integration is the best remedy for racial harmony," she said and never talked of preserving identities or remembering our roots. She just wanted to see us comfortable in the new world we have made our own.

"Why do you remain single? Haven't you met anybody whom you like still? Why won't you get married?" she had directed these questions at me not once but many, many times. I cannot tell her about Sanjeev, however friendly I was with mother. I feel I cannot give her that satisfaction of saying, 'I told you so!' Instead, I tell my mother that I have chosen a life with a promising career, a career that I find fulfilling. I tell her that there are virtually more than a million single or divorced women in their thirties in America and I am no exception. Then, my mother's eyes widen and her head shakes in disapproval and she tells me, "Your generation—they are all mad. We shouldn't have brought you here!"

My mother thinks I talk too much and too loud and waste my life in libraries.

"You are a born bookworm," she told me once. What does she want of me? This is the life I chose for myself and I like it. Isn't this the life father wanted for himself and failed to find his way up to it. If this was good for my father and that was what you yearned for him, why are you grudging it to me, Mom? Sometimes, I still cannot understand her attitude, her double standards, but I dare not open my mouth for fear of offending her. I dare not open an argument that would lead to unpleasantness.

My mother thinks that my life is so programmed, that each day begins with the counting of the number of calories that should be consumed for the day, and most importantly the number of pages read and written.

"Your life is so dull and empty," she says and compares mine with the overflowing fulness of the life led by my cousins, Shiran and Maya.

One Sunday morning, while sitting on the aquarium steps and reading out loud a *Chicago Tribune* women's page article on, Women pursuing careers sacrificing their lives, I noticed my mother's eyes welling up with tears.

"Mom, what's wrong?" I inquired throwing the paper on the step. Suddenly overcome by the contents of the article I read of the women in the academia growing old and living lonely lives with books to hang on to, she blurted out, "I just don't want you to spend your whole life alone."

"Please, not again, Mom," I pleaded with her not to open a conversation which led to the question of my marriage, but to no avail.

I fully realize that it's hard for my mother—married at twenty-three, pregnant soon after, raised two kids—to understand what she sees as my stubbornly prolonged singleness. Ever since I turned twenty-two and ended my college education, she'd been the eager one to see me get married and settle down. It didn't matter to her that I was doing what everyone else I know in my profession was doing. Only two of my good women friends are married and they were having immense difficulties to keep their families together—one husband is a businessman who travels all over the country almost every two weeks and the other married to a lawyer whom my friend hardly sees. My other friends live in rented apartments, and live on takeout dinners and postponed futures. We do talk about raising families but we want to do that in a few years.

"You have got into a bad circle of women. They don't want to take responsibility of raising a family," she scolded me and my unmarried women friends. Sometimes I try to argue with my mother. Truth is, she is right. All I have is an overwhelming desire to stay up until three in the morning drinking coffee and reading six hundred page biographies of women. I cannot tell my mother that I have observed their marriage and I find that marriage failed to provide them with much happiness. Through my own experience with Sanjeev I find men not disposed to commitment and not dependable.

I cannot put my mother in the feminist category, but she stands for women's rights and equality. I looked at my mother's beautiful face, pleading with me to get married and settle down and now I have trouble recognizing my workaholic mother, the one who taught me that work was essential, that having children and arranging your house beautifully was not the be-all and end-all of female experiences.

I soon found out that my mother's concerns were now turning out to be contagious and the problem of marrying me off has become a concern for Aunty Rani and Aunty Viva as well. It was only last week when I met Aunty Rani, she told me that I might as well learn to cook in preparation for getting married. Aunty Viva the other day jokingly said that if I was not careful I might turn into an ageing female! When they talk like that sometimes I get frightened for I think of a life of solitude.

XXIX

Certain people, however, seen even for the first time, work upon one's memory. At once they seem both strange and familiar and that you have known them before. Despite his formal, reserved manners, Sanjeev seemed vaguely recognizable. That was my first impression of Sanjeev when he was first introduced to me in my very first year as a graduate student at Christchurch. It was his third year. He was twenty five at the time and to me he was glamorously good-looking and elegant and I remember flirting with him straightaway as if it was my right to flirt with the good-lookers.

I should have known then, that coming events cast their shadows. It's so easy to be intelligent and see things now, but how impossible it was then—when we were young. But looking back from the perspectives of days when we were young it's easy to be blind. Now I might say that it was a tiny passing shade of feeling; but I know it was not—it was a storm of revelation that tore my life apart. Sanjeev had quite an astonishing effect on my life, in several different ways. I fell in love with him on the very first day I set eyes on him. Not too much—but enough to throw away common sense and to sacrifice my happiness for his. I remember him sitting there, in the hotel lobby that evening, elegant as always, immaculately dressed, not a hair out of place. He never said so, but I knew what he was thinking that evening, "Why did God give you both brains and beauty!" It was the way he kept looking at me with those adoring eyes.

When Sanjeev went off leaving me there alone, in the midst of the crowded railway station, waving good-bye, I was overcome with loneliness I had never experienced before; I was full of loss; as we all are when we wake up from a dream of our heart's desire and find our arms empty after all. I stood there immobilized, amidst all those people not even seeing the train, for tears were flooding my eyes. For six weeks after he left for Bombay, I sat on my bed, watching through the window, listening to the traffic coming from down the street, planning . . . six weeks is a long time, when you are young, just twenty-three. I was looking forward, with never a glance behind me. I was waiting for my future—future with Sanjeev—my real life to begin. And then it happened—behind me suddenly a door had slammed shut. My dream world fell apart.

As I remember it was mid-May. The glorious weather made me restless I could hardly keep still. I heard my voice calling Sanjeev's name again and again, as if he or I, or both of us, were at the end of the world,—the echo of my calling his name piercing through my ears. And suddenly he was there, his gentle voice saying, "What are you doing here?" and I clung to him. That was the day I received the news of Sanjeev marrying the rich girl from Bombay, the girl with the dowry. How could love that we shared so much, be more important to him than money? I refused to believe that Sanjeev had been so cruel to me—the Sanjeev I knew was so principled, so honest and fair. He kept to his word. The Sanjeev I knew was a young man of unusual intelligence, a man who showed enormous kindness and generosity to me, a man of comparable humor and most of the time, a companion of the utmost charm. It's not an exaggeration to say that Sanjeev's life became mine and I lived his life for three full years. And now that he had abandoned me, my life had come to an end. The magic he created in my life had been thrown up in flames and had ended in ashes. I laid on my stomach, my fists under my chin on the pillows and kept staring through the open window at the beautiful blue sky. I have spent two days in bed not knowing what to do with my life. The sun was breaking through the window panes lighting up my disorganized room. Why get up early? Today is Sunday. When tears filled my eyes, I turned over on my back. I felt my life, going on without me somewhere else, and I was growing older without having been young. Suddenly, I felt as if age had changed my body—my hips had grown wider and my flat stomach had disappeared and instead I felt my stomach bulging out. Looking back, it's difficult to figure out exactly where it all went wrong. Maybe it was at the very beginning when he sensed that I had fallen head over heels in love with him and that he could control my life. I should have controlled my senses—if I had done that, I would not be whining right now.

I don't believe in the power of prayer, never have. To my mind it's only an appeal to a supernatural being that doesn't exist. When my brother Roshan and I set out into the world, father told us that the world outside is a desert. I thought so too only until I met Sanjeev. Contrary to what my father said I found life pleasant and sometimes glorious. Those were the times in between the innocent years of youth and the more complicated years of adulthood. In my desperation I prayed and asked God for a great favor; I asked him to remove the bitter feeling of hatred that was coming from within me for Sanjeev, the man I loved most dearly, a man who cruelly shattered my hopes and broke and trampled my heart. I know I would live a sad life without Sanjeev. I would always be lonely.

I lay on my back and let the tears flow. I thought of my friend Susan who had told me about her wedding night with her life-long love Frank, but Susan blushed and stammered that I didn't comprehend what she said. That was about five years ago. Perhaps I was ignorant of the urgency of human desires; perhaps there were too many things I didn't know of life. But every time when Sanjeev kissed me, I felt the feeling of a fierce electric current running from my lips to my bosom; my knees gave way—and I could not even utter any words. The desire I felt was nothing I had ever known. I was passionately in love with him. I wanted to be a virgin until I got married to Sanjeev. What if I had given in to his sexual demands? Would the situation be different now? Perhaps if I had, he would not have left me—his guilty conscience would have bothered his soul. But then he never made sexual advances on me. We held hands and kissed. He touched my shoulders and felt my neck, other than that nothing happened. It's not that we did not generate passion in each other—we did, but we restrained ourselves. Both of us waited patiently until we got married—but we parted before the word ever came up.

After Sanjeev left me, my attitude towards life changed overnight. I felt as if the whole world had rejected me. I stopped laughing and was moody and angry all the time. I was twenty six years old, but felt much older than I thought I would ever be. How could I tell my mother my story of never getting married? How could he do this to me? Pretended to love me—love me with all his heart—and dumped me for money.

Sanjeev was the eldest of a family of three—two boys and a girl. I have met all of them and their parents on one of their visits to Chicago. The boys had got their good looks and their intelligence from their father, Professor Vinod Desai. He taught Economics at the University of Montreal and was a highly recognized academic there. He was tall and well-built and seemed a very caring parent to me. Sanjeev must have got his smiling eyes, his blue black hair and his flawless complexion from his mother Rajani. The first time I met her it took a while for me to realize that I was not dreaming. She was a North Indian beauty; breathtakingly attractive in a saree and quite the opposite of my mother as I remembered her at the time—unbelievably kind and patient. Sanjeev told me that his parents had left Bombay when he was just three. His father had studied at the University of Toronto and they had moved to Montreal when his father was offered a position in the university there. His brother and sister had been born in Montreal and at the time I met them, they were going to high school. They were a delight and the dream of any parent—good looking, well-behaved and academically oriented.

Tears of nostalgia fill my eyes when I think back on the three years I spent with Sanjeev. I often think of those spring Sunday afternoons, when we biked towards Wilmette village—one of the most beautifully landscaped suburbs of Chicago. We climbed the steps leading to the Bahai Temple and looked at the surroundings from the temple's door. Sanjeev talked to me about the founder of the new faith—he read the bold letters of the *Koran* painted horizontally on the walls of the temple and translated them into English for me, explaining the significance of each phrase. We biked along Lake Michigan shore as hundreds of other young couples did as the wind blew off the lake. We watched the colorful boats sailing into the deep waters. Holding hands in coffee shops and days spent in front of the aquarium admiring Chicago's magnificence cannot be erased from my memory for a hundred years.

On summer evenings we, Sanjeev and I, and our friends from university, would gather at the corner coffee shop at East Walton and Cedar and talk into the late hours. We would order coffee after coffee, for that was all we could afford then, and talked on everything that happened in the world as if each one of us were the authorities on the subject. Sanjeev very often opened the conversation wtih a controversial issue.

"Why did they have to call Jesus, son of God, instead of another founder of a religion?" he would start. Nathan, the good looker from the Netherlands, attached to the Divinity School, would respond immediately.

"So that they could believe in him—son of God is superhuman—to be a father of another religion is another human, very much like one of them. Why should they believe in another human being?" Then the others would join in, John the religious one from Indianapolis, Marian from Connecticut. We all loved those times. I was so proud of Sanjeev. I thought he stood above all others, for his understanding of Buddhism and Hinduism would enrich his questions and answers and his friends would listen to him with disbelief—at the immensity of knowledge hidden inside Sanjeev's skull. He would squeeze my hand tenderly and sip his coffee once in a while looking into my eyes with triumphant glee. George was from Los Angeles. He was the non-believer and he was a literature student. He would get bored.

"The life of the spirit, ideas like truth and beauty—these are things we make up," he said, "to glorify our little lives." To us at the time talking about knowledge, politics, career provided a sanctuary from our never-ending studies as graduate students.

Though the money we received from our parents (most of us, including me, did not receive anything from our parents) and the money we earned as graduate assistants was barely enough to exist, Sanjeev sometimes took me into elegant restaurants. I remember walking into Nieman-Marcus restaurant one evening—posh and elegant—Sanjeev and I. We were fully absorbed in each other, we didn't notice the waiter standing beside us. He interrupted to ask if we were ready to order. Neither of us had opened the menus—they lay where the waiter had put them. Did we really come here to eat? Who has the money to spend ten dollars for a cappuccino? We decided we could both do with coffee. The waiter informed us there's a five-dollar minimum for sitting in the dining room! We didn't know that before we walked in, but we were fully aware that the food was expensive. We just walked in to see what the restaurant looked like and we did it for fun.

"Can you bring us both our own pots of coffee and a quart of milk, please?" Sanjeev gave the order and I giggled. The waiter gave Sanjeev a dirty look and vanished.

"Now then," Sanjeev began, laughing and shaking his head, he continued with his story. After a lapse of ten to fifteen minutes, the waiter set down between us, two elegant silver pots with steam coming out of their spouts. He put out a pitcher of cream and poured the coffee. While he did this, I found myself looking into Sanjeev's smiling eyes and felt his hand reach over and reach mine.

"Here's what happened . . ." he continued. We sat there for a long time—sometimes talking, sometimes just absorbing each other—until we saw the arm of the waiter come between us, putting the check on the table. I can go on and on talking about those carefree days when each minute we shared seemed so precious to us.

Into the second half of his final year, his manner changed completely. He developed an annoying habit of leaving his sentences and thoughts unfinished, incomplete. I thought it was the pressure of completing the last stages of his dissertation which always proved to be the hardest. He forgot to keep appointments and when he remembered he was always late; not by minutes but by hours. I bent my head and accepted his behavior because I loved him too much to make him worry about things outside his writing at the time. Now I see it as both a deliberate and a conscious effort on his part to send me a message—a message not to build too many hopes around him. Looking back, I now remember there were days when he just refused to look me in the eye when addressing me. He looked beyond my head and spoke to me as if he was talking to someone standing behind me.

"When you marry someone you marry into that family, to that whole community. That's Indian society." Sanjeev's words ring in my ears at times.

I wish that I had never picked up my phone that Friday morning. That phone call changed my whole life and transformed me into what I am today. It was Geetha on the line—my Indian friend from college days whom I kept in touch through the years. She was a good friend of Sanjeev as well and encouraged me in my relationship with Sanjeev from the beginning.

"Sanjeev has married a wealthy businessman's daughter from Bombay. The girl is educated too. I just learned that the dowry he is getting is to be given to get his younger sister married to a doctor." Geetha's voice hit my ears like a flash of thunder. It sounded so loud and cruel.

After Sanjeev left me time dragged on, but somehow time did pass. Every hour's end seemed like a huge victory for me. I had thought he was going to marry me. Now my heart's broken; hearts do break. I console myself sometimes thinking of the times, when Sanjeev criticized me. It was my personality, what I was, that he was criticizing. I was too open, straightforward, honest to the point of tactlessness.

"Nelu, sometimes you are too abrasive, I fear you will not be able to keep any friends," Sanjeev said one day.

"I am being natural," I told him. It is my style, instant intimacy with everyone I meet. Sanjeev called it the 'modern talent'. My view was anything less than perfect frankness with everyone you meet is an insult to honesty, to friendship.

"How can you be friends if you are not sincere?" I asked him. Sometimes those awful days I went through, immediately after Sanjeev left me, come to my mind. I try to put those sad days behind me, but they do appear. I remember there were times when I couldn't face the thought of entire Sundays stretching ahead of me, all by myself. I waited for the telephone to ring to hear Sanjeev's voice, but it never rang. Disasters never stopped occurring to me those days—even in teaching where I am so good at, I kept making serious mistakes.

I now find consolation thinking of the sheer awfulness of men. The idea provokes a frenzy of outrage in me. Men are stupid, smug, arrogant, manipulative, liars, and worse still they make use of women and make women look stupid. To me, at the time and even now, men exist in a culture of entitlement. 'Can you iron this shirt for me?' or 'Will you take my car and fill the tank today?'

I stopped cooking in my apartment those days and went to the fitness room of the apartment complex to buy sandwiches. There I imagined everyone's eyes fixed on me—I couldn't go anywhere, I heard them talk—'Here comes the dumped one,' 'she'll end up fifty five in a dressing gown, with a line of cats following her and imagining the mailman is in love with her!'

The past is a dangerous place. One look backward can turn your head into turmoil; thinking of the causes that led to the loss of the one you loved would make you insane. Memories are treacherous and precious at the same time. It took sometime for me to realize the inconsistency of our feelings that takes place with passing time—our feelings move from one object to the other with the dictate of our hearts. One fine day, our thoughts about the other person become a simple habit of memory, and then they fade, scattering into shadows.

As I see it now, there is one good reason for me to get married—to make mother happy. I feel my mother's hand squeezing mine and hear her say, "We did it. I am so happy for you." Is she really? Happy for me or for herself so that she could die in peace knowing that there is someone to look after me? Her dreams are shattered, she says. Her hopes are shattered, she laments. But why wouldn't my achievements mean anything to you, Mom? I am a successful academic, a published author, a respected teacher—why don't they count for something? I am a mere woman—is that it—Mom? The tears that had swelled in my eyes had evaporated like morning dew under the strong morning sun. True, I am lonely sometimes, but I've made up my mind to remain single.